SLAVE REVELATIONS

'Well then, Jilly, filly,' she said, addressing the stooping girl before her, 'I dare say you could use a bath, eh?'

Jilly managed just to nod her head, despite the pillory about her slender neck.

'Of course, such privileges as baths must be earned,' she said. 'You understand that, I suppose.' A grunt and another foreshortened nod. 'Well now, how do you think you could earn your bath, and show your gratitude to your new mistress at the same time?' The girl had sucked furiously on her gag and there was now a darkened patch about her mouth where saliva had leaked out and dampened the leather through. 'Perhaps we can think of something more suitable for that pretty little mouth to do.' Celia watched as the eyes behind the mask blinked and the pupils began to dilate slightly as the realisation sunk in.

She drew down the zip of her black leather panties to reveal her shaven pudenda – 'You understand what is required of you, slave?' – and heard Jilly swallow, a voluble exercise with the gag filling her mouth so completely. Another soft grunt and the eyelids fluttered. It was an unmistakable signal.

'Ah yes, Jilly. Very promising, very promising indeed!'

By the same author:

SLAVE GENESIS
SLAVE EXODUS

SLAVE REVELATIONS

Jennifer Jane Pope

This book is a work of fiction.
In real life, make sure you practise safe sex.

First published in 2001 by
Nexus
Thames Wharf Studios
Rainville Road
London W6 9HA

www.nexus-books.co.uk

Typeset by TW Typesetting, Plymouth, Devon

Printed and bound by
Cox & Wyman Ltd, Reading, Berks

ISBN 0 352 33627 7

Author's Preface

This is the third book in the *Slave* series and I'd like to take this opportunity to thank all of you who have bought and read the first two and say a special 'Thank You' to everyone who has since taken the trouble to write to me and say so many nice things about them: it's nice to know you're enjoying my efforts!

I should also like to pay no small a tribute to the editorial team at Nexus, who, like me, believe that the erotica market is deserving of something a little better than the 'Wham, Bam, Thank You, Ma'am' school of thought that pervaded the genre for so many years. As a result of their forward-looking approach, I am able to write the sort of books I think the vast majority of readers are discerning enough to appreciate.

And so, once again we return to our somewhat disparate bunch of heroes and heroines, having left them in a variety of situations, both likely and unlikely, and see just what they make of whatever fate intends to throw in their paths next.

One small note worth considering: some reviewers and readers alike have described this series as being set in the 'near future' – to them I ask this simple question: 'How do you know?' Because, my dears, for all we know, this may already be the present and the *near* present, too. In fact, it may be nearer than you think!

Listen very carefully and you may just hear a faint rustle, as the latex mask of destiny eases itself high above the thigh boot of fate and hovers in the cosmos of uncertainty, waiting for the untimely arrival of the stiletto heel of disaster and the harness of providence to once again do battle . . .

Jennifer Jane Pope
December 2000

NB: To those readers who e-mailed me, suggesting that Jess, Alex and Co should really be described as Shetland Ponygirls, I'd just like to say this: *I* do the corny puns, thank you, and that one was too corny, even for me! (I think.)

The Storybook World of Jennifer Jane Pope ~
www.avid-diva.com

e-mail to: jenny@avid-diva.demon.co.uk

Prologue

(Necessary – well, useful, anyway – for those of you who haven't yet read *Slave Genesis* and/or *Slave Exodus*, as well as for those of you who have, and have gone and lost the plot *again*!)

The Shetland Isles, a group of about a hundred islands off the north-eastern tip of Scotland and the most remote outpost of Britain, surrounded by possibly the most inhospitable and untrustworthy waters known to man . . .

Of the hundred islands, only fifteen are officially populated; the rest are mostly little more than near barren lumps of rock, swept by winds, rain and snow for much of the year and quite often impossible to land on, though throughout the years certain hardy and enterprising – not to say foolhardy – individuals have tried to put their very remoteness to good use.

Outwardly, Carigillie Craig, on the eastern-most fringes of the group, is now home to a respectable and very expensive health farm, patronised by the ultra-wealthy and famous, but both Carigillie and its smaller neighbour, Ailsa Ness, hide a dark and sinister secret.

For nearly two centuries, both islands have been owned and controlled by a curious race of people, whose males can live up to four hundred years, but whose females die before they are thirty – even younger once they have given birth. But the leader of the colony, known to the outside world as Richard Major, and his right-hand man, Dr Keith Lineker, have not wasted their time and have perfected the science of cloning and genetic modification to the extent that they are able to produce half-android, half-human host bodies – Jenny Anns – into which normal human brains can be transferred, and which can also live as long as their creators.

From the offspring of these clones, they can take DNA samples to produce further clones, into which the brains of their own females can be transplanted, offering them, too, extravagantly prolonged life expectancy.

Until now, the human brains for the Jenny Anns have been taken from women close to death – cancer patients, accident victims and even Jessica, whose original body was all but torn apart when an unexploded Second World War bomb finally detonated as she was walking home in 1951. After nearly fifty years in her stronger, fitter body, Jess is happy with her life as a pony-girl, living in the underground stables complex on Ailsa and kept for the exclusive use of Andrew Lachan, billionaire tycoon, who ensures that when she is not serving him on his frequent visits to the island, she can enjoy a life of relative comfort and luxury, despite her ever present bridle and harness.

The rest of the Jenny Anns are not so fortunate, for in return for their alleged salvation, they are expected to act as sex slaves for Ailsa's more discerning visitors. The reduced pain threshold of their bodies makes them ideal objects for the gratification of every imaginable lust and fetish, but most bear their crosses stoically, realising that there is no alternative and certainly no chance of escape.

One exception to this general air of acceptance is Tammy, but then Tammy is not like her sister Jay-Ays, for, until her original human body was washed up on the island after a storm wrecked one of the local trawlers, Tammy had been Tommy MacIntyre, a decidedly rugged and macho young fisherman, and the prospect of spending decade upon decade as the sexual plaything of a procession of warped masters and mistresses is too appalling to contemplate.

Meanwhile, a series of seemingly innocent and unconnected deaths elsewhere in the islands attracts the attention of Detective Sergeant Alex Gregory, local girl made good and still ambitious to do better. Why would an elderly man risk climbing on to the roof of his cottage to adjust a satellite dish that had been disconnected for a year? And why would a part-time coroner examining the bodies of the victims of a helicopter crash suddenly lose control of his car on a road known to be dangerous?

Detective Constable Geordie Walker, recently posted to the islands to keep him away from the threatened revenge of a crazed gangland boss he helped bring to justice, thinks that Alex is making too much of things and their boss, Detective Inspector George Gillespie, approaching retirement and eager not to tread on too many wealthy or influential toes, agrees. Alex, however, is a lady not easily deterred.

She recruits the aid of her old friend and former fellow member of their university skydiving club, local helicopter charter pilot, Rory Dalgleish, and makes a parachute descent on to Ailsa Ness under cover of darkness. Unfortunately for Alex, the island is about to receive other unwanted visitors, in the shape of Andrew Lachan, his former special services security adviser and a small team of hired mercenaries.

Unable to persuade Richard Major to sell him Jessie outright, Lachan is determined to abduct her to his Highland farm retreat, but their sea-borne landing attracts the attention of the islands' own security men. In trying to evade the ensuing gun battle, Alex, who is still stunned from watching the human pony-girls racing each other around the torch-lit track at the furthest end of the island, slips and falls into a narrow ravine, breaking her back and paralysing her body completely.

When she comes round, it is to find that she, too, is now a Jenny Ann and expected to adapt to a lifestyle that is as completely alien to her as are the creatures who have inflicted this humiliation upon her. But if Alex is horrified at her expected new role, Andrew Lachan, the only survivor of the ill-fated kidnap attempt, has also awoken to find himself, like Tommy before him, now in a very sexy female body, sharing a stable with Jessie, the very reason for his coming here in the first place.

Alex's original body is removed to Carigillie Craig, together with her parachute and the scene staged to make it appear that she had snapped her neck upon landing. Geordie, who knew that she was intending to land on Ailsa, not Carigillie, is instantly suspicious and suspects she has been murdered. However, despite Rory Dalgleish's assertions that Alex baled out over the smaller island, DI Gillespie concludes there is no real proof of skulduggery and not even enough evidence to mount a thorough investigation.

Meanwhile, hundreds of miles to the south-west, the death of Andrew Lachan and some of his henchmen have been faked, in an explosion aboard his luxury motor yacht, the *Jessica*. A former colleague of Geordie's, appointed to investigate the 'accident', is not entirely happy with the situation. Discovering a link between Lachan and Healthglow, the company supposedly running Carigillie, he telephones his old friend, to see if he can throw any further light on things.

Working mostly unofficially, Geordie and Colin begin piecing together snippets of information and following up even the most tenuous of leads, one of which brings Geordie face to face with the late Lachan's aristocratic secretary, the beautiful Sara Llewellyn-Smith, and leads on to the discovery of the most singular pony stable that Lachan had been preparing for his beloved, two-legged equine slave.

With the two islands definitely off-limits to further investigation, the inquiry turns towards one of Healthglow's regular clients. No longer in the first flush of youth, Celia Butler is still a striking woman and the establishment she herself runs, deep in the English countryside, intrigues the two detectives and arouses a macabre fascination in Sara.

Very shortly, Colin and Sara, adopting the roles of master and slave pony, enrol in Celia's bizarre training academy and Geordie, too, finds himself in a situation he never expected, complete with his own very obliging, rubber-clad slave girl.

Meanwhile, things on the two islands are not looking too promising, for Major has struck up a partnership with a sinister South American drugs baron, Ramon Valerez, to whom the Jenny-Ann technology offers possibilities far beyond their original roles. The prospect of genetically modified 'supergirl' ponies, capable of hauling heavy contraband packages through the precarious mountain passes of his homeland and also acting as sexual inducements for his own men, leads Valerez to invest heavily with Major and his people, providing the funding for a new breeding programme that will produce all the two-legged ponies he could ask for.

However, the two Andean Indian girls he has brought halfway across the world for Lineker's team to use as their initial guinea pigs are not quite so tame as they at first appear and soon they make a break for freedom, accompanied by Alex, desperate to be free of her new role as Jangles the pony-girl.

Unfortunately, Alex quickly realises that Major's assertions that no one can escape the islands without a boat, or even a helicopter, are not idle boasts. With the sea on one side of them and the island guards soon in hot pursuit, they are no nearer escaping than they were in the subterranean stables and cell complex, and if the bitterly cold autumn nights do not kill them, they will surely soon starve to death . . .

Slave Revelations

Amaarini Savanijuik drew the long, shiny black glove slowly up her right arm, smoothing out the gleaming black fabric as she went and flexing her fingers inside their tight sheaths with a cold deliberation that sent tremors of dread anticipation crawling up Alex's spine.

Still clad in her pony-girl garb, the heavy hoof boots weighing her cruelly arched feet down, Alex stood with her back against one of the two steel posts in the centre of the underground room, her own gloved arms drawn cruelly back behind her and secured at wrists and elbows, forcing her shoulders back and her generous breasts out through the two rounded apertures in her rubbery body suit.

The guards had secured her in this manner an hour or more earlier and now the strain was beginning to tell, even on this body they had given her, for her two nights and one day of 'freedom' had already taken their toll and now every joint ached and every muscle and sinew screamed out for relief.

'I'll ask you again, Jangles,' Amaarini hissed, placing a gloved forefinger on Alex's left nipple and pressing the engorged teat back into the soft flesh of the breast behind. 'Where is the other Indian girl?'

'Dead, I expect,' Alex retorted, repeating the same statement she had already made several times over. 'I told you, she dived into the water and tried to swim for it.' She stared defiantly back at the taller woman from between the heavy blinkers that were an integral part of her bridle.

'As you people keep telling us,' she said, 'the currents here are deadly. Last I saw of her, she was about a hundred yards off shore and looked like she was being swept north, well away from any of the other islands.'

'Stupid little animal,' Amaarini snapped. She regarded Alex steadily for several seconds, holding her gaze and then, without warning, drew back her hand and lashed out, palm first, striking Alex a ringing blow across her left cheek, the blinkers only slightly absorbing the impact.

Alex managed to stifle her instinctive cry of pain, but she could do nothing about the myriad coloured stars that sprang up before her, and only the fact that her new body apparently had no tear ducts prevented her from further demonstrating how much the slap had hurt her.

'You, on the other hand,' Amaarini said quietly, 'are supposed to be intelligent – at least, intelligent by the standards of your people. You should have tried to stop her.'

'I did try,' Alex moaned, shaking her head and trying to clear the ringing sound from her ears. 'I tried to tell her, but she hardly spoke a word of English, did she?'

'A waste,' Amaarini muttered. 'A complete waste. It will take at least ten days to arrange for a replacement to be delivered here. Sẽnor Valerez is very annoyed, I can tell you.'

'It wasn't my fault . . . mistress.' Alex added the acknowledgement reluctantly, hating herself for doing it, but there was little point, she knew, in inviting further physical punishment. A slap was bad enough, but she had seen what some of these people could do with a whip and she was not anxious to invite that sort of attention.

However, Amaarini's next words made it only too clear that it was too late for such thoughts.

'You are to be flogged this evening, Jangles,' she said. 'In case any of the other slaves get any stupid ideas, your punishment will serve as a warning to them. Your pain threshold will be reduced to a minimum, so it will not be necessary to break your skin or leave any permanently disfiguring marks, but I can assure you that you will suffer as though you were being burned alive.

'Also, your vocal links will be disabled this afternoon. You will no longer be able to speak intelligibly. The electronic device implanted in your voice box will be programmed so that you will whinny most convincingly from now on. Luckily, your body was fitted with one of the newest types, so it will not be necessary to return you for further surgery.'

She loomed over Alex, grasping her chin between forefinger and thumb, in a grip that belied even her statuesque build.

'How does it feel, horse-girl?' she rasped, pressing her face close. 'How does it feel to know that from now on you'll be no better than an animal, eh? And soon, when the good doctor has finished his latest tests, I'm going to ask him to fit you with a new synapse link, so that we can disable your arms and hands at the press of a button.

'You see, you won't need hands from now on, pony-girl, nor will you need the power of speech, not where you'll be going to eventually and, in the meantime, I'm going to make it my special task to show you just how inferior your pathetic species is!'

'You're becoming a very bad influence on me, Melinda Harvey-Johnson.' Tim Walker – 'Geordie' to his friends and colleagues – stared into his half-empty pint glass and grinned. Opposite him, in the intimate, panelled booth of the Lazy Shepherd pub, Melinda Harvey-Johnson tossed her mane of blonde curls and smiled back at him.

'Gillespie obviously didn't believe a word of what I told him this morning on the phone,' Geordie said. 'He suggested I might find myself out on one of the coast guard patrols when I finally got back up there.'

'So, how long before you have to be back?' Melinda asked. 'Can you swing the weekend down here, or do you have to make a start before that?'

'Well, I told the old bastard I'd take a couple of extra days off my annual leave entitlement,' Geordie replied. 'Not much he could say about that, but I really should make a move first thing Monday morning. The temporary replacement they sent has ended up going down with some mystery bug and I'm supposed to be standing in for poor old Alex, until the powers-that-be decide on what they're finally doing, so poor old George is a bit short-handed.'

'Perhaps I could come back with you,' Melinda suggested, 'for a few days, anyway. I'm not exactly committed to anything right now, so I've got time on my hands.'

'Well, it gets a bit damp and chilly up there, this time of the year, or so I'm told,' Geordie warned her. 'What they call autumn feels more like midwinter, if Alex's stories are anything to go by.'

'Well, I'm sure we can find plenty of ways of keeping warm.' Melinda smirked. 'Unless you don't want me to come, that is? Perhaps you've got yourself a wee Scottish lassie waiting for you up in the wild islands, eh?'

Geordie shook his head. 'Nope, no lassies, wee or otherwise,' he said. 'And yes, I'd love you to spend a few days up there with me. It'd give us time to get to know one another properly.' He laughed shortly and picked up his glass.

'Well, I suppose we have been a bit one-tracked these past couple of days,' Melinda admitted. 'And, talking of which, if you're staying down for the weekend, I've had an invitation that might just interest you.'

'Oh? What's that – a society cocktail party?' Although he had only known Melinda a few days, Geordie was already aware that her circle of friends was more the sort of thing Colin Turner was used to and that her father, if not exactly a paid-up member of the nobility, was certainly as close to the aristocracy as it was possible to be without having an actual title.

'Well, party yes, society, yes . . . cocktail, no!' she said. 'More like ponytail, I'd say.'

'Ah!' Geordie lowered his glass again and regarded her across the pitted table top. Melinda raised her elegant eyebrows a fraction.

'The idea doesn't appeal?' she asked.

Geordie hesitated. 'Well,' he began, 'I'm not saying it doesn't appeal, but all that stuff is still a bit . . . well, a bit new to me.'

'Yes, I know it is,' Melinda conceded, reaching out a slim hand to rest her fingers on his wrist. 'And that's why this weekend would be such a good opportunity. It's nothing to do with Celia's place – just some other friends of mine, at a discreet country place, friends with similar, um, tastes to my own, shall we say?'

'So, you'd be Millie the Maid for this weekend?' Geordie said. He peered down into his now nearly empty glass, avoiding direct eye contact.

Melinda chuckled. 'Well, Millie certainly,' she said, 'but not necessarily the maid. There are all sorts of possibilities, including Millie the Filly. We could invite Colin and Sara, if you like. I'm sure they'd both be very keen.'

'Well, Sara would, from what I've seen,' Geordie agreed, 'but I'm not so sure about Colin. That little experience at Celia's was a bit of a shock to his system, I can tell you! Mind you,' he added, with a lopsided grin, 'he wasn't the only one!'

'Do all girls with double-barrelled surnames have a penchant for kinky sex?' Colin Turner sat cross-legged on the end of the bed, watching Sara as she continued carefully polishing the harness leathers, working with meticulous, almost loving precision. She looked up and smiled across the bedroom at him, completely without any of the embarrassment she had shown that first day, in the stables with Geordie, when he had returned unexpectedly to catch her wearing the pony-girl rig that her late employer had intended for his unknown lover.

They had returned to Andrew Lachan's estate the previous morning, since when Sara had spent almost every waking hour sorting through the curious collection of leather tack and rubber outfits she and Geordie had discovered in the hidden stable room, hardly acknowledging Colin's presence, except for a brief interval making love in her bedroom during the early hours, an experience that Colin suspected she had found equally as unrewarding as he had himself, especially considering the passion of their earlier encounters.

He hoped she wasn't already beginning to regret her change of mind and the rather late decision not to remain with Celia Butler's assistant, the rather awesome Margot, and he knew that if he wanted to keep this delectable girl, he would have to be willing to make changes and learn new tricks himself.

'I wouldn't know,' she replied sweetly. 'I dare say there are a few, but then I suspect it holds true in all walks of life.'

'Except,' Colin pointed out, 'that your average Miss Secretary on a thirty-six-hour week and luncheon vouchers would have to save a long time to buy something like that.' He nodded at the gleaming collection of leather straps and brasses in her hands. 'How much would that cost, d'you reckon?'

'Well, you saw Celia's price lists, didn't you?' Sara said. 'So you tell me. Besides,' she added, 'I thought the idea was that the "master" paid for the tack. After all, whoever's heard of a pony with money?'

'Well, you've got a point, I suppose.' He sighed. 'And, from what I saw at Celia's, it's right out of my price bracket. I could stretch to the odd bridle, I suppose, but those gigs and traps and things, well, I've got a car and wine habit to feed anyway.' He grinned and sat back, easing his legs out straight in front of him.

'What about a removal van?' Sara asked, returning her concentration to her work. 'Could your budget run to hiring one for a day, say? Not a proper company, I don't mean, but one of those self-drive things.'

'I probably know a place where I could borrow one, actually,' Colin replied. 'Cost of a few pints and whatever fuel I used. Why? What do you have in mind? Or shall I guess?'

'Well,' Sara said, laying her burden carefully to one side and arranging it over the back of the chair next to her, 'I was just thinking. The solicitors and valuers will be here next week, just to check over my inventories and the headline prices, but when I compiled that lot, I had no idea about the stables, of course.'

'Ah, yes,' Colin mused. The corners of his mouth twitched briefly, but he maintained a neutral expression.

'And you're thinking that it would be better for your late boss's reputation and memory if we perhaps just spirited a few incriminating odds and sods out of the way?'

'Something like that.' Sara nodded. 'Of course, I did think of just making a bonfire down in that paddock area . . .'

'But that would be a terrible waste, naturally,' Colin said gravely.

'A terrible waste, yes.'

'Enough to have a Scotsman turning in his grave, assuming they'd ever recovered enough of him to need one.' Sara flashed him a dark look and he coughed, realising that his comment had not just been in bad taste. The events of the past few days had made it all too easy to forget that Sara had had more than just a soft spot for the late millionaire, even if her feelings had never been reciprocated.

'Sorry,' he muttered. 'Forget I said that.' He paused, avoiding her gaze. 'You'd need a pretty sizeable garage to keep everything in,' he pointed out, at last. 'The tack would all fit in a decent-sized closet, but some of the larger stuff – not to mention those mannequins – that's a different kettle of fish.'

'I have a cottage,' Sara said quietly. 'It's in Norfolk, not far from Fakenham. It's pretty remote and there's a small barn – really it's not much more than a large shed, I suppose, but it would be big enough.

'The cottage itself is still being renovated. My great-aunt left it to me two years ago and I haven't really had much time to devote to it, what with my duties for Andrew, but now, once I've finished here and handed it over to the legal beagles, I was thinking I could spend a few month's down there.'

'You'll not be looking for another job yet, then?'

Sara shook her head. 'Not yet,' she said. 'I've got a few bob in the bank and Andrew also left me a nice little bequest in his will, or so I've been told, so there's no rush.'

'Lucky girl.' Colin sighed. 'I'm afraid I need to work for my corn.'

'But you'd still have the odd weekend free, I guess?'

'Depends what you mean by "odd",' he quipped and was rewarded with a small smile in return. 'But yes, I do like my recreation. All work and no play and all that.'

'Good.' Sara walked slowly across to the deep bay window and stood, looking out into the gathering dusk beyond. 'Can you organise the van by telephone – for Sunday, if possible?'

'Sunday would be good,' Colin said. 'Less heavy traffic on the roads.'

'And that gives us two clear days beforehand,' Sara said, without looking back at him. 'Time to get everything organised and packed.'

'Yes, plenty of time for that,' he agreed. She was standing so that Colin could see her in a quarter profile from behind; he couldn't see her eyes, but the slight twitching of the tip of her elegant nose was unmissable.

'I'll go down to the study and make a few phone calls,' he said softly. 'In the meantime, perhaps you'd better take a stroll down to the stables and see that everything is in order. It's supposed to be a mild evening, so maybe there's a pony that could do with a bit of light exercise.'

He saw the colour rising in the one cheek he could see, but her poise never flickered for a moment.

'Yes,' she said, nodding her head very slightly. 'I was thinking that myself. You go ahead and make your phone calls and I'll go down and get her ready for you. No need to hurry. She's only a pony, after all, so she won't mind standing around waiting for her master.'

For the scene of Alex's punishment, Amaarini had chosen the concourse area that ran between the two facing rows of underground stalls, which was both long and wide and afforded plenty of room for spectators, of which Alex knew there would probably be many, both guests and slaves alike, for a flogging was seen as entertainment for the former and a warning to the latter.

However, it was also considered that a significant part of a miscreant slave's punishment sentence was the tension that built up through delaying the actual moment and the ritual of preparation was deliberately unhurried, with several lengthy waits in between.

To begin with, Alex was given into the charge of Higgy, one of the senior grooms, assisted by the younger Jonas and Sol, who between them made sure that Alex was never in a position to even consider resisting. They began by stripping her totally, removing her hoof boots, harnesses and finally her form-fitting pony suit, after which she was propelled into the tiled showering area and hosed down with two icy cold jets of water.

Halfway through the ordeal, as she gasped for breath and writhed and staggered under the onslaught, Higgy produced a small black box, aimed it at her and thumbed one of the controls. Instantly, Alex's squeals and gasps changed and, to her horror, she realised that she was now whinnying like a frightened mare and snorting in a very non-human way.

The three men exchanged delighted grins and began laughing, altering their aim and narrowing the jets to increase their intensity, so that now Alex felt as if her entire body was being lashed by small whips. Another adjustment with the control unit and the pain from the impact seemed to double, so that Alex was forced into the furthest corner, cowering and trying to cover her most sensitive parts and all the time unable to prevent herself from making even more of those humiliating, horse-like screams.

'That'll do, lads,' Higgy announced, at last. Alex felt like crying with relief as the water pressure died, but her eyes, as ever, remained the only dry part of her as she staggered out of the shower bay, now shivering uncontrollably and barely able to stay on her feet. To add insult to injury, Higgy dealt her a sharp slap across her left buttock, which again brought forth a neighing squeal of both protest and pain.

'Aye, I reckon you'll make a pretty noise this evening, lassie.' He chuckled. He looked down at the control unit and smiled. 'Amazing, the way these little things work.' He flicked another switch, the small red LED light faded and he tucked the little device away in a pouch that hung from his belt.

'Give her a good rub-down and make sure she's well and truly dry,' he instructed his two assistants. 'I'm going to find another pony suit for her for tonight. How'd you fancy being a pretty white pony, eh, Jangles?' Alex stared sullenly back at him, her lips pressed firmly together, and for a moment considered trying to leap on him and rake his face – and in particular his mocking eyes – with her long nails. She would suffer for it, she knew, but then what else could these bastards do to her that they weren't planning already?

However, while she was still weighing up the consequences against the inner satisfaction she knew she needed, the choice was taken from her, for the two younger grooms moved quickly up behind her, seized her arms and dragged them behind her back, cuffing her wrists together. Higgy grinned and shook his head and, in that moment, Alex knew that the three of them had been simply toying with her, allowing her just long enough to consider whether to try to make use of her brief moment of freedom and then depriving her of the opportunity just as she was on the point of making up her mind.

'Aye, I know what you'd love to do, pony-girl,' Higgy said quietly. 'You're one with plenty of spirit, that's for sure, but you'd do better to keep it under control, I promise you. The quicker you learn, the better it'll be. The moment they gave you that fine new body, you lost your right to individual choice, or pride.

'You're a slave now, Jangles – and a pony-girl slave at that. I can understand how that's come a bit hard for someone like you, but you can't do anything about it and now you don't even have a voice to argue with, do you? Well, there's still time for you to learn, I'm sure. It'd be a waste if they do decide to ship you off with that dago fellow's ponies, when the time comes, but I reckon they'll probably do just that. They don't like trouble here, girl, that much I can tell you.'

Ramon Valerez turned away from the monitor screen at which he had been staring intently for the past several minutes. There was the hint of a smile on his swarthy Latin features, but it was a mirthless smile that did not reach as far as his hooded eyes.

'The girl has spirit, Ricardo,' he said. Richard Major regarded him impassively, ignoring the Spanish form of his name that Valerez had recently taken to employing when the two men were alone together. He smiled in his turn, but in his case the humour glittered in his curiously shaped eyes and lent a certain degree of additional menace to his almost serpentine face.

'In her former life,' he replied evenly, 'she was quite the independent spirit. My enquiries and contacts suggest that she would very soon have been promoted to the rank of inspector.'

'So, there can be little doubt that it was she behind the escape attempt?'

Major shook his head. 'I think not, Señor Valerez,' he said, in a voice that suggested he was barely tolerating his guest, though the South American, to whom English was a second language, would not pick up on the inflection, he well knew.

'I can show you footage from several of the interior cameras, which proves that Jangles, as she is now called, was in a totally helpless state when she left the complex, which completely bears out Amaarini's story.

'Somehow, your two little savages managed to get away. The groom, Sol, claims that he was hit over the back of the head whilst checking around outside the main entrance, though I suspect there is more to his story that he is not telling.'

'You think he helped the little bitches?' Valerez demanded, his eyes narrowing. Major's features remained as inscrutable as ever.

'It depends upon your definition of the term "helped",' he said. 'If you mean did the lad purposely let them loose, then the answer is no; however, if you take the expression in its widest sense, then I must say that, in my opinion, he undoubtedly was of great assistance.

'I am not a betting man, señor, but if I was, I would be inclined to wager a reasonable sum on young Sol having taken one or other of your savages outside, in order to avail himself of the pleasures of her body. Then, unfortunately for all concerned, I imagine he allowed himself to become careless and somehow the girl got the better of him.

'After several years working with our Jenny Ann females, I fear Sol may have fallen into the trap of assuming all females are as placid and accepting as the majority of our stock.'

'The mountains at home breed a vicious and basic people,' Valerez retorted. 'Thcy are little more than animals – savage and violent.'

Major raised one eyebrow slightly. 'You surprise me, Señor Valerez,' he said smoothly. 'I was given to understand that the aboriginal Andean peoples were, by nature, a peaceful breed. Of course, even the most tranquil of races can revert to instinct when their home territory is threatened, I suppose.' Momentarily, Valerez's eyes betrayed annoyance, but he quickly regained control of his temper and smiled again, revealing a set of perfect and just too white teeth between his thin lips.

'You will punish this groom, this Sol, of course?' he said, turning back to watch the ongoing preparations that were being relayed from the stables on the adjoining island. 'His carelessness – not to mention disobedience – has cost us the life of valuable breeding stock.'

'You have arranged for a replacement, though?'

'I have,' Valerez confirmed. 'In fact, I have issued orders for three females to be shipped across by the most expeditious means. I should, perhaps, have had more than two sent in the first place, except that your Dr Lineker assured me that two would be sufficient.'

'Under normal circumstances,' Major said, 'the two girls you brought across would have been perfectly adequate. We did not expect to lose one, but then I must take the responsibility for that myself. The fact that the island is escape-proof should not have blinded me to the possibilities that a lower intellect might be prepared to accept impossible odds and sacrifice her life in an attempt to get away.'

'I understand that, Ricardo,' Valerez said. 'However, it would not have happened – the girl should not have been afforded the opportunity to make that choice – had your groom acted correctly. I demand that he be punished and punished most severely.'

'I see.' Major pursed his lips slightly. 'And what form would you suggest his punishment take?'

'At home,' Valerez snapped, 'such insubordination would be deserving of only one punishment.'

'A bullet in the head, señor?' Major suggested, with just the merest hint of irony. 'Immediate execution, *pour encourager les autres*, as the French would have it?' He shook his head. 'Sol is one of our own,' he continued. 'He is second generation and born of one of our slave women, but he has our blood in his veins, nonetheless.'

'And you cannot, or will not, kill your own, eh, Ricardo?'

'No.' Major turned away and paced slowly across the width of the room until, reaching the wide window opening that afforded him such an excellent panoramic view of the North Sea beyond the island, he paused, staring out at the greying horizon, where sky and water blended in an indistinguishable murk of pending dusk.

'Killing any living creature is a waste, Ramon,' he said at last, without looking back at Valerez. 'Sol has been a very efficient worker for a good many years now, despite his apparent youth. However, I agree with you that he should be punished for his error and I believe I have the perfect answer and one that will also appeal to your own particular tastes.'

Despite the fact that he had known what to expect, the sight of Sara, standing waiting for him in the middle of the little stable room, still took Colin's breath away and he remembered how Geordie Walker had described the way she had looked when he had found her that first night, only an hour or two after the pair of them had discovered Andrew Lachan's secret tack room. Very much, Colin presumed, the way she looked now, with the flickering lantern lights shimmering on the studding and buckles of her harness and bridle.

She had begun, he saw, drawing back her hair and tying it into a high ponytail, emphasising the style by drawing the thick golden tresses up through a stiff leather tube, that held them up and away from her head, before allowing them to cascade down again like a plume and leaving her perfectly shaped ovaloid features completely unobscured – or so they had been, until she had added the intricate leather bridle.

Looking at her, Colin guessed that she must have started her self-costuming from the feet upwards, for the elaborate tack assembly comprised a myriad fastenings and lacings and the thick blinkers and broad bit gag would surely have hampered her efforts to prepare herself.

The boots were of highly polished red leather, long and reaching well above the knee, laced tightly, so that they followed every contour of her shapely legs. Like the boots Colin had seen – and indeed experienced himself – at Celia Butler's singular establishment, they were high-heeled and arched the insteps dramatically, though the way in which the soles and heels were moulded into heavy hoof shapes disguised any semblance of human feet.

Above the boots, Sara had buckled and laced herself into a stiff corset of matching leather, the golden studs contrasting with the crimson background and from this basic girth several other straps ran in different directions, so that her entire upper body was encased as if in a red spider's web.

Two straps descended from the front of the corset, forming a V-shape, the base of which sat so that it just covered her shaven sex. Without looking closer, Colin knew that these two straps were there joined to each other and a third strap, which then ran back up between her buttocks to buckle to the lower hem of the corset at the rear.

Above the girth, more straps, this time ascending, forming loops – cages almost – about either breast, lifting them and separating them, yet without covering them for any modesty; rather the way in which the two heavy steel rings at the centre of each complex cone sat about the two engorged nipples, forcing them forward in twin, hardened peaks, made Sara's bosom seem even more naked than if it had been left entirely unhampered.

By her sides, her arms hung limply, encased in long leather sleeves that she had managed to lace herself, though not as tightly as they were designed for, Colin realised, for in that case her arms would have been too stiff about the elbow joints for her to bend them. He nodded to himself, appreciating the dedicated effort it must have required for her to achieve even this effect.

About her neck was buckled a high, stiff collar, beset with three rings of golden studs, which forced her to keep her chin up and her head held high, the rquired pose for what Celia had taught them both was a 'show pony'. The haughty bearing contrasted starkly with the rest of the image, for the bridle that encased her head and the thick, rubber padded bit that filled her mouth gave Sara an air of humility and suffering, her cheeks bulging, her beautiful eyes framed by the leather, the blinkers preventing her from seeing in any direction other than straight ahead.

'Very nice,' Colin said quietly. The observation was totally inadequate and they both knew it, but he needed a few more moments to compose himself. Trying to control his shaking hands, he stepped forward and lifted her right arm. Sara stood immobile, staring at the end wall, apparently not seeing him and made no effort to resist as he began tightening the lacing. After a few minutes, he stepped back, allowing the arm to fall free.

'Can you bend it now?' he asked. Sara gave a curt shake of her head, which set her fair mane swirling and lifted her arm to demonstrate. Colin saw the sinews at the very top of the limb twitch, as she attempted to bend it at the elbow, but there was scarcely any movement of the joint. Stepping forward again, he repeated the process on her other arm and, as he stood back for a second time, he heard her let out a long, deep sigh. From now on, he realised, as did she, there was no way she could remove anything: for all practical purposes, she was now helpless and dependent upon her 'master'.

'I think that girth looks a little loose,' Colin observed, fighting to keep his tone as neutral and expressionless as possible. One thing he had learned – among the several other things he had learned during their short visit to Celia's – was that the ambience, the mood, the entire effect of the ritual, could be destroyed in a moment, just from a single poorly chosen remark, or even by an unguarded snicker. He moved behind her and began working on the laces.

In truth, Sara had laced herself into the girth pretty strictly and Colin felt a pang of guilt as he began to tighten it yet further, but he knew that it was expected of him, that Sara had already fallen under the spell of this bizarre scene and that every millimetre by which he managed to reduce her waist was adding in some inexplicable way to her ultimate responsiveness.

Finally, the task was completed and Colin retreated a few paces, looking her up and down, yet all the while avoiding direct eye contact, as he watched the way in which her breasts now rose and fell with the rapid, shallow breathing that the corset enforced upon her. Inside the tightish leather breeches he had donned in the bedroom earlier, he could feel himself beginning to grow hard and he turned away, not yet wanting to display the effect that the sight of her virtual nakedness was having upon him.

'I think we'll use the gig this evening, Sassie,' he said, using her pony-girl name. He walked past her, to where the two-wheeled cart lay half hidden beneath the dust sheets, but his eye was immediately caught by the further array of leatherwear and implements that hung from the wooden rack on the wall beyond it. He stood, motionless, for several seconds and then made a decision.

The gloves he selected were short, reaching only to the wrist and were, in fact, more like mittens, tapering to a point, from which dangled a heavy steel D ring, and holding the thumb and fingers tightly together inside, so that any likelihood of Sara being able to perform tasks that required even the most basic dexterity was removed with cunning simplicity. There was a zip up the back of each, which purred closed effortlessly and a sturdy strap that then buckled about the wrist, hiding the zip tag from view. There were also, he saw, several small holes through which a padlock could be fastened, preventing anyone but the keyholder from unbuckling and removing the mitt, but that, he decided, was quite unnecessary under their present circumstances.

'Nice and secure,' he murmured and then paused, standing just to one side and slightly behind Sara, so that the blinkers prevented her from seeing him. For several seconds, Colin stood, just watching her, biting thoughtfully on his top lip as he studied her more closely, trying to see beyond and inside the fantastical image, the fetishistic icon that she had so willingly become. Tentatively, he reached out one hand, letting his fingers run gently over the taut flesh of her splendidly naked buttock. He saw her muscles tense, felt them twitch just slightly beneath his touch, but apart from that, she made not a move, made not the slightest sound, even.

Breathing in deeply, Colin moved slowly back in front of her and stood again, this time deliberately staring into her eyes, which shone back at him, unblinking, unflinching, wide and innocent, deep and unfathomable. Again he reached out, this time with both hands, thumbs and forefingers taking her burgeoning nipples in a gentle grasp, rolling the stiffened flesh softly between them. He was rewarded by a flaring of her nostrils and a slight and barely perceptible intake of breath, which Sara then let out again in a long and soundless sigh.

'I'm still not sure I really understand all this, Sa– . . . Sassie.' He corrected himself in the nick of time and, just for the briefest of instants, Colin thought he detected a flicker of humour in those deep green orbs, but then it was gone again and Sassie the pony-girl stood as mute and unemotional as was befitting her status.

'This really does turn you on, doesn't it?' he whispered. Still no response. He smiled crookedly. 'Well, I can't say it doesn't do anything for me, either,' he said, 'but you'll have to give me a bit of time to come to terms with it all. Celia said a few things that set me thinking, but I don't pretend to be any sort of psychologist.'

He released his grip on her nipples and let his hands fall to his sides, considering his next move and wondering if perhaps he may not have spoiled the mood for Sara, but, as he backed away and turned towards the shrouded gig, a sudden flash of comprehension struck him and he paused, looking back at the still motionless pony-girl.

'Trot,' he said, so quietly that his voice was barely more than a whisper. 'Trot to the end of the room and then trot back again. And let's see those legs well up in the air, or I'll have to take the crop to your quarters.'

The air in the small chamber seemed to grow suddenly very still and Colin had the unnerving sensation of time stopping. It seemed an age, an age in which he wondered whether perhaps he had not gone just a little too far and then, as if in slow motion, he saw Sara lift first one leg, raising the knee so that it was level with her navel and then, as the steel-shod hoof boot came clattering down on to the hard flagstone floor, repeat the move with the other, so that she pranced forward, buckles and brasses jangling, breasts bouncing proudly inside their leather cages.

Alex had known that the escape bid was doomed to failure from the moment the two native girls had pounced on Amaarini. If she had been given the option at the time, she knew she would almost certainly have refused to go with them, but that, she reflected, was then and this was now – and 'now' was looking decidedly unpromising from where Alex was viewing it.

It was not so much the thought of her pending punishment that was preying upon her, despite the fact that Amaarini had promised that the pain would be like nothing she could ever imagine. Pain, in Alex's opinion, was just that and, if it got too bad, she presumed her body

– even this new body that she was growing to hate so quickly – would shut down. Cloned, or even partially electronic, there were limits to the endurance of anything remotely human and, besides, Alex was only too aware that these people had nothing to gain and quite a lot of investment to lose if they pushed her too near to the point of total collapse.

For the moment, however, the worst aspect was the way in which they had succeeded in dehumanising her and the almost off-handed treatment she was now receiving at the hands of Higgy and the two younger grooms. To them, it seemed, she was no longer a naked and desirable female, but simply an animal, a creature in their charge that had to be prepared in accordance with precise instructions. Worse still, although they seemed in no hurry to bit or gag her again, she had been rendered completely unable to protest her treatment, or even to reply to the coarse asides they directed at her as they worked.

Having dried her thoroughly, they quickly moved on to clothing her again, this time in a skin-tight suit of the same rubbery-feeling fabric, except that now her new skin was pure white, as Higgy had promised it would be. And this time, as the boots, harness and bridle were brought out, Alex saw that they were all of a deep golden colour and set with jet-black studs and brasses.

'Going to have you looking as pretty as possible for this, Jangles.' Higgy smirked, as he eased her right foot into the first hoof boot. For a brief instant, Alex wondered about trying to kick his grinning face, but with the other grooms holding her with her arms pinioned behind her it would have been a gesture of the utmost futility and the fleeting feeling of satisfaction such an action might give her had to be weighed against the consequences it was sure to invoke.

She was, she realised, already in big trouble and although part of her brain was telling her that she was in so deep that things couldn't be made any worse, the larger and more practical section of her reasoning suspected that here there was never any such situation. Worse things could certainly be made for her and there seemed little point in trying to find out by just how much.

As if by way of reinforcing Alex's cautionary analysis, she now realised that these new boots were even higher in where the heel would have been had there been one and that the elevation of her feet was such that her feet were now actually being forced into an *en pointe* position. Under normal circumstances, she knew there would have been no way in which she could have stood with her feet in such a tortured contortion and even her new and stronger body would have struggled with it, but for the fact that the boots themselves laced so rigidly that they acted as supportive splints to her ankles and drew in tightly to give extra support to her calf and thigh muscles.

'Very nice.' Sol snickered, when Higgy finally gave them the order to release their hold on Alex. The young man walked slowly around Alex, looking her up and down with evident relish. Just for a few seconds, she saw, the mask of disinterest had been allowed to slip and she knew, just from the look in his eyes, that it would not be too much longer before he manoeuvred a situation where he would be able to take full advantage of her.

'Pay attention to your duties, laddie,' Higgy snapped at him. It was obvious to Alex that Higgy had detected Sol's 'unprofessional' interest and that he disapproved. To Higgy, the pony-girls down in this stable complex were only ever to be treated as if they genuinely walked on four hooves. He might well avail himself of their helpless favours too, as Alex knew he did, but compliments were only ever handed out as a groom would do to a favourite dumb animal.

'Stand, Jangles,' he commanded. 'Hooves together now and no shuffling.' Alex stared unblinkingly at him, her lips pressed tight together, wondering if the man had any real idea of what it was like to be made to wear such hideous footwear. Shuffling, walking – it was as much as she could do to retain her balance and moving about was the furthest thing from her mind at this moment.

'See to her forelegs, laddie,' Higgy instructed the other groom, Jonas. 'Wing style for this, I reckon. The sleeves are over there, on that bench.'

The sleeves to which he referred did not look particularly different from others Alex had worn, or seen being worn, during her still brief experience of the stables. They were white, to match her 'pony skin', rather than the gold of her tack and made of what appeared to be a very soft and surprisingly supple leather, though whether the leather was genuine or synthetic, she had no way of telling.

One at a time, they were drawn up her arms, her fingers and thumbs guided into the tight mitts at the ends, rendering her hands useless for all practical purposes, but even that was not enough. Once both sleeves had been laced tight to fit over her arms as closely as the basic body suit, each arm was folded up and back in turn, tiny metal snap clasps on the inside of each wrist then clipped to small metal rings set at the top of each sleeve, so that, when the grooms stepped away from her again, Alex was left with her arms folded up double and sticking slightly out from her torso.

She grimaced as she saw now why Higgy had referred to this method of securing her upper limbs as 'wing' style, for they now resembled nothing less than chicken wings and added an air of the ridiculous to her already humiliating position.

'They'll make you flap them for sure.' Higgy grinned, nodding his approval at what he saw. 'That Amaarini wants to see you do the dancing pony routine and she'll have quite an audience down here to watch it, you can be sure of that, Jangles!'

The remainder of their preparations were what had by now become fairly routine to Alex, though the girth corset was drawn much tighter than anything she had been made to endure before. Despite herself, she let out a sharp breath when Sol hauled on the adjusting straps yet again and was mortified to hear the high-pitched whinnying sound even that produced.

'Make sure that's as tight as you can make it,' Higgy instructed. 'If her ladyship thinks you've left even half an inch spare, she'll have your guts for her garters and probably your balls for earrings!' Sol snorted and looked up at Higgy, but decided to say nothing, but then, to Alex's horror, he began again on the line of straps, determined to tighten her girth even further . . .

Sara allowed Colin to back her between the shafts of the little gig trap without the slightest flicker of emotion, though he did notice how her breathing now seemed to be coming a little faster. Of course, he reflected, as he began fiddling with the buckles and straps that were provided for attaching her to the vehicle, that could have been in part due to the restrictions imposed by her corset girth, thanks to which her already trim waist now looked almost impossibly small.

There were two main traces, one on either side, that buckled to rings set conveniently to either side of this corset girth and these straps were designed to take most of the strain when Sara began to pull the cart and its burden. Along the length of the shafts there were other rings and staples, none of which appeared to have a particular purpose, but all of which had been provided, Colin reasoned, to permit the lucky pony owner to secure his 'animal' in a wide variety of ways.

Taking two tough-looking spring clips, Colin guided each of Sara's mitted hands back in turn and connected the rings at her fingertips to the most conveniently placed rings on the shafts, so that her arms were held out behind her, but at the same time imposed little real strain on them, unless she wished to use them to share in the burden when she finally began to move.

Working in silence, he uncoiled two much longer straps, each of which was fitted with a clip at one end and thus, he assumed, intended to be attached to either side of Sara's bit and stretch back to act as driving reins. Looping the free ends about the thin rail that rose up in front of the driver's pillion seat, Colin walked back across to the doors and then turned to study the overall effect that had now been created.

Immediately, he felt his pulse quicken and a definite stirring in his groin and he had to turn away, pretending to busy himself with the latch, for fear of betraying his growing excitement far too soon and ruining the ritual and atmosphere that he now knew had become so important to Sara. And, with that thought in mind, once he had pushed the doors wide open, he crossed back to the tack rack on the wall and took down the long coachman's whip and flicked it through the air experimentally.

The sharp cracks it produced sounded unnaturally loud in the confined space and although Sara stoically remained staring straight ahead, Colin saw her start in genuine surprise.

'Well,' he said quietly, 'you want to be a proper pony, don't you, Sassie? A few reminders from this little beauty will keep you up to your work.' He was just about to pull himself up on to the narrow seat when he saw the lanterns, sitting still half under the sheet that still covered the second buggy. How he had not noticed them properly before, Colin had no idea, for they were not exactly hidden and the light glinted off their brass finish quite brightly. Crossing the room, he stooped down and picked one of them up for closer examination.

'Oh, very neat,' he said, half to himself. 'Very authentic-looking finish, but much better than the originals would have been.' The lanterns were, in fact, fashioned to work more along the line of torches, powered by heavy batteries in their bases, the bulbs throwing out a powerful directional beam. Turning the lamp over and flipping open the hinged base, Colin saw that the battery pack was rechargeable and could be removed and replaced quite simply. As to where the charger unit was, if indeed Lachan had got as far as purchasing one, he had no idea, but when he flicked the switch on the side, Colin saw that the unit appeared to be near enough fully charged, so he dismissed that problem for the time being.

Taking the lanterns back to the gig, he now saw that there were two brackets, one set to each side of where the driver's rail supports rose up and that the lamp cases slotted into place quite simply. The brackets were angled just slightly, so that when the two beams were activated, they pointed gently inwards and merged together at a point some twenty metres in front of Sara.

'Well, you shouldn't fall over anything in the dark now, Sassie.' He grinned, finally mounting the gig. 'We'll just have to hope this place really is as remote as it looks, otherwise these lights might just bring someone nosing around.' He chuckled and paid out the whip, dangling it forward from its long handle, so that the tip hung just in front of Sara's face.

'Mind you, Sassie,' he continued, wrapping the driving reins carefully around his other hand, 'I dare say you'd like to find a nocturnal admirer or two, wouldn't you? Such a proud and pretty pony you are, eh? So, let's have ourselves a little evening drive, shall we?'

He flicked the whip, cracking the tip just to the right of Sara's head and then flicked it again, closer this time, so that the leather just brushed across her bare shoulders.

'Hey-hup, girl!' he cried, shaking the reins at the same time. 'Walk on! Walk on, I say!'

Geordie sat cross-legged on the end of the bed, trying not to smile as Melinda paraded back and forth across the room. Quite how she had succeeded in getting herself into the form-fitting red latex catsuit he was not sure, for she had insisted on retreating to the privacy of the bathroom to change and had not reappeared until she had donned the entire outfit, including the broad, studded leather belt, the steepling heeled boots and the gloves.

Except that they weren't gloves, Geordie saw, now that he looked closer. True they had fingers and thumbs and each one fitted its hand perfectly, but they were actually extensions to the catsuit sleeves and could not be removed separately. The hood, too, appeared to be part of the main garment, though at present it hung down across her breasts, limp and shapeless and swinging slightly to and fro as Melinda's body swayed in rhythm with her exaggerated promenading.

'What do you think?' she demanded, twirling around on one tiptoe. 'Pretty basic, compared to some of the outfits I've got, but perfectly adequate for what I have in mind.'

'And what might that be?' Geordie asked warily. He turned and leaned back and across the bed, reaching for his cigarettes and lighter, which he had left on the bedside cabinet. Whatever was coming, he had a shrewd idea that he was going to need a smoke first.

'Well,' Melinda replied, placing her hands on her hips, 'that depends very much on you and just how adventurous you feel like being. We don't have to travel over in costume, of course, but sometimes some of us do, just for the thrill of it.'

'Thrill?' Geordie queried. He took out a cigarette and placed it uncertainly between his lips. Melinda grinned at him.

'Well,' she said, her voice sounding huskier than before, 'there's always the chance of the car being pulled over by the police. It doesn't happen very often, of course, especially as we'd be driving in the dark, but you never can tell.'

'You've been stopped before, then?' Geordie asked. The thought of being pulled over by a couple of uniforms in a traffic car and with someone in the car dressed the way Melinda was now defied contemplation. Melinda nodded.

'A couple of times,' she said. 'The first time I was in the back of a friend's car, all dressed up as Millie the Maid, vinyl skirt round my armpits and a plunging neckline like you wouldn't believe. My friend was wearing all black rubber, though it was a fairly conventional-looking skirt and jacket, unless you looked at it from close up.

'The two cops were so taken with trying to look up my kilt that they nearly missed what was right in front of their eyes, but then one of them smelled the rubber and his eyes nearly popped out of his head. I thought he was actually going to start dribbling there and then.'

'I can imagine,' Geordie said. He lit his cigarette and took a lungful of smoke down. 'What did your friend say? Wasn't she even a tiny bit embarrassed?' Melinda giggled and slowly turned her back towards him, rotating her latex-clad buttocks with slow deliberation.

'That's the trouble with all policemen, in my experience,' she sighed. 'They always assume the obvious.'

'Oh?' Geordie let the smoke out in a long stream. 'I'm not sure I follow you.'

'Well, for a few minutes, neither did those two young coppers.' Melinda laughed, looking back over her shoulder at him and winking. 'But then the penny dropped and it was they who were embarrassed. You see,' she continued, turning slowly back again to face him, 'same as you just said, they assumed that because my friend was wearing a skirt –' She paused, letting her words hang in the air between them, where the smoke now curled lazily around in a shifting blue grey cloud.

'You mean your friend was a man in drag?' Geordie suddenly exclaimed, as the penny dropped. Melinda's grin grew even wider.

'Well,' she said, 'he wouldn't have liked the term "drag" particularly, but he was definitely male. Though,' she added, with a little snort of mirth, 'he made a pretty convincing woman until he opened his mouth to speak. Oh, you should have seen their faces!'

'Did they nick you?'

'What for?' Melinda looked genuinely shocked. 'We weren't breaking any laws. Keith – my friend – was well within the speed limits all the way and he doesn't drink alcohol at all, though they did ask him to blow in their little breath-testing thingie.'

'Well, maybe, but . . .' Geordie paused, confused and trying to unscramble his thoughts. 'They must have been able to do you for something. For fuck's sake, they were traffic cops and they can *always* find an excuse!'

'Well, they did look over the car pretty thoroughly,' Melinda admitted, 'but mostly I think they just wanted to get a longer look at Millie the Maid. They asked me to get out and I thought they were going to search me, but then I think they realised there wasn't really anywhere I could have been hiding anything in that uniform.'

'But your pal, this Keith? Surely they could have pulled him in for whatever – causing a public disturbance, or behaviour liable to, or something?'

'Nope.' Millie shook her head firmly. 'He had all his driving documents, plus other ID stuff and he wasn't breaking any laws at all. Once upon a time, maybe, in the dark old days, coppers could pull in blokes for wearing women's clothing, but not nowadays, not unless they're deliberately causing a potential nuisance in a public place and, as Keith pointed out, sitting behind the wheel of his car, he wasn't hurting anyone.

'After all, as he told them, *they* hadn't realised he was a man, not until they had stopped us and come right up to the window and even then it took them the best part of a minute. Of course, the fact that he was – and still is – a High Court judge probably helped him get the point across.'

'Well, if you think I'm going to drive to this weekend with your friends, dressed as a woman in a rubber dress, et cetera, you can think again, young lady. And I'd rather you travelled a little conservatively, if you don't mind. Acting detective constables don't carry the same legal clout as judges, but they still have careers and reputations to think about.'

'Whatever you say, master dear.' Melinda pouted, eyes shining. 'But that still gives us all night and, who knows, maybe I can persuade you to live a little and loosen up?' She reached up and took hold of the dangling hood, stretching it and raising it up to her face.

'Perhaps you could just put me in the boot of your car and pretend I'm your little rubber dolly, eh?' Geordie closed his eyes and took another drag on his cigarette. If his brief experience at Celia's bizarre farm had been somewhat educational, the coming few days promised to be revelational!

The grooms were taking their time with Alex now, first pulling the close-fitting pony hood over her head and threading her hair through the crown opening, tugging the awful ears until they sat correctly at either side of her head and drawing the elongated snout extension so that it fitted over her nose.

'Actually, I think I prefer them without these stupid pony-face things,' Jonas observed, stepping back whilst Sol disentangled the bridle straps in readiness for fitting them.

'She looks too much like a real animal now and that's a shame, if you ask me, seeing as how pretty she's been made.'

'Well, nobody *has* asked you,' Higgy snapped, 'and anyway, you're missing the point, laddie. The whole point of this muzzle,' he said, reaching out to pat the nose extension, 'is to help the silly mare understand just what she is now. Sooner she forgets about what she used to be and what she thinks she might still be, the better for all of us.

'She'll discover the alternatives this evening, of course.' He looked steadily into Alex's eyes and she thought she detected just a glimmer of compassion, a suspicion that seemed to be borne out by his next words.

'The thing to remember, Jangles,' he said softly, 'is that your punishment won't really last that long, no matter how it might seem to you at the time. And then, after it's all over, just you try to make sure that this is the last time you upset her bloody highness.' He leaned closer and his left hand gently cupped one of Alex's rubber-clad breasts.

'You try your best, Jangles,' he whispered, 'and I'll see if I can't put a word in for you. From what I hear, you wouldn't want to end up going over with that bloody dago git. Even *that* body would struggle to stand up to what he has in mind, I can tell you. Whatever you might think now, you take my word for it, Jangles – you'll be better off here, understand?'

Alex stared back at him impassively, unwilling to open her mouth, for fear that another of the hideous whinnying sounds would escape from it, but she nodded, nevertheless. Higgy mimicked her action and winked.

'You've got potential, Jangles,' he said. 'Old Higgy knows a pony-girl with potential, don't you worry about that.' He turned suddenly, as if he had only just remembered that the two younger grooms were standing so close, and fired an instruction at Jonas.

'Get her bridled and bitted now, you idle little bastard,' he snapped. 'Flat flange plate bit, mind you – the spiked bit can wait till nearer the time. No point in paining her too soon.' He wheeled around to Sol.

'And you,' he said, prodding a finger at the lad's chest, 'you can wipe that smile off your face and go and get the punishment stand ready. She wants it over there.' Higgy pointed again, this time to the centre of the concourse between the two rows of stable stalls. 'And bring the widest stand base, too. We don't want the poor filly toppling over halfway through proceedings. She's got enough to contend with, without that.'

'You worry too much,' Sol muttered, almost under his breath, but not quite quietly enough that Higgy did not hear him. However, although he opened his mouth to reply, the senior groom suddenly changed his mind and turned away.

'Just make sure you do as you're told,' he called back over his shoulder, as he retreated towards the stall where he knew Alex would eventually be returned after the evening's proceedings. 'And if I were you,' he added, in a whisper that was deliberately too low for Sol to hear, 'I would be the one who did all the worrying around here.' He shook his head and unlatched the top half of the stall door, turning to glance back at where the two lads were now fitting Alex's bridle as instructed.

'After all,' he muttered savagely, 'I ain't the one whose arse is gonna be in a sling, am I?'

The night air was crisp and clean, but not overly cold and Sara's shivers were more of anticipation and desire as she trotted along the bumpy mud track. What little breeze there was made her engorged nipples tingle and the fat dildo she had strapped inside herself – had her master realised it was there, she wondered vaguely – rubbed and rippled against her swollen clitoris with every proud, trotting step she took.

The hooves she had selected were steel shod, but not at all heavy, the horseshoes themselves thin and the filling of her raised hooves themselves clearly of some specially lightweight compound. In addition, the gig she pulled was perfectly balanced, the wheel rims covered in a thick, hard rubber, so that they seemed to skim over the uneven surface with little friction. As a result, she found she was able to keep up quite a good pace without tiring herself unduly and the occasional flicking of the whip across her shoulders served only to heighten the complete feeling of being possessed that had begun to overwhelm her from the first moment she had stripped off her everyday clothes in the little stable room.

She shook her head, forcing all thoughts of her normal existence from her mind. Now was not the time for such things, she knew. Now was the time of freedom, freedom in captivity, freedom away from everything mundane and supposedly normal. Her legs flexed and stretched; her hooved feet rose and fell; her nostrils flared, as she sucked in the virgin night air and, at the command of her driver master, bent anew between the shafts and picked up the pace from a trot to a loping canter . . .

'We can't know for certain that the Indian girl drowned, Rekoli,' the man the outside world knew as Keith Lineker said. 'Some of these primitive types exhibit amazing resilience.'

Richard Major – Rekoli only to his most intimate circle – shook his head.

'You're worrying far too much again, Ikothi,' he said. 'How long have we been in these islands now? You know as well as I do that the tides and currents here are lethal and the water temperature, even at this time of the year . . . if the girl managed to stay alive for even two hours, it would be nothing short of miraculous, especially considering how her body was used to much warmer climes than these.'

'And what about the body itself?' Lineker demanded. 'The sea rarely keeps what it claims. It could be washed up anywhere.'

'And probably will be, old friend,' Major agreed soothingly. He crossed the room and opened the drinks cabinet, taking out a large crystal decanter and two elegant glasses. 'I spoke with Boolik on the matter earlier. He has studied the local waters for many years now, as you know.

'According to his calculations, if the girl's body does resurface, it'll be washed up somewhere on the Swedish coast and by the time that finally happens, there won't be a lot of it left for the authorities to worry about. They'll ask a few questions around, no doubt, probably try to see if any ships have reported losing a passenger overboard, but it will be like looking for the proverbial needle in a haystack and they'll have far more pressing matters.

'One naked female, dead from drowning or hypothermia – what is there to interest anyone in that? I should imagine the newspapers in whatever area she finally washes up will play it up for the sensationalism of the nakedness, but it won't last more than a day or two and we are miles away from anything.'

'Except that if Boolik has worked out the prevailing currents,' Lineker pointed out, 'then so could someone else. It might just occur to someone that this naked female could have come from these islands.'

'Perhaps.' Major sighed. He replaced the stopper in the decanter and passed one of the glasses to his companion. 'On the other hand, she could have come from any one of more than a hundred islands hereabouts, or even from the mainland itself.

'If anyone asks, then we simply say that all our personnel are accounted for. Besides, our friends in the appropriate places will ensure that nobody takes too close an interest in us. They soon put a stop to the local police nosing around, didn't they?' He raised his own glass and sniffed delicately.

'Relax, Ikothi,' he said. 'And do try this new brandy. It really is excellent. Our little islands are perfectly secure, so do try to stop worrying. In another few days, the replacement stock will have arrived and you can get back to your work and all this will be forgotten.

'And on the positive side,' he added, glass still poised in mid air, 'this will serve to teach us to be even more careful in future. Discipline among the grooms must be reinforced with a sharp lesson. The lad at fault will be severely punished, as an example to the others. He can spend a week or two between the shafts himself and then he'll think twice before he steps over the line in future.'

Lineker raised on eyebrow. 'You want me to –?' he began, but Major raised a hand.

'No, not that,' he replied. 'He'll be of little real use to us if you swap him into a Jenny Ann body. I want to punish him, not turn him against us and fill him with resentment. No, let him suffer his punishment in his own body. I have already given Amaarini the necessary instructions.'

Geordie stretched back along the bed and sighed, peering up at the red vision from beneath half-closed eyes. Melinda was now covered in red latex from head to toe, the hood mask covering everything except for her eyes and mouth, with only two small openings beneath her nostrils to assist her breathing. Her hair emerged from a crown opening to cascade down across her shoulders, but that apart, Geordie thought, she now looked more like a crimson serpent than a human being.

'What do you want me to do?' he whispered, as she stood at the foot of the bed, looking down at him. He saw her lips curve into a broad smile.

'Nothing,' she replied flatly. 'Just stay as you are. Just as you are.'

And 'just as he was' in this case now was completely naked and with his manhood already more than half erect. It was curious, he reflected idly, as Melinda eased herself on to the end of the bed and squatted astride his feet, how this quite stunning woman seemed to become even sexier when covered with her tight rubber skin than she was whilst completely unclothed. It was something Geordie had spent little time dwelling on in the past, for his needs and desires had always been fairly uncomplicated, if not to say basic.

Stockings had always been something of a turn-on, to be sure, as were high heels, for they always added something to even the nicest legs, but rubber? He thought back briefly to the few hours he had spent at Celia's, recalling his first encounter with Melinda – or Millie the Maid, as she had been at that particular juncture. She had automatically assumed that Geordie was just another of the guests at the farm, but then the outfit he had found in the attic changing rooms had completely fooled her and it was a natural enough mistake for her to make.

'You can close your eyes, if you like,' Melinda said, inching further up the bed, so that she now straddled his knees. Geordie grinned back at her.

'But then I'd miss the best part, wouldn't I?' he countered and then shivered slightly, as she lowered herself just sufficiently so that the insides of her thighs brushed against the lower part of his own upper legs. The latex felt cool and smooth, despite the heat that he now knew from experience her body was already generating inside the impermeable skin.

'The best is yet to come,' she said, running one hand slowly up the outside of his thigh, the other resting in her own lap and then slowly burrowing in, seeking the flap of rubber that covered her sex. Geordie shivered again and reached up to cup her gleaming red breasts, shaped so stunningly by the rubber cups of the body suit. Melinda made no effort to stop him and he saw her stomach draw in even more tautly at the first contact. Her tongue appeared between her lips, following the rubber opening.

'No?' he asked, opening his eyes wider with the question. She sighed, very gently.

'Whatever you want,' she whispered. Her wandering hand found his stiffening shaft and gripped it gently. The coolness of the rubber should have been expected, but it still seemed to come as a surprise to Geordie. He groaned quietly and increased his pressure on her captive orbs.

'That's nice,' she whispered, peering downwards. 'Look, it's growing bigger and bigger.' She began to manipulate his erection with gentle precision and within seconds the head of his penis was bulging as if it must surely burst. Geordie steeled himself, trying to think of anything that might help him fight against the urge that was now threatening to overwhelm him. Melinda sensed his problem and stopped her ministrations.

'Steady now,' she teased. 'I don't want this going off prematurely. On the other hand,' she added, 'perhaps it would be for the better. Then we can concentrate on doing things properly afterwards.' Before Geordie could respond, she suddenly bent forward and, still gripping his organ, took the head fully into her open mouth, at the same time masturbating him once more with her fingers.

Instinctively, Geordie opened his mouth to call out and his hands started reaching for her shoulders, but it was already far too late. Even as he started to grip the slippery rubber, he felt himself lose all semblance of control and, with a gurgling cry, he ejaculated, to be rewarded by her full lips clamping themselves even more firmly to his rampant flesh, as Melinda greedily gulped his spendings to the very last drop.

As the grooms brought out the punishment stand, Alex quickly understood what was intended and a cold knot began to form itself in her stomach. Images of herself, perched on that stand, with probably that bitch Amaarini whipping her in front of however many people would be gathered to watch her punishment, crowded into her mind and she closed her eyes, fighting to shut them out.

Meantime, the two younger grooms went about their work with silent efficiency. First, they dragged out a shallow timber dais. It stood about ten inches high and measured approximately six feet square and from its centre rose a stubby metal post, perhaps eighteen inches high and an inch and a half in diameter, secured to the decking by means of a round metal plate and several bolts.

Over this elongated stud was slipped a much longer pole, sleeve fashion, this time rising to a height approaching four feet, Alex guessed, and not really one single pole, for as she peered at it with morbid curiosity, she saw that it appeared to be two poles of roughly equal length, joined at their centre by another inner tubular sleeve, a few inches of which was visible between the ends of the outer tube.

Quite what the purpose of this was, Alex could only imagine, though the most obvious guess she could make was that it afforded the facility for adjusting the overall height of the post and the awful seat that was now being affixed to the top of it. The term 'seat', Alex thought grimly, was not the right one, nor even would it have been accurate to describe the narrow, leather padded bar as a saddle, though that was far closer to the truth and she was reminded of her brother's racing cycle she had occasionally ridden as a teenager.

However, uncomfortable as Alex had found that, at least her brother's saddle had not been fitted with the awesome-looking phallus that projected up from the centre of this particular piece of equipment. The thing was eight or nine inches long, easily two inches thick and made from a black, shiny material that glistened under the overhead lights. Seeing Alex's horrified reaction to this, Higgy could not resist taunting her.

'Aye, y'll be well filled for your flogging, Jangles.' He cackled. 'Your own stallion to ride, eh? I'll wager my best boots y'll whinny a pretty song, all right.' Alex regarded him unblinkingly as ever, trying to hide the fear that was now beginning to overwhelm her, for she knew that he was almost certainly correct. Pain or pleasure – even pleasure of such a hideously enforced nature – would break through her determined silence eventually and she could imagine the reaction that would bring from those who Amaarini was gathering to watch her humiliation.

Jonas was now kneeling at the base of the structure and Alex saw that he was fitting a further refinement to the stand, about a foot from the wooden decking. A steel collar bolted around the tube, from which projected two horizontal metal bars, one on either side. They were only a few inches in length and at the end of each was fixed a circular metal shackle, obviously intended to be secured about a booted ankle.

It was both simple and horribly effective, Alex realised, for even though the height of the saddle and dildo was such that anyone impaled and seated upon it could not in the normal course of events dismount her perch unaided, the shackles removed any lingering danger of her managing to throw herself off in her agony and perhaps inflicting real injury upon herself.

'The woman wants you mounted half an hour before everyone starts gathering down here,' Higgy said. He consulted his wristwatch. 'That gives us nearly an hour and I'm hungry.' He turned to his two assistants. 'One of you go up and double-check the outer doors are secure,' he instructed. 'There's no one left on the outside, except the usual security patrol. Then you can decide between you who's going to stand watch at the top of the main corridor.

'Nobody is to come down here until I get back, understand? That's madam's own instructions, if anyone queries you. Any complaints, tell 'em to take it up with her.'

'I'll take the watch,' Jonas volunteered. 'I'm not particularly hungry at the moment. But what do I do with *her* in the meantime? Do you want me to put her in a stall till you get back?' Higgy shook his head, grinning.

'What's the point?' he said. 'She ain't goin' nowhere like that, is she? Those new hoof boots of hers will stifle her wanderlust and, besides, where is there for her to go? No, let her stay here and get a good look at what's in store for her. And while we're at it, open up the top doors of all the occupied stalls. Let some of the other mares and fillies see her.

'They'll be brought out to watch her being whipped, so they might as well enjoy the wait with her, eh?'

'I do not trust these people one single millimetre, patron.' Manuel Jesus Parillez regarded his employer with the look of a sullen child and the fingers of his right hand played lightly over the bulging left breast of his designer jacket. Even the clever cutting of the best tailor could not quite disguise the presence of Manuel's Magnum .357, Ramon Valerez observed, managing to hide his smile.

'You mean you do not *like* them, Manolo,' he replied pleasantly. 'It is not the same thing.' Parillez, stocky, swarthy, slightly balding and fiercely devoted to Valerez, curled his top lip back into a snarl.

'I do not like them, because I do not trust them,' he spat. 'So it is much the same thing, señor. I worry for you. Would you have it otherwise?' Valerez extended a hand to touch Parillez lightly on the arm and now he did smile.

'Of course not, my faithful Manolo,' he said softly. 'I know that you have only my well-being in that great heart of yours. However, you must trust to my judgement in these matters.' He paused, looking around the wooded glade, as if to reassure himself that they were still alone and unobserved. The entire island, he knew, was infested with bugging and monitoring devices and Richard Major's security team kept a constant watch on everything that happened within its approximate three square miles of windswept outcropping, but here, along one of the narrow paths that were too overgrown to be used for their outdoor mania with the pony-women, Valerez knew they were safe from eavesdroppers.

'Manolo,' he continued, turning aside to walk towards the stump of a long fallen tree, 'we must bide our time and try to remember our manners whilst we are here. These people are, after all, our hosts and, like them or not, trust them or otherwise, we must observe the proprieties.

'Whatever we may think of them, their so-called guests, or even their curious and even perverted obsessions, it does not alter the fact that they have something that we want, something we *need* even.'

'These robot women, you mean?' Parillez said the words as if they stung his lips on passing them and left a bad taste in his throat afterwards. 'It is not right, patron. It is against the will of God.'

'Manolo, Manolo,' Valerez said, sighing heavily, 'I have long since ceased to concern myself with the will of God, if indeed such an entity does exist. I concern myself purely with the benefits of this life and leave the afterlife, should there be one, to take care of itself and, if necessary, of my soul, which must surely be beyond saving by now in any case.

'Besides, do not your priests tell you that everything is the will of God? Good, bad, evil, corrupt – are we not supposed to have the gift of free will, eh? If your God was so against what these people have discovered here, would he not have stopped them before they found it?

'No, my old friend, there is nothing ungodly about this, even as there is nothing godly out there in the big wide world. Neither is there right nor wrong, simply what is possible and what is not. And these women are not robots, either, Manolo.

'They are little different from the men and women we take from the mountain villages back home, except that they are stronger and fitter and, thanks to the science of our friend Lineker, a lot easier to control. And the tough little animals friend Lineker will soon be producing for us will be better still, for they will come to us unburdened with previous existence, fresh and simple as newborn babies, but each girl with the strength of two men.

'Strength, Manolo, that we can harness and control at the touch of a few simple buttons, don't forget. Once we have Lineker installed in our nice new facility, we will have an almost inexhaustible supply of labour. Indeed, we could have our own army, if we needed it.'

'An army of women?' Parillez pulled a derisory face. 'Pah! Leave the women to the work and leave men to men's work. Or will this doctor fellow start breeding male slaves, too?'

Valerez lowered himself carefully on to the stump and sat back, reaching inside his jacket for his cigar case.

'Apparently not, Manolo,' he replied. 'It would appear that Dr Lineker is, as yet at least, unable to reproduce male clones, at least not ones that live beyond a few weeks. He did try to explain the reasons for this, but aside from something about genetic weaknesses, I'm afraid I was unable to understand a word he was saying.

'Besides,' he added, flipping open the lid of the case and extracting a slender panatella, 'it is scarcely important, from my point of view. The female clones are stronger than any normal-born male, so why worry ourselves that we have no bananas when we can have our fill of juicy avocados?'

'Yes, patron,' Parillez agreed sourly, 'but a man can give himself a stomachache from eating too much fruit, whatever it might be. And we have survived thus far because we have guarded our secrets closely, I remind you, much as these people seem to have done. We are opening doors here, patron, doors which once opened may not close again so easily.'

'Indeed, Manolo.' Valerez nodded. 'But then so are they, my old friend. So are they!'

Sara had been left far behind by the time Sassie reached the top of the rise. Gone was the smart, intelligent, fashionably dressed executive with her portfolio of degrees and business qualifications; gone was the articulate right arm of one of Europe's richest businessmen; gone too was the cool and haughty detachment that had been the hallmark of Sara Llewellyn-Smith. In her place now loped a gloriously naked pony-girl, free as the wind, despite the strictures of her harness and bit.

'Whoa, girl, whoa!' From behind her, she barely heard her master's command, but felt the steady tug on both reins that drew the rubber-covered bit deep into her mouth and slowed quickly through a trot, to a slow walk and then stood, panting for breath, vapour from nostrils and mouth forming small clouds before her face, her proud breasts rising and falling within their spiderweb leather lattices.

She felt the weight shift on the shafts at her sides and then lift almost completely, as Colin's boots landed on the packed mud of the pathway with a reassuringly solid thump. Deliberately, Sassie forced herself to remain looking straight ahead, as he walked up, first alongside her and then around to face her. In the pale moonlight, she could see that he was smiling, yet there was something else in his eyes and it troubled her that something seemed to be troubling him.

In his right hand, he held a water canteen and now, with his left hand, he tried, unsuccessfully, to spring the clip that held her bit to the main bridle. Snorting his annoyance, he placed the bottle carefully between his thighs and concentrated the co-ordinated efforts of both hands. This time he succeeded and he drew the spittle-soaked rubber bar from between her teeth and held up the bottle to her lips.

Gratefully, Sassie gulped several mouthfuls, oblivious to the cold splashes that rained down on her exposed bosom. Eventually, she managed to shake her head, indicating that she had drunk enough and Colin lowered the bottle and replaced the screw cap. Obediently, Sassie opened her mouth to receive the bit again, but he shook his head.

'Not yet, Sara – I mean Sassie,' he said, sounding unexpectedly hoarse. 'Or *do* I mean Sara? Dammit, I don't know.' He looked both confused and embarrassed and, as if to find something with which to cover his embarrassment, he stepped back past her and switched off the two battery-powered headlamps. Coming back once again, he did not stop until he had walked three or four paces in front of her and then he turned his head away, staring out to the distant hill line that ran black now against an almost black sky.

'I think I'm Sassie tonight, master,' Sassie whispered. Colin remained looking away from her and she waited, knowing now, she thought, what it was that was bothering him. 'Would you rather I wasn't?' she asked, eventually, when it became clear that he was either unwilling or unable to voice his misgivings. She saw him shrug, but still he didn't speak and she wished she had the use of her hands, if only to be able to touch him reassuringly on the shoulder or cheek.

'This whole business still doesn't sit too well for you, does it?' she said. 'Perhaps we should have talked about it more, but I thought – after the time at that farm that is – I thought you were starting to understand, the same as I think I came to understand what it was I really needed.'

'Nah, it's not your fault,' Colin said, but he still refused to meet her gaze, or even to look at her. 'It's me . . . all me. It's just that this all seems so weird. Here we are, out on some wild bloody moorland, me a damned policeman and you . . . well, what sort of money did Lachan pay you, eh? You're . . . well, whatever you are, I don't suppose you come cheap.'

'Maybe not,' Sara replied. Sassie seemed to have become subdued again for the moment, though her spirit was still very much present. 'And, to satisfy your policeman's inquisitiveness, Andrew paid me ninety thousand a year. Plus expenses,' she added, permitting herself a small smile behind his back.

'That's more than twice what I earn,' Colin retorted. At last he turned back, though only half-way, so that now she could see him in silhouetted profile. 'But that's not the point,' he continued. She tried to decide whether he was actually now looking at her from the corner of his eye, but it was impossible, for the moon was completely in the wrong place and his features were in deep shadow.

'The point is,' Sara said for him, guessing what was coming and impatient for them to get to the point as quickly as possible, 'is that you're not sure quite how come we've ended up in this situation, nor whether I really am quite happy like this.'

'Something like that,' he muttered. Now, finally, he did turn back to face her. 'I mean,' he said hesitantly, 'is this what you *really* want?' Sara gave a little laugh.

'Not permanently, no,' she replied evenly. 'But there's something about being like this that – well, it's hard to explain, but I felt it the first time I tried on one of these harnesses and then, out here on the moor and along the hillsides, especially in the darkness like this . . . I can't even begin to describe it, honestly I can't.

'And if you find all this a bit hard to take in,' she added, grimacing slightly, 'then how do you think I feel about it? I can imagine the looks on several hundred faces, if they saw me here like this, but I can also imagine some of the things that would be going through their minds.'

'Well,' Colin conceded, 'it'd be hard to blame any man for whatever he might think looking at . . . well, you know what I mean,' he finished lamely, with another shrug.

'So you do fancy me like this?' Sara challenged. Even in the darkness, she saw the mixture of expressions as his features kept changing. At last, after what seemed an interminable age, he formed a reply.

'Sara, I'd fancy you no matter how you were dressed,' he said slowly. 'Or undressed, for that matter. And this . . .' He made a gesture that encompassed both Sara and the gig and, she presumed, her harness and bridle. 'This is something between the two, I suppose. And yes, it's bloody erotic, if you must know.'

'Then why don't you just fuck me?' she demanded, with a bluntness that surprised even herself. 'I mean,' she added hastily, 'that's your privilege, if you choose. I willingly gave myself to be your pony-girl and that's supposed to be what happens between a pony-girl and her master, isn't it?'

'Yes. Yes, I had it all from Celia and I've seen all that stuff on the computer.' He sighed and placed his hands on his hips. 'The thing is, it all seems just a bit, well, cold almost.'

'I'm quite warm, actually,' Sara reposted. 'Though I'm going to start feeling cold if you're intending to keep me just standing here much longer.'

'Perhaps we should go back,' Colin suggested. 'I'll walk beside you this time. You must be pretty tired, pulling all that weight.'

'I'm all right, now I've rested a few minutes,' Sara said, shaking her head slightly. 'This cart is surprisingly well designed and it's not that heavy, not even with you in it. Of course, if you choose to lead me for a while, that would be your master's perogative.' She tried very hard not to smile as she spoke and almost succeeded. 'And of course,' she added, 'if I'm presuming too much, you could always replace my bit.'

'Yes, I suppose I could,' Colin conceded. 'And maybe I will – in a while. But first,' he continued, 'I want you to answer one question.' Sara nodded and, after another short delay, Colin asked her. This time she made no attempt to hide her smile.

'That's an easy one,' she said. 'The first time, when I was with your friend, Geordie, I felt as if I was bound to do anything he wanted of me, as he was my master, for want of a better word, even if he was a bit taken by surprise. If he had been the one to take me to Celia's, then things would maybe have turned out different, but he wasn't and they didn't.

'So, you're now my master – Sassie's master – and unless you actually give me to someone else, then that's it, I think. I'm yours, whenever I'm Sassie.'

'And what about when you go back to being Sara?' There was a short pause and the air between them seemed to grow thick.

'When I go back to being Sara,' she replied deliberately, 'I don't know. If it's anything like before, then I doubt I'll belong to anyone at all and I wouldn't want to make you any promises I know I might struggle to keep. However, the one thing I can say for sure is that you will always be Sassie's master now – or at least for as long as you still want to be.'

'I see.' Colin remained motionless and Sara could see that he was weighing her words carefully. Suddenly, and without any further warning, he stepped towards her, grasped the bit and pressed it between her lips. Sara made no effort to keep the rubber tube from passing between her teeth, but he had moved so swiftly that it would have been all the same if she had tried to, she realised. She heard the snap fastener click into place and then he stepped back again.

'Well then, Sassie,' he said and now his voice sounded more certain, 'I think we'll have another little trot and then we'll see just how willing you really are to please your master, right?' He smiled at her as he finished speaking and Sassie, now back in her rightful place, nodded her head in arrogant and excited agreement.

'Be very careful, Amaarini,' Richard Major warned. He stood with his back to the bank of monitors and the two security men who mounted watch over them. Amaarini, tall and resplendent in a tight-fitting catsuit of shimmering silver, her hair now dark with reflective silver streaks swept upwards to give her even more height, met his gaze unwaveringly.

'Something is worrying you, Rekoli?' she asked. 'You do not usually concern yourself in these disciplinary matters.'

'Disciplinary matters are usually internal matters,' Major replied. 'We do not usually involve our visitors, other than in the role of spectators. This is something quite different, I think.'

'I disagree, Rekoli,' Amaarini returned. 'The stupid escape attempt cost us half of Valerez's breeding stock, which in turn will involve him in a great deal of inconvenience and expense, not to mention the delay. I thought it would be a nice touch to offer him the opportunity of punishing one of those responsible.'

'Perhaps,' Major said. 'However, Señor Valerez is not our usual corrupt human, in case you had not noticed. He tends to regard much of what happens here with no little contempt.'

'Corrupt?' Amaarini echoed, wide-eyed. 'The fellow sells drugs that are responsible for death and misery over half this damned planet. If that is not corrupt, I'm sure I don't know what is!'

'I agree.' Major nodded. 'However, Valerez is one of those inexplicable examples of so-called humanity who is able to divorce values. Yes, he and his kind kill thousands and inflict misery on millions, but they would not see it that way, not for one moment. Their argument would be that people have a choice and that if they did not supply the wherewithal, someone else most certainly would, an argument I cannot really refute.

'What Valerez does is business, my dear, at least as far as he is concerned. He is in it for the money and the power that that money will buy him.'

'He is also a very dangerous human,' Amaarini growled. 'Very dangerous indeed. He is only human, it is true, but he is very cunning and totally ruthless.'

'He is what he is and we are what we are,' Major replied smoothly. 'As long as we are aware of his capabilities and motives, he should never be in a position to cause us any problems.'

'Neither should Lachan have been,' Amaarini reminded him. Major smiled.

'Touché!' he conceded. 'But Lachan has been dealt with now and we should be grateful to him for teaching us a much needed lesson. We allowed ourselves to become too confident, too complacent. It will not happen again. If and when – and I am certain it will be the latter – Señor Valerez tries whatever he ultimately has in mind, I am certain we shall be more than ready for him.'

At first sight, the stall was no larger, nor different, than most of the others on the south side of the concourse, but its spartan interior – straw-covered floor, steel drinking trough and the usual simple wall rack from which dangled a variety of bridles, bits and harnesses – did not tell all the story, nor did it reflect the special status of its two occupants, for the wall rack served a dual purpose and its second function was to disguise that section of the timber partition behind it that served as the door to an inner sanctum that was as unexpected as it was different from the outer chamber.

Here, two low beds replaced the straw-covered floor as sleeping arrangements and a flat television screen mounted in the white painted wall gave access to a myriad satellite television channels, whilst the twin speakers mounted to either side of this were connected to the music system that was likewise flush-mounted a few feet below the screen. There were also books, arranged in neat recessed shelves and a spotless vanity unit, the top of which was cluttered now with an assortment of shampoos and gels, waiting to be taken into the shower cubicle that was tucked away behind a sliding glass screen in the furthest corner.

The newcomer, or casual observer, might be forgiven for thinking they had wandered into a not inexpensive hotel room, albeit a room that shared one thing in common with the outer stall: a lack of windows, but one look at the occupants would have dispelled that thought in an instant, for their mode of dress – or rather lack of it – was not greatly different from that of the dozen or so less fortunate pony-girls who resided in the less well-appointed quarters elsewhere along the outer concourse.

There were two of them: tall, dark-haired, superbly proportioned and with perfectly sculpted facial features, each girl the mirror of the other, as alike as two peas in a pod and therefore, it would be supposed, identical twins, probably in their late twenties. However, on both counts, such a supposition would have been wrong, for not only was there a gulf of some third of a century between their birth dates, but the younger of the two had, in fact, been born male and had lived as such until only a few weeks earlier, carving out a career in business that had set him in the top few per cent of the world's richest men.

However, Andrew Lachan, billionaire entrepreneur and lifelong devotee of the cult of human ponies (female) had finally made his first real mistake in life and one that there could, it seemed, be no coming back from, regardless of all his wealth and influence, now left far behind in the outside world. Perched awkwardly on the end of the bed that had been allotted him for those nights when there were no other calls upon his time, Andrew – except that they now called him Bambi and he had quickly learned that not to respond to that new appellation brought swift and painful retribution – gazed sorrowfully towards his dopplegänger.

Jessie had been his Achilles heel and no mistake, he reflected mournfully. Beautiful, compliant, seemingly so satisfied with her curious lot in life, she had been only too willing to serve him with a dutiful devotion that had bordered upon compulsion and she had also, Andrew/Bambi knew, loved him more completely than he had ever thought it possible to love another human being. In return, he had come to love Jess just as fiercely, just as protectively, until she had become the most important single thing in his life.

The only drawback had been Richard Major's refusal to permit the beautiful creature to leave the island, no matter how much of a financial inducement Lachan had offered. True, because Lachan had paid such a handsome retaining fee, no other guest was ever permitted to enjoy Jess's favours, nor even to sit behind her whilst she pulled their cart and the Lachan money had ensured that she was kept in these luxury conditions when she was not serving her master, but it had somehow never been the same.

Andrew Lachan was a man who needed to own things outright, to possess completely, and he was not used to finding problems that his wealth could not solve. In the end, understanding that Major would not let Jessie go, no matter how much the offer was increased, he had resorted to other means, but the nocturnal raid on Ailsa Ness had been a disaster, despite the best efforts of his hired mercenaries, who had paid for their folly with their lives.

Andrew had expected Major and his followers to exact a similar revenge from himself, but as Major had been at pains to point out, his people were not murderers. Bambi's cute nose wrinkled now and her full lips formed into a sulking pout; it would have been better for Andrew if they had killed him then and there, rather than consigning him to this.

The unwilling pony-girl stared morosely down at herself, at the splendid female body that would hold her in its captive grasp for perhaps another three centuries, always a reminder of what the former Andrew had craved, a mockery of his weakness every time she looked at herself in a mirror, every time she was forced to listen to the jingle of the tiny bells that now hung from her ears and nipples, or the soft creaking of her body harness that whispered its taunts with every breath taken, with every rise and fall of her magnificent breasts.

'How could you stand being like this for so long?' The large eyes would have been tear-filled, had that been possible, but Andrew/Bambi now understood the reason why Jess's eyes had always been so free from expression, never blinking, even in the strongest sunlight or the fiercest sea breeze. 'Why did you never complain to me? You always seemed so content, Jess.'

Even the voice, identical in timbre and pitch, sounded like her and the resonance of it, inside Bambi's skull, was as much a cruel mockery as her physical appearance. Jess smiled thinly, and stared back at her stablemate.

'I *was* content,' she replied softly. 'I was perfectly happy, especially being *your* pony-girl. Not that it was ever bad here before you first came,' she continued. She turned half away and her lips set themselves into a pensive expression.

'I've tried to explain this to you,' she said. 'Even before, I tried to explain, but now I realise there's no way you could possibly understand and I feel so guilty that it's come to this.'

'No.' Bambi shook her head and the dark tresses that had been left hanging like a mane after the hair at either side of the head had been shaved away, swung in time with the movement. 'No, it's not your fault. It's mine, all of this. I could – no, I *should* have done something more. There were other, better ways and then we could both have been away and free of this place, these people . . .' Her voice tailed off and she lowered her head, gazing down at the heavy hoof boots into which her now delicately shaped feminine feet had been locked almost continuously since she had woken up in her new body.

'They've always been kind to me,' Jess said simply. 'And they saved my life, don't forget. My old body may not have been much to write home about in the first place, but they didn't just take me out of it for no reason. That bomb blast shattered just about everything. How it didn't kill me outright, I'll never know and I know the doctors at the hospital couldn't believe I was still alive.

'A miracle, they called it, but then I can remember thinking, as I was lying there, it wasn't much of a miracle and if that was the best God could do for me then he shouldn't have bothered. I just kept thinking I'd have been better off dead.

'And then, one day, I woke up to find there had been a real miracle. I wasn't just still alive, I had this.' She waved her hand to indicate her own body, the lightly tanned skin framed into erotically shaped sections by the heavy leather harness that was her perpetual identity. 'I had this beautiful new body, younger, fitter even than my old body before the explosion, and without pain.

'I was beautiful, And– Bambi,' she corrected herself, conscious of the fact that the room was bugged and that they could be being monitored, 'I was truly beautiful and for the first time in my life, men actually desired me.'

'And abused you,' Bambi muttered. 'And I was as guilty as the rest of them, wasn't I? How could you have loved me for that, eh?' Jess turned back to face her and smiled.

'I told you,' she replied, 'I could never hope to explain it to you, but I did love you and I wanted you to love me back, to possess me, to own me and to show me, in the way that you did, that I was something special to you. Never before in my life had I know anything like that.

'For the first years I was here, it's true, I was only supposed to be an object of desire and yes, I was abused in many ways, though even that I scarcely minded. The rules here are quite clear, as I'm sure you know, and besides, I was made to feel and understand just how much I owed my new masters. I'm not saying I was happy with everything that went on, but it quickly became an easy enough life and I was content.

'Then you came here and, for the first time in my life, I began to experience love. When you weren't here, I spent my every waking moment yearning for your return. I craved your touch, I longed for the sound of your voice and I lusted – yes, *lusted* – for the caress of your whip and for the feel of the wind in my mane and then finally for the warmth of your body.

'If you'd asked me,' she added, her voice dropping to the faintest whisper, 'I would probably have laid down my life for you.'

'I know.' There was a protracted silence, which Bambi finally broke. 'I realised how you felt,' she went on, finally. 'And I felt the same way about you. I offered Major more money than most men could ever hope to see in a lifetime, just so I could have you with me all the time.'

'In my nice warm stable, with all my nice new tack?' Jessie said, arching her eyebrows. Bambi looked away from her again, unable to answer. 'Well, despite what you may think, I think,' Jess said wistfully, 'it would have been nice. Oh yes.' She nodded, seeing the look of disbelief forming on Bambi's face. 'I would have enjoyed it totally. I *wanted* you to own me, don't you see?

'People outside of here will probably think I'm insane for thinking that way, but then why should I care what anyone else thinks? After all, what am I now, if not a simple pony-girl, eh? I had spent years learning how to be nothing else and even after this,' she said, her arm swinging round to take in the television, the books, the beds and the carpet on the floor between them, 'even after all this came along, I'd have swapped it all gladly, swapped it all for a bundle of straw in a bare stable, with you as my master.'

'And now it's all too late,' Bambi said flatly. 'It's all too late and it's all my fault. You must hate me, Jess. Now you'll be made to serve other masters again and who knows how they'll treat you.'

'You'll be made to serve too,' Jess pointed out. 'Amaarini says that we are to be a pair.' Bambi shuddered, for she had been trying to keep certain thoughts well to the back of her mind, even though she knew that what Jess said was inevitable. 'But at least,' Jess said, crossing the room now and laying a soft hand on Bambi's naked shoulder, 'we'll be together all the time.'

'That's little consolation, now.' Bambi looked up into her face. 'I'm no use to you now, Jess, not like this. I can't believe you can even bear to look at me any more.'

'You mean *you* can't bear to look at *me*,' Jess retorted. 'Well, I'm still the same person, still the same pony-girl. And I still have the same needs, as you'll eventually find out you have.'

'And that'll do me a lot of good, I'm sure,' Bambi snapped, pushing her hand away. 'This body is good for one thing and one thing only and that's not a thing I think you need.'

'Perhaps,' Jess said. She turned away and walked slowly and deliberately back across to her own bed. 'On the other hand,' she whispered, lowering herself gently and slowly lying back so that her weight was resting on her elbows, 'who can say what I might need? And, as my old grandmother used to say, do we want to die wondering?'

Ramon Valerez fingered the braided strap carefully, turning it over in his hands with a very dubious expression on his swarthy features.

'*This* is what you suggest I punish the bitch with?' he demanded. 'This is the sort of thing I would use to beat an errant child – it is no more than the belt with which to hold up a pair of breeches.'

'It does not look very dreadful, I agree,' Amaarini conceded. Her high brow and carefully arched eyebrows emphasised her look of contempt, but she made no effort to disguise it. 'However, *señor*,' she continued, emphasising the title with a curl of her lip, 'I was given to understand that you knew the exact nature of these later-type Jenny Ann bodies. I see, however, that you evidently do not.'

Valerez regarded her with barely concealed anger, for he was unused to being addressed in such an openly superior manner, least of all by a female. Back home, he would have had her flogged and then left to hang from her wrists for a day afterwards and if she died in the meantime . . .

However, although he would not admit it, not even to himself, there was something about the exotic woman that made him less than easy in her company and it was not just the fact that here, in the two islands, she had several somewhat unnerving security guards never far from her call. She was tall – very tall – it was true, but there was something more than just her sheer physical presence that made his stomach feel just a little cold. These people were possessed of some extraordinary technology: their weapons, the fabrics they used for their clothing and in the construction of certain other artifacts and, not least of all, whatever it was that Lineker used down in his underground laboratory or hospital, that enabled them to create new human life and in such an unbelievably short period of time.

Quite who or what they were, Valerez was not quite sure and it served his ultimate purpose to take Major at his word that they were descendants of a lost civilisation who had managed to keep their existence from the world at large for many centuries. But without being sure of the absolute truth, Valerez had no idea just how far he could go in his dealings with them, nor indeed how far he would have to go in order to succeed in ultimately gaining control over them. And, in Amaarini, he was dealing with one of their more powerful number; in time, he consoled himself, he would repay her for her thinly veiled insults and general impertinence, but for now he would simply have to bide his time.

'Your Dr Lineker and Señor Ricardo have told me certain things,' he replied, carefully, 'but there is clearly much that I do not yet know. Perhaps you would be so good as to enlighten me?' He forced himself to smile and Amaarini mimicked the expression, but he noted that her smile did not reach her cold, almost reptilian eyes (any more, in fact, than his own smile reached his eyes, a fact which Amaarini did not miss and that Valerez himself was unaware of).

'I'd be delighted, Señor Valerez,' Amaarini replied. She reached out and took the strap from him, wrapping one end of it tightly about her right hand and then, with a quick flick of the wrist, sent it hissing through the air to strike the outstretched palm of her left hand. The noise of the impact was startling, but Valerez saw that she did no more than slightly flinch. She offered the strap back to him.

'Would you like to try that yourself?' she asked. 'I can assure you, as you so rightly said, that there is very little pain beyond a mild stinging sensation. It would, as you observed, serve to discipline a child, but certainly it would hold no real terrors for a normal adult human.

'However,' she continued, her lips twitching into the semblance of another smile and one which did, this time, reach those eyes, 'we are not dealing with normal human beings here, as we are all aware. You know, of course, that the cloned host bodies are used to house the brains of fully developed humans and that the connections between those brains and the various nerves in those bodies is made electronically?'

'Of course.' Valerez nodded. 'That much was explained to me some while ago now.'

'The technology for achieving such a remarkable feat is very complicated,' Amaarini continued. 'Even *I* do not pretend to understand more than the basic idea, but then that is hardly my field, nor is it my concern, but I did make a few small suggestions, some of which the good doctor has been able to incorporate in the later bodies.

'For instance, in the earlier versions, the sensory system was boosted in certain areas, in particular the clones' responses to both pleasure and pain, especially the first, though their ability to withstand pain beyond the tolerances of an ordinary human has proved quite useful when it came to a certain number of our more overly exuberant guests.'

'And some of the less energetic found their girls' ability to respond eagerly to even the mildest of sexual stimuli also to their tastes?' Valerez suggested. Amaarini nodded.

'The problem was – if one could call it a problem – that it has sometimes been difficult to incorporate just the right levels of responses in any one body, in order to satisfy the requirements of many of our visitors. I'm sure I do not have to draw you pictures, señor?' Valerez grinned and gave a curt shake of his head.

'Well, I then thought how absolutely handy it would be,' Amaarini said, without the slightest hint of irony or sarcasm, 'if the various response levels could be made variable, so that pain tolerance could range from very high to very low and pleasure responses adjusted likewise.'

'Ah, yes,' Valerez said. 'Señor Ricardo has mentioned this to me, of course.' He paused, scratching at his chin. 'So, you are telling me that this – this Jangles, the one who was in the British police, that she will have her pain tolerance lowered for the purposes of her punishment?'

'Yes, exactly so,' Amaarini replied. 'The punishment will also serve as something of a defining experiment. The doctor has carried out some laboratory trials, naturally, but the variable units have never been fully field-tested, so it will be interesting to see just how the subject reacts under operational conditions.'

'You will reduce her pain tolerance to the minimum?'

Amaarini pursed her lips and frowned. 'That very much depends,' she said slowly. 'It has not yet been tried, even under laboratory-controlled conditions, so we really don't know just how much the different females can tolerate. It is not just a case of not damaging the bodies, you understand – they are stronger than normal anyway, as you well know – but of what the psyches can endure and also the physical strains on the brain itself.

'Unfortunately, until Dr Lineker can find a satisfactory way of cloning a fully functioning brain unit, we are still restricted by the brains we take from the donor bodies and their ability to withstand certain neurological shocks. And I regret to say, that in this one matter at least, the brains from our own gene stream are no better developed.'

'You mean these brains are likely to explode, or something like that?' Valerez laughed harshly. Once again, Amaarini shook her head.

'In a manner of speaking,' she said quietly, 'though not in any way that you would be able to see physically. The brain itself would remain looking largely as it does, so the doctor informs me, but everything within it will – well, it would be something like an electrical fire, with many areas melted and fused within the outer mass.'

'And the subject would then die?'

'Quite possibly.' Amaarini's eyebrows twitched almost imperceptibly, as they seemed to do whenever she was concentrating on mental images. 'Death would be one logical result, or madness, or a vegetative state. As I say, we do not yet know.' Valerez lifted an arm and consulted his watch.

'Well,' he drawled easily, 'perhaps we soon shall, eh?'

Sassie's breasts now rose and fell majestically, as she stood between the shafts, her lungs sucking in the sharp evening air, small droplets of perspiration reflecting the moonlight from her shoulders and chest, as they formed on her heated flesh. Before her, Colin stood now, holding the shortened lead rein and breathing heavily himself, although in his case it was for an almost entirely different reason.

'Beautiful!' he gasped. 'You are really beautiful, Sassie!' He stepped forward, leaning in to kiss her cheek, where it bulged above the bit strap, and then stooped slightly, this time kissing each swollen nipple in turn and drawing a muffled moan from behind Sassie's gag. Colin felt a cold ripple of desire rising up through his body and had to fight to keep his knees from trembling.

'I think there's only one thing I can possibly do now,' he rasped. Sassie's eyes were wide open, but her pupils seemed incredibly dilated and she hardly seemed to be seeing him. Colin caught his breath and hesitated for a moment, with his right hand already resting on his belt buckle. It seemed impossible that this could be the same woman who – but then, for the past half an hour he had been sitting up there behind her, watching her perfectly proportioned buttocks and legs, the curved back and the long neck, as she had run and run, seemingly with energy reserves that were superhuman.

He took half a pace back and bent to begin fumbling with the buckles that held the V-shaped crotch strap assembly to the bottom edge of the girth corset. His fingers pressed into her soft but taut flesh and again he heard her moan, watched transfixed as she thrust her still harnessed crotch towards him and now he could smell her, almost taste the lust as it oozed from her body.

'My God!' he gasped, as the two straps fell loosely away to reveal the flanged rubber base of the dildo with which she had plugged herself. 'Oh, my unsainted uncle!' Tentatively, he reached for the flat rubber disc, his fingers slipping as they encountered the juices that had long since been trickling out past the obstruction and it took Colin several awkward attempts before he was able to establish sufficient purchase to begin withdrawing it, but then, as he was able to grasp the base of the shaft itself, it slipped completely out and Colin half imagined that he heard a soft plopping sound.

The insides of the tops of Sassie's thighs were now thoroughly soaked and even though Colin could not see the evidence of her wild arousal in the poor light, the aroma was now stronger than ever and, as he dropped the rubber cock to one side and reached out for her opening again, his fingers slid at every contact and entered her without the slightest obstruction or resistance. He quickly found her clitoris, but it would have been harder not to, he realised, for the usually quite small nubbin was now swollen unbelievably and seemed to have grown in length, so that, in Colin's inflamed imagination, it felt like a small and very erect penis.

From behind the bit now came a most inhuman whinnying wail, which tore the still night asunder, before descending in pitch to become a roar and then a rattling growl that was at once awesome and terrifying in its intensity. Sassie's entire body arched forward in a stiff bow, with every muscle and sinew tensed and bulging beneath her pale flesh.

'Whoa, steady!' Colin whispered. 'Steady, gal!' He withdrew his fingers from her and returned his attentions to his belt buckle and this time it yielded to him first time. As he began to peel his breeches down his thighs, he realised that he had forgotten his riding boots, but there was no time now, for Sassie's need was even more desperate than his own and as his rampant shaft sprang free, he knew that the time for niceties was long past.

Shuffling forward again, awkwardly because the fabric of his breeches was now about his knees, he took himself in one hand and with the other grasped Sassie firmly by the hip. She peered back at his face from beneath hooded eyes, her face, white in the moonlight, framed and half obscured by the intricate straps and blinkers, but leaving no doubt in his mind as to what she wanted from him.

He flexed his knees, moved forward to stand between hoof-booted feet that had been obligingly parted for him and then rose again, guiding himself into her slippery, pulsing sex, gasping himself as her internal muscles gripped and sucked at his length with an unbelievable ferocity. Both his hands now came up, gripping her distended breasts, kneading them as he pulled himself closer to her.

'Steady, gal,' he whispered. 'Yes, that's better. Steady now, steady . . . aahhhh!' His strangulated scream of premature release merged with Sassie's most inhuman wail yet, and he fell forward against her, only her bondage between the shafts preventing her from toppling back and falling. Even so, the entire cart began to roll to the rear, so that together they began to descend in a slow arc, until Sassie lay suspended between the timbers as they dipped to touch the ground at their forward extremity. Colin found himself virtually lying on top of her, only his last ditch flash of comprehension and his reflexive action in grabbing at the shafts himself preventing his full weight from bearing down on her and perhaps dislocating her shoulders.

However, as the cart settled and he regained a measure of composure, Colin now saw that the couplings between Sassie's corset girth and the shafts were supporting most of her weight without too much discomfort, the weighted hooves keeping her feet down on to the ground and her captive hands in their leather sheaths, needing only to give her a measure of control over her lolling head and shoulders.

It was, he realised, an almost perfect position and one that he would remember for a very long time yet to come . . .

'I still don't quite get it, this fixation with rubber and pony harnesses,' Geordie said. He sat up on the bed, his back propped against a pile of pillows, his shoulders resting against the bedroom wall above the headboard. Melinda lay alongside him, but with her head in his lap, a head that was still tightly encased by the tight rubber hood, as was the rest of her body still sheathed in the matching catsuit and boots.

'Maybe you will,' she said drowsily, 'or maybe you won't. You've not made a bad start, I must say,' she added, opening one eye wider and peering up at his face, 'but then I do know it's not everyone's cup of tea.' Geordie breathed out a stream of cigarette smoke and looked down at her. She could, he realised, have been almost anybody, for the gleaming eyes and pouting red lips were the only humanising features left uncovered by the mask.

'But you must be feeling very . . . sweaty in that lot by now?' he ventured. 'I was absolutely boiling in that outfit at Celia's and we were outside in the open air for most of the time anyway.'

'*Very* sweaty,' Melinda confirmed. 'Very sweaty, very hot and very satisfied and I thank you most sincerely, kind sir, if not for your choice of expressions, then certainly for seeing to my most pressing needs.' Even with her features obscured, Geordie could tell that she was grinning widely and he reached out a hand, leaned over her and delivered what should have been a stinging slap to what he could see of her latex-covered rump; certainly the sound of the impact was quite spectacular, but Melinda hardly seemed to notice it, other than to tremble slightly and crane her neck so that she could reach his now flaccid organ with her tongue, which suddenly appeared, snake-like, from between her lips.

'You're incorrigible,' Geordie said, shaking his head in disbelief. 'Tell me, would you prefer I tied you up and took my belt to your backside?' He heard her snigger, though her face was now muffled by his lower stomach. 'Well, would you?' he persisted. 'I mean, I'm the first one to admit that I've got a lot to learn about all this, so I don't want to go putting my boot into something by mistake, so you'll need to tell me a few things.'

'Later,' she said, raising her face for a moment. 'There's no rush and you're going to need a bit of a recovery period, unless you're Superman, of course. You just lie back and relax, my lord and master, and let your little Millie doll say a proper thank-you for a damned good fucking – both the one you just gave her and also the one you're going to give her in a little while.'

After a few minutes on her own, Alex found that her leg muscles were beginning to suffer from being kept in one position for so long and, despite the extreme height of the new hoof boots, she concluded that the only way to relieve the cramping pains was to try to walk about a little. In any case, she reasoned, it was almost certain that her tormentors would expect her to be able to walk in the tortuous footwear before too long.

To her surprise, it proved to be less difficult than she had first assumed; this new body was still capable of surprising her with its resilience and basic strength, but then, as she peered down at the extreme bondage in which she had been placed yet again, she knew that very few ordinary human bodies would have been able to endure such treatment for more than a few minutes at best.

She shook her head in pitiful resignation. Such a miracle, such fantastic scientific achievement and yet what had it been consigned to? These people, whoever or whatever they were, surely they must see what a tragic and criminal waste it was to confine their fabulous knowledge to such narrow and perverted ends? Alex turned slowly to stare back at the punishment stand awaiting her and she knew that she would have been crying, had these eyes been capable of such a basic human reflex.

Yes, they knew all right – they not only knew, but they had made a deliberate choice, prostituting their science to the lowest common animal denominator, as surely as they prostituted their helpless victims, selling, or leasing, both to any bidders who could afford their asking price, the brooding, leering, emotionless 'visitors', who prowled the island complex in their leather, rubber, silks and satins, strutting in their heels and their boots, making use of the Jenny Ann girls as if they were nothing more than animals.

Where these visitors came from, who they were, what sort of corrupt thoughts invaded their minds, Alex had no idea. One or two of the faces seemed familiar, if only vaguely so, for those visitors who did not mask or hood their features with rubber or leather generally disguised them with outlandish make-up. However, one thing Alex was certain they all had in common was money. Whatever the 'going rate' was for a day's unhindered immorality here, it was plainly not cheap.

Bastards, she thought, bitterly. Inhuman bastards. I wonder if you'd still feel the same if you spent a few days in something like this? But then that's the whole point, isn't it? None of you is ever likely to find out what it's like to have these bloody boots on the other feet, are you?

She turned away from the stand and her gaze travelled slowly along the line of stalls, the top halves of the split-level stable doors mostly hooked back in the open position, though none of their inmates seemed to have so far been interested in taking advantage of this to look out at the lonely figure, as she walked slowly and precariously along the central concourse.

Probably only too glad that it was her and not them, Alex concluded. She wondered how she would react in their position, if it was her safe inside one of the spartan cubicles and some other unfortunate trapped and trussed and awaiting a horrific punishment from which she knew there could be no escape. Would she be able to turn away from the sickening scene? Would she be able to retreat inside her tiny prison and resist the urge to watch the poor creature's torment as she waited?

Alex closed her eyes and stood still, listening to the sound of her heart, as it beat soundly and solidly inside her chest and to her rasping breathing, as that same chest fought against the strictures of the girth corset and those awful, horribly enlarged breasts rose and fell in time. Suddenly, she felt very cold, but it was not a physical cold, nor did it have anything to do with the temperature here in this subterranean hell; rather it was a chill detachment that slowly began forming itself into an icy anger – not the heated rage of frustration and humiliation she had felt so often since first awaking in this caricature of a body, but a freezing, patient distillation that she knew now she could control and nurture until one day, however far in the future that day might yet be, she would unleash it upon these devils incarnate in a revenge so unspeakable that even she could not, as yet, imagine it.

Back in the stables once again, Colin quickly released Sassie from between the shafts, but when he raised his hands to remove her bit, the look in her eyes and the cursory shake of her head brought him up short.

'No?' He was unsure of quite what was expected of him next. Sassie fluttered her long eyelashes and managed to convey the fact that she was smiling, even though the bit obscured most of her mouth's ability to perform such a gesture. Colin smiled himself, took hold of the short-lead rein instead and led the unresisting pony-girl across the floor to the far wall, where he quickly looped the leather trace about a conveniently positioned hook.

Looking about him now, it was several seconds before he saw what he wanted next, a pale brown towel, one of two that were draped across the shafts of the second cart. Separating it from its twin, he brought it back over to where Sassie stood waiting patiently and opened it out between his hands.

'You've raised a good sweat out there, girl,' he said softly. 'Better give you a good rub-down and get you dry, otherwise next thing we know it'll be the vet for you. Equine flu, or whatever they call it.' He laughed quietly and began working his way up the uncovered portion of her left thigh.

She really did have the most beautiful skin, he told himself, lightly tanned and glistening under the sheen of her perspiration. Impulsively, he bent further, leaning forward to brush the skin lightly with his lips. To his surprise, despite everything, it felt cool to his touch and he saw her shiver slightly at the gentle contact.

'Better get you dried off first,' he muttered, redoubling his efforts on that front and within three or four minutes the task was completed. Putting aside the towel, he reached out a hand and touched her lightly on her crotch strap, immediately over where he knew the flanged base of the dildo would be, the dildo he had replaced after their frenetic love-making. Immediately, Sassie tensed and her eyes closed, as every visible muscle stiffened and strained again.

'I can't believe you've got the energy left,' Colin said, grinning. He pressed harder and even through the thick leather he could feel the rubber phallus pushing further inside her still. A muffled squeak escaped from behind the bit and her breathing rate increased yet again, but that apart there was no real reaction. As before, she was waiting to follow his lead, Colin realised.

'It may be against all the rules of this game,' he said softly, reaching over to unhitch the lead rein from the hook again, 'but I think this is one little filly who deserves a bit of home comfort. C'mon, Sassie, my beauty – time we domesticated you. Harness and hooves, I don't care, but the next time we're going to do it in a nice soft bed and, if you're still so full of beans, I reckon you can do the mounting.'

Higgy returned with just Jonas accompanying him, but the two grooms were more than enough to deal with Alex in her helplessly bound state and complete the final stages of her punishment preparations. Whilst Jonas held her head, Higgy moved across to where they had left the punishment stand and wheeled it slowly over the slightly uneven surface, stopping once or twice to gauge distances from either end and each side.

At last, it seemed that he was satisfied with its position and he motioned to Jonas.

'Bring her over,' he instructed. 'We'll put her up now and give her time to settle, before all the spectators start arriving.'

'Poor little mare,' Jonas whispered, half under his breath. Alex cast a look of surprise sideways, but the blinkers prevented her from getting a clear view of his face. Louder, he called out. 'We gonna lubricate that thing, or not? Don't wanna damage her, do we?'

'Lubricate her?' Higgy laughed. He reached into the pocket of his breeches and withdrew the now familiar control unit, aimed it at Alex and pressed for some adjustments. 'Just stroke her pussy a couple of times, lad.' He chuckled. 'She'll give herself all the lubrication she's likely to need now.'

To her horror and humiliation, Alex realised that this was no idle boast, for the moment the younger groom's fingers made contact, even with her swollen outer labia, she felt a thrill of what felt like lust shoot through her, though the reactions within the conscious part of her brain were more loathing than anything else. Almost immediately, she felt herself growing hotter and then the sensation of her juices oozing from her now gaping sex and beginning to seep on to the flesh of her inner thighs confirmed the efficiency of their dreadful manipulations of this now detested body in which they had imprisoned her. Jonas was visibly impressed.

'These new girls are something else!' he cried. 'How many more of them have been adapted like this one, Higgy?' The senior groom grunted and shook his head.

'Not many, so far,' he said. 'And don't you go getting carried away with no ideas, Jonas. Sol's already in the shit for trying to tup that little native filly, so you make sure you get all the right permissions before you think of trying to mess with this one. Besides, Amaarini's got her own plans and you don't wanna go treading on her toes, not unless you fancies a spell in harness yourself, with her driving you.'

'No thanks.' Jonas grinned. 'Still, maybe when her haughtiness gets tired of her, eh?' He moved in front of Alex, fondled her right breast gently and then ran his thumb across her nipple, which immediately began to grow even larger still. 'Maybe not too long, eh, beautiful?' He grinned. 'Don't know why, but there's something about you that I really like. What do you reckon, Higgy?'

'I reckon we ought to get her up and mounted,' Higgy snapped. 'If Amaarini comes down here early and her little prize attraction ain't ready, we could find ourselves up there instead and I don't fancy something that size stuck up me, thank you very much.'

'She wouldn't go that far, surely?' Jonas said. Higgy raised his eyebrows.

'You reckon not?' he retorted. 'Well, I'm not going to take the chance, me. She's in a funny mood at the moment and it ain't just that she's angry. Something's in the air, I tell you, and it ain't just seagulls. Now, shut your jabbering and get around on one side of her.'

They took station at either flank and gently but firmly guided Alex forward, up on to the raised portion of the dais, until she was standing immediately behind the upright pole, with its tiny saddle and awesome projecting dildo.

'Now, lass,' Higgy said, speaking to Alex in a very calm voice, 'this can be easy, or it can be hard. If you try to struggle, it makes it harder for us and harder for you. Stay quite still whilst we lift you and it's not that bad, I promise you.' Biting into the bit, Alex found herself wondering how he could possibly know what was bad or what wasn't, but she could see the logic of what he was telling her, so she nodded, trying to signify that she understood.

'That's a good girl.' He turned to Jonas, nodding. At the signal, Jonas bent slightly, hooking his left arm under Alex's right thigh, whilst on his side of her Higgy mirrored the action, right arm under left thigh. With their free hands, each of the men grasped at one of the straps that ran up from the back of the girth corset and held on tightly, effectively to keep Alex steady when her feet were lifted clear of the floor, which they now quickly were.

They raised her easily and she realised it was an exercise they must have carried out between them many times in the past and, as they poised her above the waiting phallus and then began lowering her smoothly on to it, she wondered just how many unfortunate females had sat this terrible saddle before her. However, as the thick shaft quickly filled her, sliding easily into her moistened sheath, her thoughts quickly turned away from such speculations, for already the presence of the intruder was taking its toll on her deliberately heightened senses.

Dimly, she was aware of them placing her booted ankles into the waiting fetters, clicking them shut and adjusting the heights so that her legs were held down perfectly straight, but by now she was past caring about anything, other than the heat and the turmoil that was beginning to rise and rage within her. As if from a distance, she heard Higgy's voice.

'Reckon I'd better turn the level down just a bit.' He snickered. 'If I leave her like this, she'll either boil over or blow up long before the main event starts.' Alex heard Jonas's higher-pitched laugh, but thankfully, as Higgy began to regulate her control unit, her fevered brain began to clear a little and she felt the heat in her body reducing until it finally became little more than a steadily throbbing warmth and the noise in her head a mere background buzzing.

* * *

Colin lay back on the bed, the upper half of his body propped up slightly by the heaped pillows and gazed up at the apparition above him. Sassie, still harnessed, bridled and with the bit still firmly between her teeth, kneeled straddled above him, the tip of his erection held firmly between the lips of her now burning sex. Her arms were free now, but she made no attempt to use them, concentrating instead on her legs and the quite staggering control she had over her vaginal muscles.

'You are stunning, Sassie.' Colin sighed and gritted his teeth in an effort to fight back the climax that was threatening to bring their latest coupling to a close. Desperately, he tried to blot her image from his mind, concentrating on boats, cars, fields, anything that would help him regain some semblance of control and eventually the threatened moment passed again. He opened his eyes and saw her eyes twinkling down at him, filled with amusement, as well as desire now.

'Naughty pony,' he whispered and reached up for her engorged nipples with both hands. 'Perhaps I should put you back in the nasty cold stable.' Except that they both knew there would be no nasty cold stable for Sassie this night. She rotated her hips and thrust herself down on to him, accepting his entire length and then gripping it tightly inside her.

'Whoa, girl!' Colin gasped, only too well aware that his regained control was of an ephemeral nature only and could be blown away in an instant if she kept this up. 'Good girl. Relax,' he ordered and sighed again as she obeyed. Lovingly, he ran his hands over her breasts and then slowly down her sides, fingers skimming over stiff leather and soft flesh alternately. He closed his eyes and let out a long, slow breath.

'Wherever we go after here,' he whispered, 'it's gonna break my bank book for sure. It's not enough I have an expensive car and a cruiser to maintain – now it looks like I have to build and run a bloody stable!'

The crowd of spectators that began to gather in the stables concourse was a typical cross section of what Alex had seen throughout the island since her arrival and she was reminded of that first fateful night, when she had watched from her hiding place as the pony-girl races took place.

As far as she could see – for some of their costumes could have been hiding all manner of truths – they were roughly equally divided between the sexes and, as ever, there was a great deal of leather and latex in evidence, with at least half the crowd wearing masks or hoods of one kind or another. Whether these masks were intended for fetishistic effect or pleasure, or whether they were being worn to protect the wearers' identities, Alex thought, was open to conjecture, for she already knew that more than one well-known celebrity made frequent use of the island's singular facilities and services.

Since Higgy had adjusted the controls for her pain and pleasure levels, Alex had managed to recover a degree of self-control and awareness and, as the little groups began to form a rough circle around the stand, she was able to overhear some of the conversations, especially as there were one or two voluble individuals intent on voicing their observations for general consumption. As on earlier occasions when she had come into contact with the paying visitors, Alex found it quite astonishing that none of them seemed to realise the true nature of the girls provided for their diversions, or, if any of them were privy to Ailsa's secret, they certainly gave no indication of the fact.

'I see what Amy meant,' one unusually tall female observed, nodding towards Alex. She was clad from neck to toe in a black leather catsuit and wore a highwayman-style mask across the upper half of her long features, with her black hair drawn back into a long ponytail. Amy, Alex knew, was one of the names by which the guests knew Amaarini.

'Splendid-looking filly, isn't she?' the leather-clad woman said. Her two companions, a man in a similar outfit, except that the leggings were looser fitting, and a shorter female in a full-length evening dress of shimmering red PVC, with matching half mask, nodded in agreement.

'Wonderful tits,' the man remarked. 'High and firm, despite their size.'

'Lovely body altogether,' the second woman interjected. 'Terrific muscle tone and really long legs.'

'Makes you wonder where they find them,' the leather woman said, her lips curving around into a smile that told Alex quite a story in itself. 'I mean, this one could be a model, if she wanted.'

If only you knew. Alex tried to ease her tongue beneath the bit, which moved slightly in her mouth as a result. This brought a further observation, this time from the man.

'They handle the bit so authentically,' he said. 'Just like a real pony. And I do so love the way that mask has been moulded. Horsey-looking, but still retaining that definite air of humanity.' *Humanity? You'll find little enough of that here, you stupid bastard. What would you know about humanity anyway? You're just waiting to see me flogged and perform that cow Amaarini's so-called Pony Dance.*

'I wonder how soon she'll be available again?' the tall woman pondered. She took half a step forward and looked up into Alex's face. 'I think I'd enjoy having you pull my buggy for a few days,' she announced, her smile widening still further. *Among other things. I just bet you would!*

'Is it right they don't let the pony-girls up into the bedroom levels?' the other woman asked. The man grinned. Unlike the women, his features were undisguised and Alex could see that he had a rather florid complexion. At a guess, she thought, he was in his late forties, starting to go to fat and probably drinking far too much into the bargain.

'Not the permanent ones,' he said. 'They like to keep them in character all the time they're here, so they tell me. Letting them up above can break the concentration, they reckon. Did you know they won't even speak down here when their bits are removed?'

Won't? Can't, more like. Paralysing sprays were used to disable the girls' vocal cords whenever they were let out alone with visitors, Alex knew. No chances were taken that a girl might let the truth slip and now, of course, she was one of the new generation, for whom the simple press of a button replaced anaesthesia and reduced her vocal abilities to those of the pony she had been attired to represent. *Science gone mad!*

'I wonder what she's thinking,' a woman to Alex's left piped up. She was petite, with hair so white blonde it had to be artificial, Alex decided, and dressed in a rubber version of a circus ringmaster's outfit, except that she wore skin-tight leggings in place of the usual riding jodhpur alternative, with spike-heeled, knee-high boots to complete the ensemble. Her face was not masked, but her make-up was so extreme that it effectively disguised what she must look like in everyday life.

'Probably thinking about that cock she's sitting on,' the man next to her said. Whether they were actually a couple was hard to tell, but his garb was completely at odds with the woman's theme. Leather trousers and heavy biker boots were topped with a sleeveless leather tunic and he wore a parody of a uniform cap, the entire outfit being in pristine white leather. He wore pale lipstick and soft eye shadow and Alex suspected he would have been more impressed if it had been a male subject about to be punished, rather than herself.

'I must ask where they got the rather ingenious stand from,' he continued. 'I rather think I'd like to get one of those for my special barn and I can think of just the person to give it a try-out.' He ended with a girlish snigger, a surprisingly feminine sound considering his heavily muscled build, though perhaps not so when given his overall appearance. The ringmistress chuckled with him.

'Me too,' she agreed. 'Mind you, I think they make a lot of this stuff in-house, so we'd probably need to look around for a specialist manufacturer. I have a couple of phone numbers in my room, if you'd like them. Excellent craftsmanship, reasonable prices and no questions asked,' she finished, tapping the side of her nose with a meaningful forefinger. The man nodded eagerly.

'Yes, please,' he enthused. 'That would be absolutely darling of you.'

His earlier observations were not far off the mark, Alex was forced to admit to herself. Even with the threshold control set lower, the presence of the dildo within her could not be ignored and whilst there was no real stimulation at the moment, she could feel her vaginal muscles pulsing steadily against it and a steady, if low heat between her thighs.

The various conversations continued for several minutes more and Alex now found herself wishing that Amaarini would make her entrance. Whatever horrors were still to be endured, the waiting seemed interminable and she knew that the longer she was left to imagine what was to come, the worse things would be in the end. The sooner her punishment began, the sooner this dreadful humiliation would be over, but then, she realised, this delay and public display was probably all part of Amaarini's overall scheme.

The bitch would be here when she was ready and not before, Alex knew, and then her real trial would begin. Trying not to move her head, she cast her gaze across those people she could see within the limited field of vision permitted her by the blinkers. Yes, that would be the real punishment, she reflected grimly. The pain would be bad, but it would fade and go in time. Worse than the pain was the now certain knowledge that, in what could only be a matter of minutes now, she would be made to display her total helplessness and surrender to her body in front of these gawping, perverted voyeurs, who would then probably carry away the image of her sufferings and use it for their private gratification for a long time afterwards.

Geordie flipped off the mobile phone and tossed it on to the end of the bed. Melinda, still dressed for one of her 'Millie' roles in the red catsuit, but now minus the matching helmet mask, lay back against the disorderly pile of pillows and looked up questioningly.

'Problem?' she asked.

Geordie pursed his lips and scratched his jaw with two fingers. 'Not as such,' he said. 'More of a curiosity, really.'

'Oh?' Melinda smiled encouragingly. 'Going to tell me about it,' she asked, 'or is it some terrible police secret?' He shook his head.

'No, not a secret,' he said. 'In fact, it's not really even official, though the governor thought I'd like to know about it.'

'The governor?'

'Gillespie,' Geordie said. 'Detective Inspector George Gillespie. My governor up there.'

'Ah, yes. Of course.' Melinda chuckled to herself. 'You mean you really do call each other things like "guv" and "skip"?' she said, clearly amused by the idea. Geordie mirrored her grin.

''Fraid so,' he admitted. 'Though "sarge" is more usual than "skip" in most nicks. That tends to be more the Met and the Sweeney in particular.'

'The gung-ho boys, you mean?'

'And girls, these days,' Geordie said. 'Some of the women are even more gung-ho than the lads, or they were when I worked there.'

'Sounds like you've been around a bit, my bonnie Geordie lad,' Melinda teased. Geordie snorted.

'Just a bit,' he agreed. 'Anyway, old George just heard something he thought might be of interest to me. Something that might be relevant in the Alex Gregory case.'

'The policewoman who died? But I thought that was supposed to be an accident?'

'Supposed to be,' Geordie agreed. 'Probably was, if the truth ever be told, but I still keep getting these little nagging feelings. Can't explain them, nor why, but Alex had her own suspicions and the accident theory could be just too pat. Call it the male equivalent of women's intuition, if you like.'

'So, what's your guvnor's latest news, then?'

'Well, it was all a bit garbled,' Geordie said, perching himself on the foot of the bed. 'Something about a Norwegian trawler and some foreign girl. He said it was too involved to explain on the phone, but that there's some Norwegian copper arriving up there tomorrow night.

'It's actually part of our regular liaison swaps, but this particular guy was there when the trawler arrived back at its base and he's also bringing the video tape of some interview that good old George reckons I might like to see. He knows Colin and I have been pursuing our own private inquiries, so this is all a bit on the quiet still.'

'Sounds intriguing,' Melinda said. 'Does that mean we have to forget about our wicked weekend?'

'Would you mind too much?' She shook her head and sat upright, swinging her long legs over the side of the bed.

'No, not really,' she replied. 'Hopefully, there'll be plenty more wicked weekends, if you haven't lost interest in me by then and I enjoy a good mystery. Is it still all right if I come up with you? I can pay my own air fare, if we're flying.'

'Well, I can pay it for you,' Geordie said. 'I can claim mine on expenses, but I don't think they'd wear me putting in for yours, not even if you were Miss Marple herself.'

Alex's eyes narrowed as she saw the sallow figure of the South American close on Amaarini's heels. Behind him again was another man, heavier in build and clearly another Latin, probably some sort of personal bodyguard, she guessed. Obviously Valerez was intent on witnessing her punishment, probably because one of his precious native girls had been lost as a result of their abortive escape bid.

Poor little Samba. Taken out of her own world, out of her depth, unlike her companion, the quiet and plainly petrified girl they called Gypsy, she had the sort of spirit that wasn't easily crushed and it had been she who had engineered the opportunity for the three of them to get away, and the young groom, Sol, had probably been lucky to escape with no more than a bruised skull when she tried to brain him with that stone.

Not content with that, the diminutive girl had then tackled Amaarini herself, filling a long rubber glove with stones and using it as a makeshift and very effective club. It was probably as well for her, Alex thought, that she hadn't survived the adventure, for Amaarini would surely have made her continued existence a living hell for what she had done to her. Maybe Samba had realised that and that had persuaded her to make her desperate attempt to get off the island by braving the deadly waters around the place.

There was no way she could have survived, Alex knew. Even small craft got into difficulties in those treacherous currents, with razor-sharp rocks lurking inches below the surface and temperatures that could numb a body into paralysis in less than an hour – minutes even, during the winter months. Even taking Gypsy's rubber catsuit to wear over her own would offer only limited protection against the cold, though Alex had to admire the uneducated lassie's ingenuity in working that one out for herself.

She wouldn't have let Samba even try it, had she known what the girl was planning, but then Samba probably knew that also, which was why she had slipped away from the tiny cave whilst Alex was sleeping. It hadn't taken Alex long to work out what had happened once she woke up, despite Gypsy's total lack of English and then, seeing the remaining girl hunched there, shivering and naked, there had only been one sensible course left to them.

Gypsy had been reluctant, but Alex could see that she understood, that she would die of exposure herself, unless they found proper shelter and food and there was only one place they could find that, even though it meant giving themselves up to the guards who had been sent to scour the island for the escapees. She wondered what was happening to Gypsy now. Without her more robust friend, she would be feeling totally abandoned, scared out of what wits she had, as like as not. She would be paying for Samba's defiance and attempted mutiny and yet she was no more than the innocent stooge in it all and the loss of her friend would hurt her more than anything Amaarini or her cohorts could think up, Alex was sure.

What a waste. What a terrible, terrible waste. She thought back to her all too brief acquaintance with Samba, recalling the native girl's cheeky grin and dancing eyes, the way in which she would draw herself upright, thrusting her firm little breasts proudly out and her comical attempts at mastering English and the few phrases she had picked up so quickly.

Alex peered down at herself as Amaarini and her small cortège approached, the circle of spectators parting respectfully to allow them through. She knew exactly what Samba would have said about her current situation. It was the one phrase she seemed to be able to make fit a variey of circumstances, including Amaarini's condition after she had whacked her over the head with her deadly weighted glove.

'Well fucked!' she had exclaimed gleefully. Well, Alex thought, she wouldn't have been so gleeful about all this, but her words seemed to sum Alex's own plight as succinctly as any others she could think of.

Sara emerged from the bathroom, swathed in towels, her hair still dripping and her arms still showing faint red marks from the tight gloves, but her face glowed with vitality and her eyes were still bright. Colin looked up from his notebook and smiled at her, now feeling somewhat sheepish.

'Everything all right?' he asked. Sara nodded, ran the fingers of one hand through her damp tresses and grinned back at him.

'Any reason it shouldn't be?' she said. Their eyes locked for several seconds and then she relented, crossing the remaining distance between them and stooping to plant a wet kiss on his forehead. 'Don't worry,' she urged him. 'It was absolutely wonderful – all of it.'

'Yeah, I know,' he conceded. 'I thought so, too. It's just that afterwards, now, well, you know what I mean?'

'Of course I do,' she said consolingly. She back-pedalled the few feet to the bed and sat down, bringing one corner of the top towel up to rub a particularly wet area of her hair. 'I feel a bit that way, too,' she confessed. 'A bit silly, I suppose, but then I'm determined not to even think about it. I intend to go on being Sassie and I want to be Sassie for you and no one else, all the time you still want me, that is.

'So, the one thing we have to get straight is that Sara and Sassie are two entirely different creatures, right? And the normal you – this you – is different again from the man who is Sassie's master. So, when we're like this, we won't even mention Sassie and her master, if that makes it easier for you.'

'Would it make it easier for you, too?' Sara frowned, considering the question and then nodded.

'Yes, it would,' she replied eventually. 'All we need to do is work out some sort of code we can use, so we each know when the other fancies playing stablemates, yes?'

'Yes.' Colin closed the notebook and leaned back in the chair. 'Two different worlds,' he mused. 'And now the outside world is trying to interrupt.' He tapped the mobile phone that lay on the table before him. 'Geordie phoned, while you were in the bath.'

'Oh?' The memory of Geordie finding her in Lachan's stable that first time, she resplendent in the tack and bridle he had intended for his Jessie, whoever she was, flickered into Sara's mind, but she quickly thrust it aside. 'What did he want?'

'Wanted to know if I could make it up to Scotland for a few days, to the Shetland Islands, to be more precise.'

'And can you?'

Colin shrugged. 'I can manage most things,' he said. 'My job gives me a lot of personal discretion. We don't just guard important people, we're supposed to go out and look for possible future dangers.'

'And you both think you might find one up there?'

'Possibly. We do know that Healthglow crowd is decidedly moody, though we don't actually have too much proof as to what they might be hoping to achieve, aside from making a small fortune out of people like –' He stopped in mid-sentence, realising what he was about to say.

'Anyway,' he continued, changing tack abruptly, 'I can make it up there, no problem. I was wondering if you fancied coming along for the trip. Lovely scenery up there, so I'm told. Melinda's going, by the way.'

'Quite remote, those islands,' Sara mused. 'Got room in the car for a few bits and pieces?' Colin grinned, but shook his head.

'We'll need to fly up and then take the ferry across,' he said. 'There's someone Geordie is going to meet and he reckons I should be there too, so we don't have a lot of time to spare.'

'Oh well.' Sara sighed. 'It was a nice idea, but maybe those Shetlanders aren't quite ready to meet up with Sassie in the middle of the night. So, what time's the flight?'

'This particular pony-girl has been specially conditioned,' Amaarini announced to the eager gathering. 'A combination of hypnosis and a recently developed prototype drug ensures that she will now be particularly receptive to even the slightest sexual stimulation, whilst at the same time her perception of pain has been altered.'

Obviously the majority, if not all the crowd were not in on the big secret, Alex thought to herself. She looked to where Higgy now stood just to Amaarini's right. In his hand he held the little black control unit, but he was keeping it close to his side, not making it obvious. Alex drew in a deep breath; any moment now he would be using the device and then it would all start.

'Our pony-girl here – her name is Jangles, for those of you who do not already know – will find even the mildest slap, even a simple flick from something as innocuous as this,' Amaarini continued, pointing to the strap that Valerez now held up for all to see, 'so apparently painful that she will react as if she were being flogged by two lead-tipped bullwhips simultaneously.

'She will writhe around as if she were being immersed in scalding water and, in doing so of course, she will simply stimulate herself more.' Amaarini cast her gaze from side to side. 'Presumably you have all noticed the nature of her little perch,' she said smugly. There was a general murmur and a few laughs.

'She is, of course, properly bitted, but the doctor has earlier administered a drug to her larynx, so that all the noises she can now make will be appropriate to her condition as a pony-girl. Our special guest here, Señor Cortiga,' she continued, indicating Valerez, 'has agreed to undertake her punishment himself.' So, Señor Valerez was keeping his true identity under wraps, Alex mused. Not totally surprising.

'So now, ladies and gentlemen,' Amaarini said, lifting one arm in the air in a grand gesture, 'if you are all ready, Señor Cortiga will begin.' As she spoke, Alex saw Higgy make a few discreet adjustments to the control unit and instantly she felt the changes inside her body. From being an almost passive presence, now the dildo suddenly seemed to have grown and even felt as if it were somehow alive, as even the slightest pulsing of her muscles sent supercharged messages to her brain.

The abrupt change in perception had caused Alex to momentarily forget about Valerez, but now the first blow from the flimsy-looking strap landed across her lower stomach. Valerez barely seemed to have put any effort behind the swing and the thin leather itself looked so improbable as an implement of punishment, but the effect was like an electric shock.

Alex let out an agonised whinny, her head jerking backwards, her entire body lifting as far as her fettered ankles would allow and every muscle in her body tensed and screamed in sympathy with the wounded area. At the same time, the sudden movement caused the dildo to trigger a set of equally intense impulses, whose message to the receptors was diametrically at odds with the first ones. A huge wave of sexual pleasure spread outwards and upwards, lust battling with agony, so that any remaining logic or control was smashed aside.

Only dimly was Alex aware of the impassive figure before her, standing, waiting, observing, as the uncontrollable orgasm shook her to her very core and the spectators, initially agape at what they were seeing, broke into spontaneous applause and cheering.

'There is no rush,' Alex heard Amaarini saying in the distance, as the tide began to ebb again. 'Each stroke of her punishment will bring her to a new peak of agony, which will almost immediately become a tremendous climax. Pain and pleasure, ladies and gentleman, the ultimate demonstration of a dichotomy that I know fascinates you all.'

Valerez's arm rose and fell again and once more the searing agony thrust Alex to the very precipice of existence, only for her to tumble back into a spiralling abyss of a totally different nature. Unashamedly now, for she was past caring, she heard the whinnying of her own pony voice as she rode the twin crests of desire and abandon, no longer caring for anything except that which her now captive mind conceived within its cruelly altered state.

'Is this *it*?' Melinda stood on the quayside, looking towards the cluster of buildings that marked the beginning of Lerwick itself. 'It's a bit, well, *remote*-looking, isn't it? Whatever happened to civilisation?'

'Don't say things like that too loudly.' Geordie grinned. 'The locals don't take too kindly to that sort of talk. There were civilised settlements up here when most of England was still full of bog dwellers, so they tell me. Besides, the ale's good and the whisky is out of this world.'

'It'd need to be.' Melinda drew her jacket closer about her and shivered. 'Christ, but it feels cold up here.'

'Well, we're well into autumn now and we're also closer to Norway than we are to London,' Geordie pointed out. 'A hell of a lot closer, as it happens.'

'How far north of here is Norway, then?' Melinda asked. Geordie laughed and turned, pointing out to sea.

'North?' he echoed. 'Try east. Over that way. We're roughly level with southern Norway, if you look on the map, and further north than most of Denmark, if I've got my geography right. This place was Viking territory once, which is why so many of the locals have Norse-sounding names. Mind you, they'll tell you that the old place hasn't been the same since the soft Jocks started infiltrating and then the English, like me.'

'And me?' Melinda grinned at him and Geordie smirked.

'You might get special dispensation,' he said. 'Your average Viking has always had a soft spot for blonde females.' He bent down and picked up their two travelling bags. 'C'mon then,' he said. 'Let's get you off this jetty before you freeze your bits off. I've got a place about a mile and a half over that way.' He nodded in the direction of the town.

'No taxis?' Melinda raised her precise eyebrows. Geordie shook his head.

'Not this time of the year,' he said. 'Not regular, anyway. Besides, the walk will do us both good. And don't worry,' he added, 'I do have a little car, if I can remember where I parked it.'

'This is Miz Johnsson,' Detective Inspector George Gillespie said. 'Our guest from across the waters,' he added. Geordie and Colin did simultaneous double-takes, but quickly recovered their composure; though when the tall, blonde Norwegian policewoman unfolded what appeared to be endless legs from beneath the desk and stood up to greet them, two sets of pulses went into impromptu overdrive.

'Nice to meet you, Miz Johnsson,' Colin said, extending his hand. Long fingers grasped his own, a cool palm, to match the cool blue eyes.

'Do call me Anna, please,' she said. 'And you must be Colin?'

'And I'm Geordie,' Geordie said, pressing his own hand towards her. Anna Johnsson smiled and nodded.

'From Newcastle,' she said. 'My father was a great supporter and follower of your football team. The Magpies?'

'Aye, you've got it,' Geordie said. 'H'away the lads.' He stepped back. 'But, a bit of footie aside, the boss tells us you've got something you think might be of interest, like?'

Celia Butler regarded the two waiting figures and smiled contentedly to herself. She had spent a lot of time preparing the current tableau, but now, as she surveyed the black-walled room, there was little doubt in her mind that the effort had been worthwhile and the five discreet video cameras would produce some excellent footage. Afterwards, a few hours of expert cutting in Basil's well-equipped editing suite and the finished result would be one of their best productions yet.

The films were still a relatively new venture for Celia, but already she wondered why she hadn't thought of it a lot earlier. Few, if any, of the players featured in most of the films were aware of it, but as they were almost invariably masked in some way or other, this hardly seemed to be an ethical question as far as she was concerned. Loin knew the truth, of course, but then Loin was a special case and, besides, part of his original contract had specified that he waived all rights and agreed to obey Celia in all matters.

In return, when he finally grew too old to continue to fulfil his current duties authentically, there would be the steadily growing bank deposit for him to retire on and always, Celia had promised him, a place for him to live within her small network of establishments.

Looking at him now, she found it almost impossible to imagine that time coming and, given the difference in their ages, Celia was realistic enough to acknowledge the fact that she would be classed as fairly elderly herself when it did. Surgery, cosmetics and diet could help arrest most of the outward signs of ageing, but there was no denying to herself the little aches and twinges that betrayed the truth on the inside. The clock continued to tick and its irrevocable influences could not be held at bay indefinitely.

Loin, however, was still in his magnificent prime, a delicate, though athletically built young man, slim yet wirily strong and with a stamina level that matched the astonishing organ that had prompted Celia to give him his name. Even in its flaccid state, his manhood was of unbelievable proportions and when excited and fully erect, many were the startled females who had writhed in squealing passion upon it. Not even Celia's penchant for dressing her young charge in a variety of effeminate costumes could disguise what he really was and so she enjoyed the paradoxes that she could create with him to their utmost.

This afternoon, she had attired him in a pair of lurex tights, from which the crotch had been carefully cut and then hemmed around, so that his massive organ was revealed in all its staggering glory. On his feet he wore one of the specially made pairs of high-heeled boots, laced to mid-calf level, so that he was forced to mince about on near tiptoe.

About his waist was a bright crimson waist cincher of gleaming satin, trimmed with black lace at top and bottom and his arms were encased in full-length gloves of more satin, their colour matching the base colour of the corset. His neck was locked into a high collar which appeared to have been made from black velvet, but a closer inspection would reveal that the velvet concealed an inner lining of thin steel, two and a half inches high, hinged at the back and locking together beneath a camouflaging bow beneath his chin.

This collar in turn secured the red, doeskin helmet which completely covered his face and head, leaving only acutely angled slits for his eyes, two tiny apertures beneath his nose and a perfectly round opening, reinforced with a hidden steel ring, which aligned with his mouth. What there was of his flesh still on display had been coloured pure white, using a new body paint that Celia had discovered in London, so that the overall effect was not just bizarre, but almost oriental in its way.

The female half of Celia's latest cast was equally as tall as Loin, but much heavier in build, due to her penchant for body-building classes. Every muscle in her body had been developed almost to the point of obscenity in Celia's opinion and but for the presence of her magnificent breasts, she might easily have been mistaken for a member of the opposite sex. Even her facial features had a square and masculine look to them, but that would scarcely matter today, for she had been masked in identical fashion to her male co-star and the rest of her costume mirrored his too, except that the colour scheme in her case was white with gold trimmings and her sparkling tights were in a powder blue.

Silently, the cameras whirred away as the action began. Pulling her own half mask into place to hide her own identity, Celia stepped forward, crop in hand and slapped the braided leather against her highly polished black thigh boot.

'Down on your knees,' she ordered, pointing the whip at the girl. With a feminine grace that belied her prominent musculature, the anonymous female obeyed. Loin, without needing to be told, moved slowly towards her, poised perfectly so that his limp shaft dangled invitingly before the rounded opening over her mouth. Once again, Celia slapped the side of her boot and two white gloved hands rose slowly, one cupping his heavy balls, the other encircling the base of his weapon and lifting it so that the dark purple knob was raised conveniently for the next stage of the ritual.

With studied deliberation, she drew him into her mouth, letting her lips slide slowly up and down his length, so that gradually it began to stir and swell. She was a natural, Celia thought, with great satisfaction, but this was the first time she had encountered Loin and any moment now she would realise just what she was being confronted with.

Sure enough, after less than a minute and with Loin still only halfway aroused, Celia saw the look of astonishment in the half-hidden eyes and heard the startled gasping choke as the burgeoning shaft took its toll. Instinctively, the woman tried to pull back, but Celia was anticipating the reaction and was too quick for her. Stepping briskly forward, she thrust the crop against the back of her neck.

'Be still!' she snapped. Surprised, the woman obeyed, frozen with her mouth agape around a flesh and blood gag that was increasing in length and girth by the second now. 'Remain as you are,' Celia ordered. She turned away and scooped up the intricate arrangement of straps from the bench behind her and, turning back again, she passed these to Loin. Further instructions were unnecessary.

With practised efficiency, he deftly untangled the web and quickly began fitting one half of the harness about his waist and thighs, drawing it snugly about himself and then, finally, looping the appropriate strap about the base of his still swelling organ, passing it behind his swollen scrotum and buckling it tightly. Celia leaned forward to check his handiwork and nodded her approval.

'Continue,' she said to him and now he turned his attention to the remaining straps and began arranging them about the woman's helmeted head to form a snug harness. 'Excellent,' Celia said, when he had finished. The eyes that peered out from the white helmet were now filled with apprehension, for their owner had at last realised the purpose of the exercise and could already appreciate the efficiency of the double harness. Now, unless she dared risk Celia's wrath in unbuckling the straps, she could no longer withdraw her mouth from Loin's finally stiffening erection and the only degree of movement left to her had been carefully calculated so that she could finally satisfy him with her distended lips.

Allowing her a few seconds to appreciate her predicament, Celia now moved in to ensure her one possible means of escape was removed. Almost before her victim had time to appreciate the full extent of her predicament, she now found herself with her wrists cuffed together, her arms pinioned securely behind her back, so that even if she had been contemplating removing the harness, it was now too late to do so.

'Gently now, Loin,' Celia commanded. She saw his head nod slightly in acknowledgement and then, deliberately, he raised his own arms and placed his hands behind his neck. Then and only then did he begin, arching himself carefully forward and feeding more of his length into her. 'Try not to choke her.' Celia chuckled. The sound would be edited into the finished film at a later stage, so her evident amusement would not matter, as long as her posture did nothing to betray her to the cameras.

The girl let out a gurgle of protest, but already she was beginning to understand and now she took up the rhythm herself and Loin relaxed, so that all the while she maintained her efforts, she was at least now able to control exactly how much of him she sucked in each time and was therefore spared the worst of it. Nevertheless, Celia thought, as she stood contentedly watching her performance, it was an impressive effort and a promising curtain raiser to the rest of the performance she had choreographed for them.

'Interesting,' Colin mused, as the television screen disintegrated into tiny white spots. They were in the small office at the end of the corridor, where Lerwick's finest technology, in the shape of a video player and twenty-two-inch television set were kept, usually undisturbed by Lerwick's finest constabulary.

'You say the trawlermen picked this girl up when?'

'Four days ago,' Anna replied. 'Well, nearer five, I suppose. They say she was all but unconscious when they found her, but by the time they got her back to shore, she was quite recovered. A remarkable young lady.'

'Canny little lass, too,' Geordie said. 'But what sort of lingo was that she was talking?'

'Well, that's the interesting part,' Anna replied. 'There were a few words of English, as you undoubtedly picked up on, plus she appears to have a limited Spanish vocabulary. As for the rest, it would appear that it's a quite obscure Indian dialect, spoken only among a few tribes in the Andes.'

'As in South America?' Geordie asked. Anna nodded.

'Exactly,' she said. 'One of my colleagues had a moment of inspiration and we contacted a professor from the University of Oslo. Unfortunately, although he is an expert in the languages of that part of the world, even he struggled with her particular dialect, though he was able to give us a very rough translation of what she was trying to tell us.'

'And that was?' Colin interjected.

'Well,' Anna said carefully, 'it's still very vague, you should understand, but it would appear that she and another girl from her tribe were abducted and brought across, almost certainly in a submarine, although her language has no word for that, of course.

'They were held prisoner, apparently below ground, and then they managed to escape. There was a man, she says, and he tried to rape her. To be brutal about it, he did rape her, but she then managed to grab a rock, or stone, and laid him out with it.' Anna's expression betrayed nothing less than admiration.

'She then managed to free her friend and then another woman. She calls her "pony-woman", though what that means we cannot be sure. The three of them then made a run for it, but found themselves trapped. The girl – her real name is a complete soup of unpronounceable letters, but she now calls herself Samba – told us that they were on a small land about which was a big river on all sides.' There was a momentary silence and then Colin spoke.

'An island,' he said. 'Big river equals sea.'

'That's what we thought,' Anna agreed. 'From what we've been able to establish, this Samba girl would never have seen the sea. Her home village was in the mountains, in an area somewhere near Colombia, so the only words they have for water are river and lake.'

'Amazing,' Colin said. 'And they say the world is shrinking.'

'There are still little enclaves that have survived the onslaught of technology,' Anna Johnsson said. 'Samba was obviously from one of them. But she is a resourceful girl, nonetheless. When the fishermen found her, she was wearing a rubber catsuit. At first, they thought it was a wetsuit, but it was quite different.

'She also had a second, identical suit, which she had managed to use as a life preserver. Somehow, she had contrived to inflate part of it and knot it off so that the air was trapped in the legs and lower portion and she then used the arms of the suit to tie it to her. As a result, she stayed afloat until the trawler found her.'

'Nice one,' Geordie said. 'Very clever.'

'*Very* clever,' Anna agreed. 'It saved her life.'

'And very interesting indeed,' Colin agreed. 'But what's in it for us?'

'Ah,' Anna replied, smiling. 'Now we come to it. Remember this "pony-woman" character? Well, according to little Samba, the pony-woman's real name was Alex and she was some sort of soldier, as near as the language translates.'

'Soldier?' Geordie echoed.

'Girl soldier who keeps the peace,' Anna said. 'As near as it translates, this Alex was a policewoman.'

A heavy silence descended on the room. After several very long seconds, Geordie broke it.

'Impossible,' he whispered. He looked across to Colin, who merely shrugged and then turned back to Anna.

'Nah,' he said. 'No way.'

'Probably not,' she said. 'But Samba says that this Alex told her that she'd jumped from this big iron bird and then the people on the island had turned her into a different woman. She also mentioned a name.'

'She did?' Geordie could feel the hairs on his neck starting to prickle. 'And what name was that?'

'Well,' Anna replied carefully, 'the nearest translation we could get was Jodie. But what do you think?' Geordie blinked and then shook his head.

'Nah,' he said again. 'No way.'

Sol stared at the semi-circle of faces, his own features deathly pale.

'No!' he cried. 'You can't do this to me. OK, I made a silly mistake, but this is crazy.' Higgy shrugged.

'Rules are rules, laddie,' he said simply. 'And you broke 'em. Madam reckons you've got to be punished for that, so that's it.'

'It's not fair!' the young groom wailed. 'It could have happened to any of us. The stupid little bitch was a psycho. How was I supposed to know that?'

'Aye, you're right,' Higgy agreed. 'It could have happened to any of us – but it didn't. It happened to you and *she* has decided you need to be punished.'

'Not like this!' Sol screeched. Higgy shrugged again.

'Could be worse,' he said. 'And it ain't like it's for ever. One month, she said.'

'No!' Sol screamed. 'No, I won't! Let me talk to her. Let me explain!'

'Won't do no good,' Higgy replied. 'Better you accept it and let us get on with it.' Sol's eyes darted from side to side. He saw the pony-girl watching him from behind the door of her stable, her eyes blank. 'No,' he whimpered. 'You can't do that to me.'

The girl caught her breath and fought back the reflexive urge to gag, closing her eyes and trying to relax her throat muscles. The size of the erect organ that filled her mouth and was threatening to choke her was incredible and Jilly had never imagined a man could be so well endowed until now.

The two short straps that joined her head harness to the straps that encircled Loin's waist and thighs were apparently not made of leather at all, but thick flat strips of some sort of elasticated material, allowing her just enough movement back and forth to fellate him efficiently, while not quite sufficiently slack to remove her lips from his erection completely.

How long she had been kneeling there, head bobbing, she had no idea. It seemed like for ever, but she realised it was probably only a matter of minutes so far. Desperately, she tried to peer sideways, tried to catch a glimpse of Celia, the mistress to whom she had so willingly surrendered her freedom for the weekend, hoping the woman would realise that she was reaching the end of her endurance abilities, but Celia was now somewhere behind her, it appeared, and a sudden flick across Jilly's shoulders with the braided crop confirmed this.

'Get working harder, slut!' Jilly heard her amused voice order. 'Call yourself a decent slave. Come on, work on him. Let's see you drain that giant cock, if you're up to it!'

Unfortunately, as Jilly had realised quite early on in the proceedings, bringing the incredibly endowed Loin to a climax was not going to be an easy challenge. Despite the steady pulsing she could feel against her soft lips, there seemed little imminent likelihood of him losing control; his ability to achieve the maximum enjoyment from her efforts without coming remotely close to an orgasm was almost superhuman.

Eyes bulging, Jilly managed to swallow some of the saliva that was collecting in her mouth and then, breathing deeply through her nostrils, she redoubled her assault, realising that there was no way she was going to be released from her ordeal until she succeeded in breeching his iron defence mechanism.

This was not what she had anticipated when she answered the discreet little advert, she thought. Neither had Celia given her any true indication of the lengths to which she would be expected to go, but then, she thought desperately, sucking furiously and working her tongue against the underside of his shaft, she realised now that she hadn't really had any idea of just what she was committing herself to.

It had long been a dream that needed satisfying, a longing that none of her relationships had ever been likely to fulfil; not one of the men in her life previously had been capable of understanding just what it was she wanted from them, just what it was she was prepared to give to them. But then, she was now starting to comprehend, neither had she truly understood what it really meant to surrender one's self completely into the control of another.

She let out a stifled moan and was rewarded by the light pressure of Loin's hands on either side of her hooded skull. Her eyes flickered upwards and she could just make out his own masked visage, the exposed mouth curving upwards into what could only be a smile. He held her motionless for several seconds, preventing her from continuing her oral masturbation of him, and the groan that welled up inside her this time was born of sheer frustration.

'You don't think it could be her?' Colin sat back in the deep armchair and looked across at Geordie, who in turn looked back at him blankly.

'Well, there's no way it could be, is there?' he replied. 'I mean, we saw her body and we went to the funeral. No, Alex Gregory was dead all right.'

'So who was this pony-woman?' Colin challenged. 'She knew your name, don't forget.'

'Fuck knows,' Geordie said. 'It's got to be a coincidence. It can't be anything else, can it?'

'Search me,' Colin said. 'I never knew the woman, don't forget. You *are* sure it was her body, I suppose?' Geordie nodded.

'Yes,' he said simply. 'It was Alex all right.'

'So who was this pony-woman called Alex, this lady soldier, policewoman, whatever?'

'How the fuck should I know?' Geordie stood up, walked slowly across the room and picked up the whisky bottle. 'I don't know, Col,' he said. 'All I do know is that there's no way it could be our Alex. Our Alex is dead.'

'So you said,' Colin murmured. 'So you said. So how many Alexes are there up here?'

'Listen,' Geordie said, looking back over his shoulder. 'We don't even know that was really her name and we don't know for sure it was an island, even. And even then, we don't know it was one of these islands.'

'Well, the Viking princess showed us the charts,' Colin pointed out. 'If it was an island – and it sounds like it had to be – it was almost certainly one of this group. If the gal had gone into the waters off the Orkneys, there's no way she could have survived the cold long enough, even if the currents had been right.'

'So,' Geordie said, pausing to take a sip from his recharged glass, 'what are you saying? You reckon Alex Gregory has come back from the dead, eh?' Colin sighed and leaned back even further into his seat.

'I'm not saying anything,' he said. 'I agree with you, none of this makes any sense. But I do think we should look into it further, maybe go over to Norway and see the girl for ourselves.'

'And what good would that do?' Geordie retorted. 'She doesn't speak English; she's obviously traumatised from her ordeal . . . Colin, what can she tell us that we don't already know?' Colin held up his hands in a gesture of surrender.

'Don't ask me,' he conceded. 'But what else can we do? Forget the whole thing? If nothing else, we have a girl who was abducted, held against her will on one of these islands and talking about other women who were also held in the same place.

'It may amount to nothing, obviously, but it might at least give you an excuse to get a warrant and go and have another look at that bloody island. And this time, at least, we've got a much better idea of what might have been going on there!'

'You will now spend one full month in the stables,' Amaarini said, smiling vindictively at Sol. 'You will live under exactly the same conditions as the pony-girls and you will also be available to the guests, for whatever purposes they require you. If you fail to perform as befits your new role, extra time will be added to your stay here. Do I make myself clear?'

Sol nodded miserably, the only way he could now communicate, for the flanged bit in his mouth precluded all intelligible speech. He stared down at the ground, although the stiff collar prevented him from seeing properly the heavy hoof boots into which his feet were now laced and neither could he quite see some of the other refinements that Amaarini had ordered for him.

He could, however, feel the persistent pressure on his erect penis and scrotum, which had been laced into a soft leather sheath and then strapped up against the triangle of stiffer leather that now covered his entire groinal area, leaving a steel-ringed opening through which his genitalia had been squeezed out.

The upper side of this inverted triangle was affixed to the lower edge of the front of the tight corset girth and the pointed end tapered into a strap that had been passed between his legs and drawn up tautly between his buttocks to buckle to the back of the girth, at the same time holding firmly in place the rubber butt plug that Amaarini had insisted be part of his punishment. The long dildo felt even larger than it had looked and provoked a curious sensation of fullness in his stomach, but he knew there would be nothing he could do about this until someone decided to permit him a temporary respite to perform his necessary functions.

His arms had been laced into sleeves identical to those he had helped lace on to Alex only a few hours earlier and bent double in the same way, forming similarly ridiculous little wing shapes. Bridle and blinkers were of the standard pony-girl design and the only difference in his overall tack was that, not having breasts, the need for the usual complicated webbing harness above the girth was removed. His nipples, however, had been pierced, and now from the two rings dangled two small bells, which added to his sense of total humiliation every time he moved.

'Remember, Sol,' Amaarini warned him again, 'this could be prolonged indefinitely and if you give me cause to suspect that this isn't teaching you correct discipline, then I could just as easily speak to the doctor. Think about that, before you try any ideas you might have. Think of what it would be like to wake up back here one morning, with breasts and no manhood.'

Sol's eyes opened wide in horror and he made a muted gurgling sound behind the bit. Standing beside him, Higgy gave his lead rein a sharp tug and Amaarini's vicious smile widened still further.

'It's a great pity that the doctor can't produce genuine male clones,' she observed. 'Looking at you now, I suspect that there could be quite a demand for your services, both from our female clients and certain of the male ones. The subject has been mentioned before now, as you may have heard.' She stepped forward and patted Sol's imprisoned genitals.

'But I'm afraid this isn't going to get much exercise for the next few weeks,' she said drily. 'You'll be dosed every day, of course, to make sure it stays nice and hard, but it's only there for show whilst you're down here.' She stepped back again. 'Yes,' she said, raising her right hand to cup her chin, 'I should think most of our visitors will find that quite erotic, don't you, Higgy?' The senior groom nodded solemnly.

'I reckon so, ma'am,' he agreed. 'I can think of one or two of those women would fight over him now. But what do I do if they ask to, well, you know . . .?'

'Explain that he's under punishment,' Amaarini replied firmly. 'He is under strict punishment and is to be permitted no relief. Of course,' she added thoughtfully, 'it may be possible to fit some sort of prosthetic sheath over everything, something hard enough so that he feels no sensation at all. Do we have anything suitable?'

Higgy shook his head. 'Nothing on the shelves, ma'am,' he said. 'But I could take him up to the workshop level and see if they could make something special to fit.'

'Yes, do that,' she said. 'That would be even better. If they take a cast first, or perhaps use a holo-scan, it would ensure a perfect fit and thus no unwanted friction from movement. How about that, Sol? You're going to become a stallion who never tires and yet doesn't feel a thing when he covers a mare. Maybe that will teach you to respect your privileges here and make you a little more careful in the future.

'Yes, take him straight up, Higgy, and let me know when the prosthesis is ready. I think I'd like to oversee the fitting in person. Meantime, put him in with Jangles when you get him back here. You can exercise them as a pair and use my personal gig, if you like. The shafts can be adjusted to have them run side by side, as you know.'

'You want him worked out the same as the girls, ma'am?'

'Exactly the same. No privileges, no exceptions. Give them an early run out, so he gets used to his nice new hooves, just in case we get any early enquiries for him. I'll arrange for a notice to be put in today's guest bulletin, so he could get very busy later on this afternoon.'

'I'm sorry, laddie, but there's no way.' Detective Inspector George Gillespie turned his back on Geordie and Colin and stood staring out the window of his office. Out in the harbour, an assortment of masts swayed as the tide began to turn and the wind started to pick up. On the horizon, heavy rain clouds had begun to gather with unbelievable speed – unbelievable unless one had experience of the weather conditions in this most northerly part of the British Isles.

'There's no way you can even think I'd sanction a warrant application for another trip out to Carigillie,' Gillespie continued, after a heavily pregnant pause. 'After all, what do we have to go on, eh? One young lassie fished out of the sea and the fact that she mentioned the name Alex.' He turned back to face into the room.

'OK, so it was me who thought you'd like to hear about her, fair enough, but then a good policeman gathers in as much as he can, even coincidental material.'

'So, you think this is just a coincidence, guv?' Geordie sat back and folded his arms. Gillespie gave him a strange look.

'Don't you?' he said. 'Didn't we both see Alex's body? Didn't we both go to her funeral, poor lassie?'

'Well, we certainly saw a body that looked like hers,' Geordie conceded, 'and yes, of course it has to be some sort of weird coincidence. All logic and common sense says so,' he concluded.

'Either way, however,' Colin interjected, 'there is the girl herself and the fact that she was abducted from somewhere in South America and held against her will on an island, almost certainly an island within this little group.'

'Well, for your information, laddie,' Gillespie rasped, 'there's more than a hundred islands in this "little" group, as you call it. The vast majority of them are little more than barren lumps of rock, but no one knows for sure what could be going on on any of them.

'Wanna know something else? Well, our great and good lords and masters and the clever sods who keep the records of these things can't even decide amongst themselves just how many of these islands actually are inhabited. Don't believe me? Well, try looking it up in a few reference books and see for yourself. I've seen one book where the guy reckoned it was thirteen, which even I know is bullshit, and another that reckons twenty-five, plus about one estimate for every number in between.

'So, if you reckon I'm going to get you the go-ahead to go stomping all over that Healthglow place again, just because some poor little native girl reckons she jumped into the sea off an island that *probably* is one of the Shetlands, you can think again. You need much more than that. That place has friends in high places, too, don't forget.'

'And you're only weeks away from your pension now,' Geordie sniped back. 'Fair enough,' he added, before Gillespie could react to the barb. 'I don't blame you. You've put in your time and now you're not going to risk your comfortable retirement on a crazy story. But do me a favour, eh, guv? Book me in as sick for another week. Say I've gone down with the flu, or whatever.

'We need time to do some more digging, because yes, I agree with you, we do need more than we've got. But we ain't going to find anything more kicking our heels around Lerwick, so I need to go see someone who might be able to help.'

'Got to see a man about a dog, eh?' Gillespie said, a slow grin spreading across his craggy features. 'OK, you can have seven days, but no more. You've been swanning around down south for nearly a fortnight already.'

'Yeah, I know,' Geordie replied, 'and I do appreciate this.' He stood up and Colin followed suit. 'But I'm not off to see a man about any dog,' he added, as he turned for the door. 'More like seeing a woman about a pony.'

Jilly gasped with relief as Loin detached the last strap from her head harness and she was finally able to pull back and allow her sorely stretched lips to slide free of his shaft. Behind her, as she stumbled unsteadily back to her feet, she was aware of Celia moving about, her heels clicking on the hard wooden floor covering and she cowered, head bowed, wondering what was coming next, for she felt as if she had failed miserably and was certain that Celia would have some form of punishment for her as a result.

Her first ordeal had seemed interminable; with no means of marking the passage of time, she had no real idea of how long it had actually continued, but of one thing she was now convinced. The man, Loin, for all the effeminate way in which he had been presented, was all but inhuman.

No mortal man could have withstood the efforts she had made for so long and still not capitulated in the ultimate fashion, and yet here he still was, his massive weapon still undischarged and rearing proudly before him, ready for the next stage of whatever Celia decreed.

Jilly felt herself beginning to tremble and her crotch – exposed so blatantly by the way in which the lurex tights had been cut away around it – started to grow very warm, the heat radiating upwards throughout her entire body as she started to imagine what it was going to be like to be impaled by such an incredible pole. Her stomach muscles tensed at just the thought of it and inside the soft leather helmet she could feel the perspiration beginning to trickle into the corners of her eyes.

She bowed her head further, trying to keep the salty moisture from reaching the eyeballs themselves and a small cry escaped her lips as the left one began to sting from the first contact. Desperately, she shook her head and her actions must have conveyed the nature of her distress to Celia, for a moment later, she felt a small wad of soft tissue being pushed through the apertures in the mask.

'Hold still, girl!' Celia snapped. 'Don't be such a stupid cry-baby. Anyone would think you'd done something to make you sweat, instead of just sucking away like a contented baby.'

'Thank you, mistress,' Jilly mumbled, when Celia was finished, remembering how she had been told she should address Celia at all times. For a few seconds, she toyed with the idea of using the safe word she had been given. Then her hands would be freed and she could flee to the sanctuary of the room where she had left her own clothes, and from there to her car and the normality of the world she had so willingly left behind.

And yet some perverse streak of obstinacy still managed to prevail. After all, she told herself fiercely, she had not only volunteered for this, she had also paid for the experience and paid in cash, a substantial fee that she had also been required to agree would not be returnable in the event that she found herself unable to stay the course.

'Now, on your back!' Absorbed in her own thoughts temporarily, it took Jilly two or three seconds to realise that Celia was talking to her and she reacted too slowly for the dominatrix's liking. The crop rose and fell twice in succession and two streaks of hot pain erupted, one across the top of each of her thighs.

'Ow!' she shrieked, and hopped from one foot to the other in rapid succession. 'Please! It's not easy, not with my hands bound like this!' The only reward her protestations brought was a third cut from the crop, this time delivered precisely across the centre of both buttocks in a horizontal line that was only inches below her dangling fingers.

'Stop your complaining, you little cock-sucker!' Celia rasped. 'Just get down on your knees again and take it from there. Quickly now. I want to see you on your back, with your legs spread and that dirty little cunt open and ready for Loin. I think you need a further example of his potential and then we'll have to see about punishing you for your pitiful efforts so far.'

'Well, you can't really blame your inspector.' Anna Johnsson smiled. The pub was beginning to fill up as the twilight changed rapidly into darkness outside, but the booth they had chosen in the furthest corner remained safely out of earshot, at least for the moment.

'No,' Geordie conceded gruffly. 'I'd probably think the same way he does, if the positions were reversed. I mean, sanity says it can't be the same Alex.'

'Well, not necessarily,' Anna said. 'There is a perfectly logical explanation, but you never gave me time to explain earlier.'

'We were a bit eager,' Colin admitted. He pulled his pint glass closer to him and stared down into it, as if hoping to find some sort of mystical answer, but whatever other powers the local ale possessed, the ability to mimic a crystal ball was apparently not among them. 'Trouble is, this entire business is a bit strange – and that's being kind about it.'

'Yes, I understand,' Anna replied. 'Even from what little you've told me, I would say that these Healthglow people probably have something to hide.'

'Including the fact that they murdered Alex Gregory,' Geordie muttered. 'Aye, I know, I was thinking she might still be alive for a moment back there, but same as Georgie boy says, we all saw her body. It was definitely her all right, unless someone's managed to perfect the art of cloning well beyond sheep!

'So, she's dead all right and I *know* those bastards were responsible for it in some way or another. Whatever's going on out on those islands, they're pretty keen to keep it quiet and, as the man said, they seem to have a bit of muscle in the right places to keep us in our place.'

'But you aren't going to let go of it, are you?' Anna said softly. 'This Alex – she was something special to you?' Geordie looked up again in genuine surprise.

'No!' he exclaimed. 'No, not in the way you're probably thinking, but she was a colleague, my superior and a bloody good copper. I don't know how these things work on your side of the North Sea, hen, but over here we tend to take a dim view if someone takes a pop at one of our own.'

'Of course,' Anna said soothingly. 'We are exactly the same in Norway, so I fully sympathise with your determination to get to the bottom of this.'

'You said you had a rational explanation?' Colin interrupted. 'So how do you think that the woman this little Indian wench saw could have been someone who's been dead for more than a month now?'

'Well,' Anna replied slowly, 'I should have thought that the answer was quite obvious, except that everyone has put two and two together and made five. You see, the girl comes from a fairly uncivilised background, a village somewhere in the Andes, where they would tend to measure the passage of time in seasons, rather than days and weeks.'

'Ah, I see what you're getting at!' Colin exclaimed, sitting back and tapping the table top. Geordie looked from one to the other of them.

'Someone want to explain to me, then?' he said, still mystified. Anna nodded.

'Alex Gregory died about a month ago, correct?' she said. The two men nodded in unison. 'Our girl was picked up a few days ago and says something about hitting a man and a woman and then trying to escape with her friend and the one she called the pony-woman, whatever that means.'

'Well, we think we know about that,' Colin put in, 'but it's a long story. Go on.'

'Well, our emergency translator's knowledge of her particular dialect is a bit patchy, so we have to remember that the story we have could be, to say the least, a bit vague. So, given also that little Samba, or whatever her real name is, is probably also a bit vague on time, she could actually have met Alex before she died.

'Her rather clever attempt to get off the island could have taken place many days, or even weeks, after she first got away from the people who were holding her.'

'I see.' Geordie looked pensive. 'Yeah, that would make sense,' he said at length. 'But it would also back up my theory that Alex's death was no accident, wouldn't it? After all, if this Samba girl saw her alive and in one piece on the ground, there's no way she broke her bloody neck in a parachuting accident!

'So, I reckon we stick at this and keep pushing until something gives. However Alex Gregory died, it wasn't the way those smug bastards tried to explain it away and even if they didn't actually murder her, somehow or other they were directly responsible for her death and I'd stake my own pension on that, never mind George Gillespie's!'

'So, what do you intend to do next?' Anna asked. 'By the sound of it, there's no way you can just go over to the island and start giving them the third degree.'

'No,' Geordie said grimly. 'But whilst that island may be enjoying some sort of legal immunity, the same doesn't go for all the people that use the place. I reckon we should try rattling a few cages a bit further from the centre and see what we can shake loose.'

'If you want my opinion,' Anna suggested, 'you could do with finding out more of what really does go on out on those islands, but you'd need to get someone to talk.'

'Or someone to go take a close look first hand,' Geordie replied. He looked across, first at Colin and then at Anna. 'We need to get ourselves a mole, Anna,' he said, 'and I know just the person to do the job. All we need now is to find a way of getting her in there for a day or two and we also know just the person who could help us with that.

'It's simply a matter of persuading both ladies in question. One I can frighten the knickers off, no problem, but as for our mole, well, she'd have to make the decision for herself and I couldn't push her. She could be sticking her neck into a noose, after all.'

'Well, perhaps I could help in some way, too,' Anna offered. 'Of course, I'd need to know far more than you've told me, but from what I know so far, it could be, shall we say, an interesting challenge?'

'I think,' Colin replied, choosing his words carefully, 'that maybe we ought to explain just a little more of what could be involved here. If you're offering what I think you're offering, then you really ought to know just what you could be volunteering for.'

Jilly felt as if her hips were being torn apart, as her body struggled in a desperate effort to accommodate Loin's enormous penis within it. Supporting himself on his hands, arms out straight, he peered down at her, eyes glittering behind the anonymity of the mask that was the negative of her positive.

'Relax.' His voice was very soft, girlish almost, and no louder than a whisper. Jilly gasped and tried to ease her position, but whatever she did the monstrous phallus seemed intent on filling her to bursting point.

'I – I can't!' she wailed. 'You're too big for me!'

'Nonsense!' She heard Celia's rasping laugh. 'He's inside you fully now, so he can't be too big. Just raise your knees and relax, same as he said. And as for you, Loin, if you speak again without my permission, I'll gag that stupid mouth of yours with the fattest penis gag in the locker.

'Now, begin, Loin, but be slow for the moment.' Jilly let out a long, animal cry as she felt him beginning to withdraw from her again, already anticipating the return stroke, but to her surprise, suddenly her body seemed to be adjusting automatically and as he thrust forward again, his member slid into her vagina like a well-oiled piston in a perfectly fitting cylinder.

'Oooooh!' Jilly's eyes grew wide and her jaw went slack. Above her, Loin grunted with apparent satisfaction and began to repeat the procedure. Jilly felt her buttocks knot themselves and clench together, but this time the reaction was one of anticipation, not fear.

'Oh, ye-es!' She sighed, as he slid back into her. She heard Celia's whip smack against her boot.

'Silence!' she commanded. 'You don't have to let us hear what a whore you really are. We can see that for ourselves. You need to learn that a slave accepts a fucking in total silence, or else the same goes for you as goes for Loin. I can find you an even bigger cock to suck on than the one you're so blatantly enjoying at the moment.'

Jilly set her jaw, clamping her teeth together in her determination to remain quiet now, for the prospect of anything bigger in her mouth than she had already suffered was appalling enough, let alone a cock made of foul-tasting rubber, especially when what was happening to her body now demanded her lungs receive as much oxygen as possible.

'Right then, Loin,' she heard Celia say again. 'Get to it properly now. I want to see her come at least once and then I think we'll bring the pillory in!'

'So, we're all agreed on what we're doing here?' Geordie asked, in summary. They were gathered around the table in the small downstairs room that served as both sitting room and dining room in the cottage supplied to him by the police. There was a curious atmosphere between them now, an air of barely suppressed excitement, tinged with an aura of the forbidden, and he was reminded of the days when he and his brother, two sisters and their cousins who lived just across the street had crowded into the one remaining dry room of the little old house at the corner of Quay Street and Dudley Lane.

It had been their gang headquarters, that dilapidated ruin, half hidden by the untended overgrowth of a dozen or more years, the windows and doors long boarded up, the only access via the overlooked cellar door amongst the tangled blackberry bushes. There they had met to plot and scheme, to plan their adventures, evenings, weekends and all throughout the school holidays, until first approaching adulthood and eventually the arrival of the bulldozers had brought an era of semi-innocent and demi-puberty to its final end.

There was something of the forbidden in the air now, something that recalled vivid images of guttering candles and dusty orange boxes, half-empty bottles of cider and orange squash and crumpled packets of cheap cigarettes and potato crisps.

'I wish I could go too,' he said. 'It doesn't seem right, leaving the four of you to take all the risks.'

'You know you can't,' Colin replied. 'They know you, so there's no point in going on about it.' He looked across at Sara. 'You're absolutely positive they wouldn't be able to identify you?' he asked. Sara nodded emphatically.

'Absolutely,' she confirmed. 'Whatever business Andrew did with Healthglow, I was never a party to it. He made all his own arrangements in that direction,' she added. 'I didn't even know about that stuff in the stables.'

'As long as you're sure,' Geordie persisted. 'There's no chance any of the Healthglow people ever called on him without you knowing who they were? If so and they recognise you, the whole thing could be blown before it gets started.'

'I told you,' Sara replied, fixing him with a steady stare, 'none of them ever came to either the house or the main offices. I knew everybody I dealt with on his behalf, both by name and by sight.'

'OK,' he conceded. 'I'm only thinking of your own health and safety.'

'And George Gillespie's reaction if he ever finds out about this.' Colin laughed. 'Lighten up, old son. We'll be OK. There's four of us, don't forget – safety in numbers and all that sort of thing. They wouldn't dare try anything too extreme, even if they did suss us, especially with you still on the outside.' He turned back to Sara.

'You sure you can organise the money side of this?' he asked. 'Going on those figures of Lachan's we found, this could cost a fair old wedge.'

'There's money in Andrew's special account, as he called it. It was deposited under two names: mine and a false one for him, with both of us as signatories. There's also the money in the deposit box he gave me the key for. I already checked that, after he . . . died. There was over fifteen thousand pounds in cash, plus a note there to say that it was to be mine, as a tax-free bonus, if ever anything happened to him.'

'Very considerate of him,' Geordie remarked and then abruptly changed tack, as he saw the look that was exchanged between Colin and Sara. 'So now,' he continued quickly, 'all we need is to organise our passport to pleasure, as it were.' He turned to Anna Johnsson, who had been sitting very quietly for the past few minutes.

'You don't have to do this, you know,' he said. 'After all, you never knew either Alex or Lachan and it's not your case. Not even your country.'

'Could be it's my idea of fun,' Anna replied softly. 'Besides, criminals are criminals, regardless of national boundaries. I've already telephoned to tell my department head I'm feeling a little unwell and decided to take a few extra days sick.'

'They didn't ask why you wouldn't prefer to get back home as quick as possible to recuperate?' Geordie asked. Anna shook her head and grinned.

'No,' she said. 'I suspect they will think that I'm just taking advantage, or that I'm not sick at all.' Four pairs of eyes reflected different quizzical reactions. 'Perhaps I should explain,' she went on quickly.

'I spent a few years here in these islands when I was a child. My grandfather was born here, actually, and I still have some relatives here, I believe. I imagine my boss thinks I'm visiting them. A lot of Shetlanders came from Norway originally and vice-versa,' she added.

'Fair enough,' Geordie said. 'So you're an honorary Jock, sort of.' He looked deliberately towards Melinda. 'You sure you're still up for this, too?'

'I wouldn't miss it for the world,' she answered brightly. 'Besides, if there are people out there who know Celia and have been to either of her places when I've been about, I'll add an air of authenticity to the party. Don't worry,' she said, 'I doubt we'll find anything there I haven't seen or done before.'

'Maybe that's what's worrying me,' Geordie said, under his breath. He pursed his lips and then, out loud, 'Well then, I suggest Colin and I pop back south to get things moving. You three ladies can make yourself at home here, if you like. It's a bit cramped, but it's got most of the mod cons.'

'I'm coming south with you,' Sara announced. 'Part of the way, at least.' She saw the surprised reactions and grinned. 'The money?' she reminded them. 'Or had you forgotten? Or maybe you think I jaunt around the country with twenty grand stuffed in my knickers?'

Celia Butler walked slowly across the room and took up a position just behind the bent-over figure of Jilly. The girl was gagged now, her masked head and gloved wrists locked securely into the horizontal bar of the pillory, her ankles held apart by the strategically placed chains and straps that were affixed to the base board of the structure for just that purpose.

Playfully, Celia slapped her latest acolyte across the rump, the thin material of the lurex tights offering no protection from her own gloved hand. She was rewarded by the sound of a muffled squeak, followed by a deeper groan when she inserted her hand between the splayed thighs and sought out the still wet gash of Jilly's throbbing sex. Celia nodded to herself; Loin had done his usual excellent job, and though Jilly would probably be spoiled for any average man after today, that wasn't a problem – at least not as far as Celia was concerned.

If her new slave wasn't frightened away by the nature of her induction, Celia would still permit Loin to service her on a regular basis, but in Celia's book Loin didn't count as a man, despite his prodigious endowment. Loin was simply another slave, a means of satisfying her female harem's lingering requirements and priming them for her own enjoyment.

She studied the helpless form in front of her with a certain amount of satisfaction and not a little anticipation. The girl was beautifully proportioned and naturally submissive and so far she had reacted well to what she could never have fully anticipated. Too many of these sweet young things came to Celia, begging for the experience of being completely dominated and without ever realising just what that actually meant.

It was still a game, of course, still role-playing, but Celia played hard and her idea of domination and subjugation was usually far more extreme than her would-be converts were expecting. At least three-quarters of them cried off in the very early stages of their initial training and fled as soon as they were released, never to be seen again, but that was only to be expected. Too many of these girls were expecting something out of a pirate movie or cheap bodice-ripper novel and when they found themselves completely helpless and learned what that truly meant, they quickly discovered that it wasn't really what they wanted after all.

Jilly, however, showed great promise and she would almost certainly make a splendid addition to Celia's stable – even to that more literal stable, if she took to the bit and harness as well as she'd adapted to everything else so far. Celia was not necessarily an advocate of change for its own sake, but she had lost two of her more established little sweethearts recently and Lisa, the most promising of them all, was beginning to get broody. Her two older sisters now had their first offspring and poor Lisa was starting to feel left out.

Silly girl, Celia thought, smiling nevertheless. There was plenty of time for raising families later and Lisa would be wasted on any man now. Never mind, she would be back soon enough, unless she was very lucky in her choice of mate, and few men, in Celia's experience, had what it took to give a girl like Lisa exactly what it was she really needed.

Donna and Kirsten were slightly different cases, of course. Donna's millionaire father, who had doted on her with a fierceness that denied her nothing, was seriously ill – quite possibly dying – and Donna had flown out to his mansion in the Bahamas to be with him. With her mother now remarried to a Texan oil baron, the family business would soon become Donna's and it was unlikely that Celia would see so much of her in the future, if she ever saw her again.

Kirsten was now in Australia, of course, married to that idiot radio station owner Mark, whom they had met up in the Shetlands some months before. Celia shook her head, marvelling at the blinkered attitude of the male sex; Mark really believed that Kirsten had married him for himself and there was no way he would ever see that the girl's real interest was in a combination of his money and his quite remarkably beautiful step-sister, Lois. Ah well, she thought, ignorance is usually bliss.

'Well then, Jilly filly,' she said, addressing the stooping girl before her, 'I dare say you could use a bath, eh?' The grunted reply was obviously an affirmative, because Jilly managed just to nod her head, despite the restrictions of the pillory about her slender neck. Slowly, Celia walked around in front of her captive.

'Of course, such privileges as baths must be earned,' she said. 'You understand that, I suppose.' Another grunt and another foreshortened nod. 'Well now, how do you think you could earn your bath – and show your gratitude to your new mistress at the same time, of course?'

Celia had taken advantagc of the latest interval in the action in order to change and she now wore a knee-length leather skirt, beneath which her high-heeled boots reached almost to the tops of her black stockings. Her top was in the form of a bustier, black leather to match the rest of her ensemble, and she had deliberately selected another pair of shoulder-length kid gloves to complete the image. The studded choker about her throat fulfilled two purposes: it hid the few unsightly creases that the passing years had recently brought with them and it added just that final touch of command and authority that Celia knew was so important.

Slowly, she reached around and unfastened the waistband of the skirt, drawing the zipper down its few inches to loosen the garment. With practised deliberation, she began to let the material fall, spreading her thighs slowly to control its progress, until, when it finally reached her knees, it dropped quickly into a small heap about her ankles.

The panties now revealed were also of black leather and the zip that rose from between her legs and stretched up to the waistband glittered brightly against the dark fabric, its purpose obvious, its promise unmistakable. Smiling again, Celia reached down for the tab and began to lower it.

'We'll have to shave your little bush, too,' she said, as her own smooth pudenda was gradually revealed. 'I like my slaves to be soft and hairless, just like this.' She stooped slightly, pushing the zipper tab well back through the gap in her thighs and then straightened again, reaching out now to take a grip on Jilly's leather-sheathed head and lift it as far as the pillory board behind it allowed. The girl sucked furiously on her gag and there was now a darkened patch about her mouth, where saliva had leaked out and dampened the leather through.

'Perhaps we can think of something more suitable for that pretty little mouth to do?' Celia suggested lightly. She watched as the eyes behind the mask blinked and the pupils began to dilate slightly and nodded to herself as she saw the realisation sinking in.

'You understand what is required of you, slave?' she demanded. She heard Jilly swallow, a voluble exercise with the gag filling her mouth so awkwardly. Another soft grunt and the eyelids fluttered. It was an unmistakable signal.

'Good,' Celia whispered. 'But first, I think I should like to spank you a little. Such a sweet bottom is so very hard to resist.' She released her grip, allowing Jilly's head to droop again and moved gracefully back to take up her original positon. Reaching out, she stroked the thinly clad globes, one at a time, sighing as she saw the horizontal back arch in response, thrusting her intended target into even more prominence.

'Ah yes, Jilly,' she said, under her breath. 'Very promising. Very promising indeed!'

Alex stood sullenly in the centre of her stall, biting deeply into the outer rubber covering of her bit, watching Amaarini, who in turn stood in the now open doorway regarding her with barely disguised amusement.

'You were quite the attraction last evening, weren't you, Jangles?' she said at last, finally breaking the oppressive silence. 'You wouldn't believe the number of requests we've had for a repeat performance, or the number of our guests who've applied to book your services.' She laughed and stepped further into the room. Alex's immediate reaction was to retreat from her, but she stubbornly held her ground.

'Of course, I had to disappoint most of them,' Amaarini continued. 'I think you'd probably kill one or two of them and certainly cause some serious damage to most of the rest.' Again she laughed and Alex detected a subtle change in her demeanour today. 'No, I think I'm going to go back to my original idea, Jangles. Despite your defiant attitude and your stupid attempt to escape, I think there's something about you that I like. Of course, in the normal course of events, I shouldn't be even thinking what I'm thinking, but I have to confess something to you.' She walked across to one side and leaned against the tack rack that was fixed to the wall there.

'I don't know how much you've managed to work out for yourself, Jangles,' she went on, 'but you're a bright girl, for a human that is. Oh yes, that's right. Our people aren't humans, not by your definition of the term, anyway. We are a very old and much superior race, or had you realised that already?' Dumbly, Alex nodded. Whether the woman was telling the truth, whether she really was from some sort of alien culture and whether her people really were superior didn't matter; what was important was to humour her, especially whilst she seemed to be in such a communicative mood.

All information is potentially useful information – that was what she had learned in her initial CID training and it had proved to be good advice over the years. Of course, the instructors almost certainly hadn't envisaged her current situation and whether or not she was ever again in the position to take advantage of anything she learned from Amaarini was open to serious debate, but all the time the woman was talking, at least she wasn't doing anything else and that, at least, was something to be thankful for.

'I won't bore you with a history lesson just now.' Amaarini chuckled. 'Some of it you wouldn't understand anyway and a lot of it you probably wouldn't want to believe, but I'll give you a basic outline, so perhaps you'll understand things a little clearer.

'You know, of course, that we gave you a new body – that body. You also feel very resentful at the things that have happened to you since you arrived here, which I can understand, of course. However, I would remind you that you chose to come here, uninvited, spying on us and that what happened to your old body was entirely your own fault.

'You ran off in the darkness, in a terrain you did not know at all and so you fell. None of our people touched you and none of them harmed you in any way. When our security people found you, they brought you back here, very close to death. Even if your old body had survived, which the doctor tells me was extremely unlikely, you would have spent the rest of your life paralysed completely, unable to fend for yourself in any way.

'That fate, at least, has been spared you, so an element of gratitude might not be entirely out of place, whatever you may think of your current status. What happens from here on is largely in your own hands.'

Alex opened her eyes questioningly, hoping that Amaarini might decide to remove the hateful bit and restore her voice again, if only temporarily, but the tall alien made no move towards her.

'You could remain permanently as a pony-girl,' she said. 'Worse still, we are preparing to send a new consignment of cloned girls to South America. There they will be forced to work in extremely arduous conditions, from dawn until dusk and then they will also be available to a collection of human males that I think you would find even more distasteful than those who visit us here.

'On the other hand, if you prove to me that you have learned your lesson and are prepared to be more co-operative, I could give you special status. You would still continue to live most of the time down here, but there are some stalls that are a little less spartan than this one. Jessica has one, for example, and behind it are quarters – small, admittedly – in which she has a bed, television and a music system, as well as books and magazines.

'Of course, in Jessica's case she no longer has a privileged master, so strictly speaking she ought to return to a regular stall, but she has been a very dutiful pony-girl for some years now and special exception has been made in her case. At the moment, in fact, she shares her quarters with the man who originally paid for her exclusive services, but he – or should I now say she – will soon have to earn her own special status, if we can find someone prepared to pay the required retainer for her.

'Your case is slightly different, however. I don't want you mixing freely with too many of our guests, even without the ability to speak to them. You're a resourceful young lady and I wouldn't trust you not to find some way of communicating the truth to one or two of them eventually and that would not do at all.

'In case you hadn't realised it, only a very few of our visitors are privy to our real secret. The rest don't really care, of course, as long as they get what they need from you all and they probably wouldn't believe the truth if you told them, but we can't afford to take such chances, can we? There is far too much at stake here, as you will appreciate.

'No, what I have in mind for you is slightly different, Jangles. I want you as my personal pony-girl. You will pull my vehicles when I go out around the island and you will perform other services for me, which I hope I do not have to explain in lurid detail? No? I thought not.' She smiled again and now she pushed herself away from the wall and moved to stand in front of Alex.

'Like you, Jangles,' she said softly, 'I am no longer in my original body. Yes, this body is a cloned one, too, though I do have far more control over its actions than you could ever be permitted to have over yours. However, it does have one weakness and that is because, although I am personally not a human, the body comes mostly from human genes and therefore it experiences certain needs, shall we say?

'It would also seem that the female whose genes were used in the production of this body was not disposed towards her male counterparts in her original life and for some reason her particular predilection has carried across to my body. Not that I'm entirely displeased at that. In fact, I count myself quite fortunate that she wasn't what you people would call normal.

'The idea of having to satisfy this body's periodic demands with a human male is quite distasteful to me, so if the price of continued life has to be the occasional dalliance with someone like yourself, then I am happy to pay it. The thing is, Jangles, are you prepared to accept my price – and my terms? It may not be quite what you would choose for yourself if you were free to do so, but, under the circumstances, I think you'll agree you could do worse.

'Far worse, in fact.'

Celia Butler looked up in annoyance. Between her wide-spread thighs, as she lay back on her huge bed, Jilly's helmeted head bobbed dutifully up and down, her tongue still lapping steadily. Hearing the interruption, she made to stop, but a quick tap on her neck from Celia together with a barked instruction and she quickly resumed her task.

Framed in the doorway, the impressive figure of Margot, Celia's chief assistant, blocked most of the light from the passageway behind her and she waited now for permission to speak further.

'What the hell is it?' Celia sighed, resignedly. She was annoyed at the intrusion, but she also knew Margot well enough to be sure that the woman wouldn't dare risk her wrath by making it without very good reason. Margot coughed discreetly.

'Visitors, madame,' she said, quietly. 'I think you ought to come.'

'What the hell do you think I'm trying to do?' Celia snapped irritably. 'Can't they wait? I'm not expecting anybody.'

'They didn't have an appointment, madame,' Margot said. 'They don't seem to think they need one.' She hesitated. 'I think they might have a point, actually.'

Celia seized Jilly's head and drew it even closer to her, grunting with pleasure as the girl's tongue responded with renewed vigour.

'You're talking in riddles, Margot,' she retorted. 'Who the hell are these people? Do we know them?'

'We know one of them, madame,' Margot replied carefully. She took a step inside the room, pointed at Jilly's back and then held a finger to her lips. 'The thing is, madame,' she continued, 'the, er, gentleman in question appears to be something more than he originally told us he was, if you get my meaning?'

'Eh?' Celia looked startled. She also looked down at the bobbing head again, suddenly understanding Margot's reluctance to be more explicit. 'Ah!' she said. 'Yes, well, perhaps you could tell them I'm just changing and I'll be right down to see them. Offer them a cup of tea or something,' she suggested and then let out a short grunt as Jilly's tongue darted into her again.

'Just amuse them for a few minutes, for heaven's sake!' she exclaimed. 'See if you can find out what it is they want.'

'Well, madame,' Margot replied awkwardly, 'I already did that and it appears they want you.'

'All right, all right!' Celia gasped. 'Tell them I'm just coming!'

'Yes, madame,' Margot said, smiling to herself as she closed the door behind her. She much preferred it when she didn't have to tell a lie.

Fiona Charles was in a particularly bad mood. Still smarting from her public humiliation and the week she had spent as a common pony-girl in the stables below Ailsa Ness, she was determined to have her revenge, especially on Miko, the man who had tricked her into her ill-fated race wager. She was also intent on renewing her acquaintance with the pony-girl who had beaten her in that same race, the girl whose insolence and rebellion had started the whole damned train of events that led up to the final indignity.

What Fiona did not know, could not know, was that the pony-girl Tammy had not actually been the girl who had competed against her and won with such ease in the end, for she also did not realise the full extent of the Ailsa Ness secret, any more than the vast majority of her fellow visitors did. Careful manipulation of schedules ensured that none of the guests was ever permitted to see most of the lookalike girls together, aside from a couple of pairs who were explained away as being twins.

Tammy, of course, was just the latest in one line of identical clones, a line that now numbered nine and of which four still remained on the island of their rebirth and whilst Tammy was, as Richard Major had truthfully claimed, a raw novice, the girl who had run in her stead had been an experienced hand and with the added advantage of a body that was stronger, fitter and far more durable than Fiona's.

But then, as we have seen, Fiona could not know that. Especially as Fiona Charles was a well-known television presenter and former reporter. Watching the woman from the shadows as she stalked through the stables concourse,

Amaarini smiled to herself. It always gave her great pleasure to see supposedly intelligent human beings acting so stupidly.

Of course, there was an element of risk in even permitting someone like Fiona to set foot on the island, but whatever journalistic nous she had once possessed now seemed to have been dampened into insensitivity by the contents of countless bottles of wines and spirits and as long as she was carefully watched. Besides, the tapes of her transformation into submissive pony-girl and the various humiliations she was forced to endure over the following seven days were a useful insurance, if ever she should start to become overly suspicious.

In the meantime, Amaarini understood her only too well. Permanently semi-drunk or otherwise, Fiona Charles was out for revenge and it might just be amusing to see how she set about it. Stupid as she could be, the woman would not dare to openly seek retribution from the girl she thought had beaten her out on the track. Major's rules were very strict concerning such things and the race, so far as all but those few of them who had been in the know were concerned, had been run openly and fairly. Even Fiona Charles would not want to risk losing face by taking advantage of her newly restored position of superiority.

'I wonder,' Amaarini whispered to herself. 'I wonder just what little scheme you are cooking up right now, Miz Charles.' She looked across to the far row of stable doors. Several were closed and those leading to the stalls occupied by Jessica, Bambi and the still unco-operative Tammy were also locked, as was the end stall, where she had not long since finished installing Jangles in her new quarters.

'I see the Charles woman has returned.'

Amaarini did not bother to turn around to the source of the interruption, recognising Boolik's voice instantly, even though he had spoken in scarcely more than a whisper. Boolik was in charge of the islands' security teams and still, Amaarini knew, smarting over the ease with which the two native girls had escaped and taken Jangles with them. Richard Major had threatened him with serious repercussions and only Amaarini's swift intervention had prevented his instant demotion from a position he had held for only a few weeks.

Boolik had been full of gratitude to her, but then, Amaarini reasoned, it would have been unfair for him to have been blamed. The fault lay initially with Sol, the stupid groom who had been so careless with the girl Samba, and Amaarini herself was still embarrassed about the way the same girl had managed to ambush her in the darkness and free Jangles from the shafts, if not from the rest of her bondage.

'She is full of anger, I suspect,' Boolik continued. Amaarini nodded.

'Of course she is,' she agreed. 'Her pride was very much damaged by what happened.'

'We must watch her carefully,' Boolik said. Again Amaarini nodded.

'I think we should do more than just watch her,' she observed. 'She is stupid enough to cause unnecessary trouble and I think the time is approaching where her continued visits here will be more trouble than the money she pays for them. Unfortunately, Rekoli doesn't seem to agree with me.'

'But you think you have a way of convincing him you are right?'

'Perhaps,' Amaarini replied. 'I'm not quite sure the best way to go about it as yet, but I feel certain that our Miss Television Personality would be far less potential trouble to us if we could get her to South America, for example.'

'I understand,' Boolik said expressionlessly. 'If there is anything I can do to help . . .?'

'I'll let you know,' Amaarini said quietly. 'I'll let you know.'

'Well, now you know what we want, Miz Butler,' Colin said easily, lounging back in the sumptuous armchair opposite Celia. Geordie had taken up a position standing in the wide bay window and had left all the talking to his friend and colleague, whose previous experience at this and

Celia's other establishment gave him an advantage that he was now pressing home. It was not over yet, however.

'You are asking the impossible of me,' Celia replied stiffly. 'There is a strict code of confidence among . . . among the people I deal with,' she finished awkwardly. Colin laughed and Geordie coughed to clear his throat.

'Of course there is,' Colin said. 'Confidence and secrecy. You couldn't hope to operate otherwise, I'm well aware of that.'

'Then you'll understand that I have to refuse your, er, request.'

'I'll understand why you think you have to refuse it,' Colin conceded. 'However, I think *you* should understand that you don't really have much choice in the matter. It's not actually a request, you see.'

'I see,' Celia replied quietly. She folded her hands in her lap and appeared to be considering them. After several seconds she spoke again, this time without looking up.

'It would appear that you've forgotten your own visit to my houses,' she said evenly. 'As I remember it, you seemed to quite enjoy yourself – you and your friend, the delectable young Sassie. She was quite impressive, for one so inexperienced, so much so that we, um, recorded her experience, just for our records, you understand. Call it a training film, if you like.' Now she looked up and there was a spiteful gleam in her eyes. Colin, however, was unmoved by this revelation.

'No doubt you recorded my experience, too,' he said smoothly. 'I wouldn't mind a copy for my own records, if you could arrange that, by the way. I'll pay for the cost of producing it, naturally.'

'I'll gladly furnish you with a copy free of charge,' Celia snapped. 'I'll also provide copies for your colleagues and superiors. It shouldn't take me more than a few days to find out where exactly to send them. I have very good contacts.'

'I assumed you would have.' Colin laughed. He leaned forward slightly and his expression suddenly hardened. 'And now let me tell you something, Miz Butler,' he continued. 'I'll give you the names of my superiors here and now and save you the trouble of chasing up your contacts, shall I? That way we'll save a lot of crap and we can cut to the chase without wasting unnecessary time.

'If you think your tapes will cause me embarrassment with my work, you'd better think again. My department looks after the welfare of a lot of very important people and we do more than just lurk around in the background with guns under our jackets in case someone decides to take a pop at one of the great and good.

'The main part of our job is intelligence – stopping things before they happen, which is far the best way, we find. And, in order to gather that intelligence, we have to do some things that fall well outside the normal police brief. Get the picture, or shall I colour it in a little more for you, Miz Butler?

'In other words, nothing you could show my bosses would surprise them in the least little bit. Fair enough, a few of my colleagues would have a grin or two at my expense, but knowing them as I do, their reaction is more likely to be one of jealousy than anything else.

'As a result of that, I couldn't say with any degree of certainty that you wouldn't get quite a lot of them paying you visits. Quite frequent visits, as it happens!' He sat back in his seat again and folded his arms, waiting whilst Celia absorbed this. Her reaction didn't disappoint him.

'That's attempted blackmail, *Constable* Turner,' she said, attempting to lay extra emphasis on what she clearly thought was the lowliness of his rank. 'I don't think your superiors would be too pleased about that, even if they did excuse your other activities. This conversation is being taped, by the way,' she added, 'just in case you wondered.'

'And the machine is sitting in the next room, in the little cupboard beneath the television set there,' Geordie added, speaking for the first time since Celia had entered. 'I, uh, took the liberty of having a look whilst we were waiting for you,' he added. 'I was interested in your film collection, you understand, not actually searching for anything, which would have been quite contrary to procedure, of course.'

'My colleague is very fussy about such niceties,' Colin added, taking up the baton again. 'Of course, now that *you* have tried to blackmail *me*, we have an actual crime to deal with, so the tape will have to be taken as evidence. My superiors certainly will be interested to hear its contents.'

'And they'll also understand that Colin made no attempt to blackmail you, as you just alleged,' Geordie put in again. 'All he mentioned was that if you sent copies of that videotape to his colleagues, there might be a few of them who'd regard it as a sort of advert. I've met some of his mates, too,' he lied happily. 'Offer them a couple of days with one of your pony-girls and watch out you don't get trampled in the stampede. Policemen's boots can do even more damage than any of those hoof things, if they stamp them hard enough, that is!'

Celia knew she was beaten, but she tried bravely not to show it.

'I suppose you also expect me to pay for this visit?' she snarled. 'You won't get a weekend at Healthglow at my prices, you know! And they'll want to run background checks on all of you before they'll even let you set one foot on Carigillie, let alone go across to Ailsa.'

'Oh, we've got all the money we need,' Colin replied airily, waving one hand dismissively. 'And as for the rest, you leave that to me. You may think you've got good contacts, Miz Butler, but you're an amateur, believe me. You just meet us in Aberdeen, the day after tomorrow.

'I'll phone you later today with all our details and you can let your friends up there know we're coming with you. And, Miz Butler,' he added, raising one eyebrow, 'don't try anything clever, please. Your telephone lines here are already being monitored and so are your two mobile phones. I'll know within seconds if you say anything you shouldn't.'

'And we're also monitoring all the phones listed either to Healthglow or their known employees and associates,' Geordie added, grinning. 'Amazing stuff, all this technology.'

When Colin's car had pulled safely away and was bumping steadily down the track leading to the tarmacadamed public highway again, Geordie took the commandeered audio tape from his pocket and laid it on the dashboard.

'For what it's worth.' He grinned. Colin looked enquiringly across at him.

'Recording no good?' he asked. Geordie shrugged.

'Recording non-existent,' he replied. 'If you look a bit closer, you'll see the tape snapped, right after she switched it on before coming in to meet us. What she doesn't know won't worry her though, eh?

'Oh, by the way,' he added, pocketing the useless tape cassette again, 'that was a good guess about the number of mobile phones she had there.'

'Guess?' Colin echoed and started chuckling. 'Like I told her, Geordie, my contacts would make hers look like a kindergarten class!'

Alex was so engrossed in the television, so relieved to be able to enjoy at least some partial relief from the deprivations she had endured for what seemed like half a lifetime now, that she did not hear the outer door open, the click of heels across the flagstone floor, or even the slight creak of the inner door being pushed open. The sound of Amaarini's voice, therefore, made her start visibly and the sight of the alien woman, when she turned to look at her, made her gasp out loud, emitting a high-pitched whinnying sound that made her cringe with embarrassment.

'You are supposed to keep this inner door closed,' Amaarini rebuked her. 'If anyone out there hears the sounds of the television or music, it will tell them that your outer stall is not quite what it appears to be. And don't just lie there, pony-girl!' she snapped. 'You should always stand in the presence of your mistress.'

Mouth gaping wide, Alex scrabled awkwardly from the bed and stood as directed, facing the only woman in her life who had ever instilled a feeling of fear and inadequacy in her. Amaarini's appearance now did nothing to alleviate that sense of inferiority, even though, in reality, she was wearing less than Alex herself.

The gown reminded Alex of a nightdress, in that it was high-necked, long-sleeved and fell almost to the floor, but there the similarity ended, for the garment was fashioned from a diaphanous black fabric that was little more than a network of almost impossibly thin fibres. It covered almost all of her magnificent body, yet hid nothing, and her full breasts pushed out now without the slightest restriction and in a way that seemed to give the lie to any theories of gravitation ever formulated.

The alien woman had also unbound her hair, which now fell about her muscular shoulders in a black torrent, reflecting the overhead lights with every slightest movement she made. Her wide, full lips had been painted a deep red and her eyes made up in a dark and dramatic fashion, so that Alex's mind flew back to cinematic images of vampires and witches. So stunning was the overall effect that Alex scarcely noticed the dark triangle of pubic hair beneath the diaphanous fabric, but even when she did, the darker patch just seemed to be a part of some fantastic designer's beautiful overall plan.

'I see you are impressed, Jangles,' Amaarini said, smiling. 'It is a beautiful body, is it not? But then your own body is a splendid specimen, too.' She raised her right arm and Alex saw the black shape of the control unit. She experienced just the slightest tingling sensation in her throat, before Amaarini lowered her arm again and turning, placed the unit on top of the small drawer unit at her side.

'You can speak now, Jangles,' she said. Alex hesitated uncertainly and then voiced the question that was foremost in her thoughts.

'Why me?' she asked. 'Is this some new little twist? There must be a dozen or more girls out there who would gladly provide you with what you want.'

'At least,' Amaarini agreed, still smiling. 'But have you never wanted what you thought you could not have, Jangles?' Alex hesitated again and then nodded.

'Ah, I see,' she said. 'You see me as some sort of challenge?'

'Do I?' Amaarini replied, tilting her head slightly to one side. 'You don't think it might be something more than that?'

'Like what?' Alex demanded. 'Rubbing my nose even further into the dirt, maybe?' Amaarini regarded her steadily for several seconds and then shook her head.

'No,' she said simply. 'That's not what I want to do, Jangles.'

'My name is Alex,' Alex said defiantly. She tensed, waiting for the retribution that must surely follow, but Amaarini simply nodded.

'Of course,' she said. 'Very well then . . . Alex, I will respect your individuality, at least whilst we are alone and until you give me cause to think otherwise. I think we understand each other on that, yes?' Alex hesitated again and then nodded slowly.

'Yes,' she said simply. 'I think perhaps we do.' She half turned and took two steps to the side, the weight of her hoof boots suddenly seeming to have trebled itself, making her feel heavy and awkward. She paused, staring down at the floor, her mitted hand raised to one side of her chin.

'You have to understand,' she said quietly, 'I don't understand anything of this. OK, I know what you expect from me, but it's not something I've ever even thought about before, so whether I can do what you want . . .' She left the sentence in mid-air and turned further, so that her back was towards Amaarini. 'I'm not sure at all,' she said at last. 'After everything else, I don't know that I should even think about it.'

'Probably not,' Amaarini agreed. 'But then, Alex Gregory, would you rather any of the other options?' The two women stood in silence for perhaps half a minute, though to Alex it felt much longer.

'Well?' Amaarini asked eventually. Slowly, Alex turned back to face her. She returned the unwavering gaze for several more seconds. Finally, she lowered her eyes and shrugged.

'Well,' she replied huskily, 'I could tell you I'd rather . . . well, you know what I mean.' She took a deep breath, the stiff corset girth digging into her ribs. 'OK,' she said, without looking up, 'I'll do my best, but I want to ask you for one more favour.'

'Yes?' Amaarini's tone was all amusement. Alex looked up at last, her features set immovably.

'I can't do it like this,' she said, spreading her sheathed arms and looking down at her stringently harnessed body. 'Fair enough, if I've got to be Jangles for the rest of these perverts, then so be it, but if you want me to have even half a chance of being what you want me to be, all this lot has got to go.'

Another silence descended between them and eventually, as it had to be, it was Amaarini who broke it.

'Agreed,' she said, in a voice that was so soft that Alex had to strain to hear her. 'Wait here and I will bring Sol to remove your tack.' She smiled suddenly and her whole face seemed to change.

'Actually, Alex, I think you will find his new appearance quite amusing. I know I do!'

'Well, this one is different, I must say!' Fiona Charles stood in the doorway to the cramped stall, hands on hips, smirking at the sight of Sol in his new role, who in turn cringed in the furthest corner, eyes lowered, head averted to one side. Fiona turned to Jonas, who was duty stable hand at that early hour.

'He looks very familiar,' she remarked. 'But I can't say I remember a male pony down here before now. I must be thinking of someone else.' She stepped further into the stall and stood in front of Sol, who still refused to look up at her. 'Is this a new idea?' she said, speaking over her shoulder. Behind her, Jonas smirked unseen.

'The bosses thought there might be some interest,' he replied, striving to keep the laughter from his voice. 'So far, though, nobody else has taken much notice of him.'

'Well, that's a shame, isn't it?' Fiona quipped. 'All dressed up and nowhere to go. We can't have that, can we? Tell you what, Jonas, bring him out and hitch him up to one of the single buggies. I'll take him for a little trot outside and put him through his paces. Does he have a name?' she added.

'Well, her ladyship calls him Solly,' Jonas offered, 'but he hasn't been given a proper name, so she told me if anyone can think of something better, then they're welcome.'

'Solly, eh?' Fiona said. 'Not that distinctive, I must –' She stopped suddenly, eyes narrowing and then stepped closer still, grasping Sol under the chin and lifting his face. He glowered back at her, cheeks reddening and she began to laugh.

'I thought I recognised him!' she exclaimed. 'Solly? Ha, I think not. You're one of the bastards who took such a bloody delight in introducing me to this place not so long ago, aren't you, Sol? Yes, I remember you. You couldn't keep your grasping little hands off my tits for more than a couple of minutes and then, when no one else was about and in the middle of the night, when I was supposed to be left to sleep, you hitched me to one of the carts and made me pull you halfway round the island.

'Yes, I remember that, my darling little boy! And then, not content with just making me run my bloody legs into the ground, you screwed the fuck out of me. Twice, in fact – once out there, in the freezing cold bloody wind and then again when we finally got back here.' Sol lowered his eyes again as she released her grip on him, but his fate, he knew, was already sealed.

'Yes, Solly,' she sneered. 'I'm going to enjoy our little trot out today. You're going to gallop like you never thought possible, my pretty pony-boy, and then I'm going to do everything you did to me – and more. Jonas!' she snapped, spinning round on her steepling heel. 'I want a really nice riding whip, something with a bit of weight to it. And I also want one of those cute double-ended cock harnesses. Yes, I know you keep them down here, so don't shrug at me. I should fucking well know, believe me.

'I'm going back up to my suite now, to sort out a nice little liquid picnic lunch, but when I get back I want to see this bastard standing between the shafts and an appropriate whip and a double-ended strap-on waiting on my seat. I'm going to give this smart-arsed little cunt a day we'll both remember for a very long time!'

'I'm not really happy about you doing this,' Geordie said. He and Melinda were sitting in the front of his car, which was parked on the edge of one of the low cliffs overlooking a deserted bay and the clock was ticking on the forthcoming mission. He looked across at her, his expression strained, but Melinda seemed quite unconcerned.

'I'll be OK,' she said, laying a hand softly on his arm. 'I doubt there's anything out there I haven't come across before. And if you're worried about – you know – well, if it has to happen, then it happens, OK? It won't mean anything to me, honestly.'

'No?' Geordie said. He turned his head away and gazed out of the driver's side window. Below them, grey waves broke listlessly on a mournful-looking beach. 'And what about us, eh? What does that mean to you?'

'Ah!' Melinda withdrew her hand, opened her bag and began searching for her cigarette packet. 'Well now,' she said, 'how come you never asked me that before now, eh?' She found the packet, took it out and flipped it open. 'How about I ask you the same question, Geordie boy? I mean, what do I mean to you, apart from the fact that I'm almost certainly the most incredible fuck you've ever had?'

Geordie squirmed uncomfortably in his seat.

'That's not very fair,' he muttered tersely. 'We've only known each other a few days, but I thought I'd made it pretty clear you were more than that.'

'Well, maybe that was a bit harsh on you,' she conceded, 'but you haven't exactly said much.'

'And you haven't exactly given me much time,' Geordie retorted. 'You seem to forget, lass, this is all still very new to me, all this deviant stuff. Fair does, you're a cracking lass in all that gear you like, but I haven't had much of a chance to get to know the girl inside all that rubber, have I?'

'So why all the concern?' Melinda said, smiling now. 'Or is that unfair, too?'

'Probably.' Geordie sighed and turned back to her. 'Give me one of those, will you?' he asked, indicating the cigarettes. 'I left mine on the table, back at the house.' She passed him the packet and he helped himself, taking the proffered lighter and flicking it into flame.

'Besides,' he said, blowing out a stream of smoke, 'it's not just *that* I'm worried about. I mean, you're right and if you want to let some bloke . . . well, you know what I mean. But you letting some stranger give you a good seeing to isn't the half of it,' he continued. 'You seem to have forgotten the reason we're doing all this. Alex Gregory died out there on that bloody island and I for one don't think it was the accident it's been passed off as. She never overshot any drop, believe me. If you'd known her, even for a short time as I did, you'd know what I'm talking about and why I'm so bloody sure.

'Those people over there are bloody ruthless, Mel lass. Alex and I – well, Alex mostly, I must admit – were pretty sure they'd already killed at least twice before she even went out there. Neither of us knew at that time exactly what was going on. Now we think we do, but it still doesn't make much sense to me.

'With the influence that lot seem to have, why kill anyone just to cover up the fact that a lot of overpaid and oversexed bastards are using their islands to indulge in kinky sex, eh? Nah, it makes no sense at all. There's more to this, I'm sure of that and you're apparently quite happy to go waltzing in there without – at least as far as I can see – without giving it that much thought.'

'Listen, Timothy bloody macho Geordie Walker!' Melinda snapped. 'If there's one thing I can't stand, it's a sexist man and being taken for granted. Alll right, I know,' she said, holding up a hand to silence any intended interruption, 'that's two things, but it doesn't matter.

'Do you think men have the monopoly on quick thinking? Is that it, eh? Well, think again, lover boy. I've thought about it and yes, it could be dangerous over there, but you and your pal need information and there's no other way of getting it, right?

'Not only that, but as we've all discussed, there are four of us going, plus dear Celia, and you're out here, on the outside, as our safeguard. Whatever else they might risk, it won't be murdering five of us, not unless they get to you first and even then, no sane person could hope to get away with covering up a total of six deaths, or explaining them away as even more tragic accidents.

'Besides, you and Colin have written that report for your inspector and it's safely tucked away with the pub landlord chappie, so that's even more insurance, isn't it?'

'Yeah, and Colin's filed a report to his personal computer in his office,' Geordie agreed. 'We've covered most of the bases, I suppose.'

'Well then, lighten up.' Melinda stared through the windscreen. After a few moments, she pointed towards the low headland that stretched out on the left-hand side of the bay. 'Can we walk out there?' she asked. 'I mean, right out to the end, where that clump of scraggy bush stuff is?'

Geordie shrugged. 'Don't know,' he replied. He looked at her, brow furrowing. 'Why?' he asked. Melinda grinned.

'If you have to ask that,' she replied, 'you probably won't want to try to find the answer with me!'

Sol staggered to a halt, gasping for breath, his chest heaving painfully, the tight corset girth seeming tighter than ever as he fought to draw oxygen into his tortured lungs. Behind him, he felt the weight shifting, as Fiona Charles stepped down from her driver's perch and he groaned inwardly as he heard her heels cracking on the hardened mud surface. Her tall boots swam into his vision and he stared down at the sharply pointed toes with a sinking heart.

'You'll have to learn to do better than that, Solly,' she chided him. 'God almighty, even I managed to run faster and longer and I'm just a poor weak female.' She extended the stiff whip and used it to lift his chin. 'You even made me run flat out after you'd spent twenty minutes fucking the guts out of me, you bastard,' she hissed.

'Well, now the hoof's on the other foot, isn't it?' She chuckled maliciously. 'And don't you look so cute there, eh?' She reached out with the whip and ran it up and down the length of his tightly imprisoned manhood. Sol let out a long breath via his nostrils and began to shake.

'Ah,' Fiona said, 'perhaps I *should* whip that thing, but then I'm sure we can find some better uses to put it to, aren't you?' She leaned in closer to him, grasping the bridle strap that ran down the side of his face and jerking his head round to face her. 'Oh yes, Solly boy,' she smirked, 'I'm going to have that proud cock of yours inside me again. Only this time it'll be on my terms and you're the one doing all the running.

'Not only that, but I've brought my own cock with me and I'm going to fuck you the way you fucked me. In fact, it's going to be far worse for you, you bastard, because *my* cock doesn't get tired out and I'm going to keep on shagging you until you squeal and wriggle like a stuck little piggy virgin, understand?'

Sol glared at her, his features distended by the fat bit in his mouth, but his attempted show of defiance simply increased Fiona's amusement. She lifted the whip and tapped him on the top of his head.

'Still a lot of daylight left, Solly boy,' she said. She turned and looked away into the distance, towards the craggy mount that formed the furthest end of the island. 'Shame this place isn't bigger, Solly,' she said, 'but then there's always the race track, isn't there?

'Remember the race track, Solly boy? Well, how does ten circuits sound, eh? And that's just for starters.' She laughed again and reached around to her side, to the small pouch that was attached to her broad belt. 'I thought we might treat this as a handicap trial, too,' she said and drew out an object that was all too familiar to Sol. She held it up and the pale sunlight caught the dull black surface to produce a purplish hue.

'Not just yet, Solly,' she growled, brandishing the slim dildo like a sword between them. 'I want you to think about this first. I want you to think about it all the time we're trotting our way down to the track and then, Solly boy, you're going to feel it inside you for every step of those ten laps. Or maybe we'll run a few first, just to make sure you're properly warmed up.

'And,' she added, her features twisting into an alarmingly distorted mask, 'if you don't run those ten – or even twenty – laps to my total satisfaction, you'll run ten more. And ten more, still.' She was cackling now. 'And ten more, and ten more and then, Solly boy, when you think you're just about fit to die, I'm going to strap on a cock that'll make this one look like a matchstick, fuck the shit out of you the way you did to me and then, my sweet little pony bastard, if we can get your cock up still, I'm going to ride that until you beg me to stop.'

Alex opened her eyes, groaned, closed them again and rolled over, burying her head in the soft pillow. Beside her, Amaarini stirred, muttering something unintelligible under her breath and threw out a long arm, wrapping it around Alex's waist and drawing her back to her. Alex stiffened, but only momentarily, before relaxing and pressing her naked buttocks tightly into Amaarini's warm groin.

I'm not doing this. This isn't me. This can't be me!

Slowly, she reached back, her right hand cupping the rounded peak of Amaarini's thigh, her fingers gently stroking the soft, yet taut flesh. Behind her, Amaarini stirred again and Alex felt the firm breasts pressing harder against her back.

What am I doing? She's a woman. No! She's not even a woman: she's a bloody alien, by her own admission. Unconsciously, Alex's other hand went to her own sex, her fingers exploring the warm stickiness, as she recalled now the events of . . . of when? She opened her eyes again, but the soft lighting in the bedchamber held no clue to the passage of time and she sighed, shaking her head.

Slowly, she turned, lifting Amaarini's arm and turning herself until she lay face to face with the beautiful alien, the beautiful alien in the so beautifully perfect human body. For several long seconds she remained frozen, staring into the perfect face, watching the long dark lashes as they twitched and fluttered and then, one hand reaching down to cup a heavy breast, Alex leaned in closer, her lips seeking those other lips, delicately sucking them into her mouth, whilst her other hand sought those other even warmer, wetter lips.

Amaarini's eyes slowly opened and for a few moments they registered surprise. Then, as Alex's fingers found their intended target, recognition dawned in them and her mouth, pulling away from Alex's, curled into a broad smile of satisfaction.

'Oh yes,' she breathed, 'that's very good, Alex. That's very good indeed.'

'I'm glad to see you're keeping well on top of things, Boolik.' The appearance of Richard Major in the central security monitoring room brought the three operators stiffly to attention in their seats. Boolik, standing behind them and overseeing the entire bank of small screens, turned and snapped his heels smartly together.

'Everything is now as it should be, Rekoli Maajuk,' he replied tersely. 'I like to keep a watching brief, whenever my other duties permit.' Major waved a hand, dismissively.

'Of course, of course,' he said lightly. 'I wasn't checking up on you, Boolik. And I've been appraised of all the facts concerning that other incident and no blame is attached to you. The young groom, however, is being severely punished, as you doubtless know.'

'Indeed,' Boolik said and pointed to one of the screens. 'I was just observing him now, as a matter of fact. There he is, out on the track circuit.'

'And who is driving him at the moment?'

'The Charles woman,' Boolik said, making no attempt to disguise the relish in his tone. Major nodded and smiled.

'I see,' he said. 'And of course, if I remember correctly, young Sol was one of the grooms in charge of her section of stalls during her little forfeit experience, no?'

'He was indeed,' Boolik confirmed.

'And, as ever, I presume that he acted towards her with all the zealousness one associates with youth?'

'I believe so.'

'Ah.' Major's smile broadened a little. 'I expect he may now be having cause to regret his former enthusiasm, eh?'

'They're coming up to something like ten laps out there already,' Boolik said. 'We can zoom the camera in much closer, if you would like to see,' he added. 'And the cart they are using is one of the ones we've now fitted with audio pick-ups, as per your instruction following the, er, incident. Would you like to follow the proceedings?' Major smiled yet again, but shook his head firmly

'I think not, thank you all the same, Boolik,' he sighed. 'There is something about the Charles female that I find quite distasteful and watching her humiliating one of our own – even if he is technically a half breed – does not really appeal to me. Not that Sol doesn't deserve such a punishment, but I'm sure I can leave it to you to keep an eye on the proceedings.

'Just don't let her go too far, that's all. Fiona Charles has a very nasty streak in her, Boolik. Most of her kind tend to accept that it's all just a form of play-acting, even though we do go to great lengths to make everything so real for them, but that woman is something different.

'I suspect that she could even kill, let alone seriously injure, if she thought she could get away with it.' He turned half away, shaking his head. 'Taking a life – even one of theirs – is a serious matter, Boolik, and should never be considered lightly. We have killed in the past – it is perfectly true – but only when there has been no other alternative in order to protect our people.

'We have even given new life in some cases, where it has been possible.' He paused, his eyes clouding over. 'These Earth humans are an inferior race in so many ways,' he said. 'They are slaves to their own bodies, most of them, and unfortunately that is a trait that seems capable of crossing the genetic boundaries, too.

'You are a true full blood, Boolik, so you won't understand fully what I'm talking about, but there are others who have the Earth human genes in their current bodies and they are only too aware of the frailties that can cause. Take even Sol out there now.

'That Charles woman will use and abuse him and try to run him into the ground. Indeed, if his body were entirely human, I dare say he would have collapsed from exhaustion well before now. Yet powerful though his Askarlarni genes are, the human gene he has inherited from his brood mother will rule the roost under certain circumstances.

'Watch and see, Boolik,' he said quietly. 'Watch and learn. Fiona Charles may well be a vicious bitch and quite probably psychopathic into the bargain, but she is also an extremely beautiful female. Even after she has beaten and run him, watch and see how his body responds to her when she is ready for it.

'He may hate her with every fibre of his being, but he will still react physically to her, even if the drug Higgy injected to keep his assets so prominently displayed has worn off by that time.'

'It is a great shame that we have had to dilute our noble bloodline with the blood of such animalistic creatures,' Boolik muttered.

Richard Major shrugged. 'The decision was taken many, many years ago now,' he said. 'Long before your time. I was quite a young man myself then, in fact, but I was privy to the counsel of the elders and I knew they were right. There was no other choice, not if we wished to survive – on this or any other planet, for that matter.'

'There are others of our people out there among the stars?' Boolik prompted. 'I have heard the tales, but there is little hard information available.'

'Indeed there isn't,' Major replied, sighing. 'And there may never be, not now. Yes, there could be others of our race who reached suitable refuges, as did our clan, but we cannot be sure, Boolik. The universe is more immense than any single mind can conceive and the stars are hard mistresses. Who knows if others were as fortunate as us?' He turned again and looked across at the screens.

'The likes of Sol should appreciate their good fortune,' he said. 'Not that I expect him to appreciate anything much just at the moment, of course.' In the doorway, he paused again.

'The Butler woman is bringing some new guests with her,' he said. 'The details have been fed into the system, as usual, but I'd like you to check the results thoroughly. Apparently the fellow concerned is very wealthy and interested in more than just the basics on offer on Carigillie, but I want a thorough clearance check before we even think of letting him across to Ailsa.

'There have been enough mishaps over these past weeks, Boolik. Let's all try to make sure we don't add to them.'

Anna Johnsson finished laying out the contents of the suitcase on her temporary bed and smiled to herself. She stooped over, reaching for the rubber corset and picked it up, raising it to her nostrils to inhale the heavy aroma it exhuded.

'I see you appreciate the same sort of things I do.' The unexpected sound of Melinda's voice from the doorway made the tall Norwegian woman start guiltily and she felt her usually pale cheeks beginning to redden. 'It's OK,' Melinda said, grinning as she saw Anna's embarrassment, 'you're among friends here. We're all over twenty-one, even if I do act like a sixteen-year-old at times.

'Of course, poor old Geordie's still a bit unsure of all this stuff, so it's probably just as well he can't come with us. First time I met him, I could tell he wasn't experienccd in the scene. You have a scene over in Norway?'

Anna nodded. 'Yes, we do,' she said. 'It's far more open in Sweden, of course, but we appear to be catching up with our neighbours quite rapidly now.'

'Do you have anyone . . . special – back home, I mean?'

'No, no one special. One or two quite special friends, but no one person in particular.' Melinda considered her reply for a few seconds.

'No one special *person*,' she repeated. 'I see.' She paused again. 'Well, that was me, up until I met that great Geordie lump.'

'You've fallen in love with him?' Melinda laughed.

'Well, I don't know about love,' she confessed. 'It's probably a bit too early for words like that anyway, but

I'm not sure what being in love with someone is really all about. I thought I did . . . once . . . but that was a long while back now and I was very young.'

'Ah. Me too,' Anna confided. 'I was very young, too.' She looked carefully at Melinda. 'I guess we must be somewhere about the same age,' she observed. 'And not dissimilar in other ways.'

'Well, you're a lot taller than me, for a start,' Melinda quipped. 'And your hair's even fairer than mine, especially my natural colour.'

'My Viking ancestry.' Anna laughed. She lowered the corset and let it fall on to the bed. 'These are very nice things,' she said. 'Are they yours?'

'Mostly,' Melinda confirmed. 'Apart from the boots, that is. They belong to another friend of mine. She was – is – tall like you. Luckily I packed them into the crate we were having sent up. Not sure why I did that.'

'The size seems fine,' Anna said. 'More fortunate that you were having the crate delivered at all.'

'Well, we left in such a hurry that we couldn't bring much with us,' Melinda explained. 'We flew most of it, to save time, so we – Geordie and Colin, that is – would get here in time to see you. The original intention was for me to stay for a couple of weeks, at least, and there was no way I was going to be parted from some of these things for that long, so I just threw in as much as I could, locked the crate and phoned for an express delivery service to come and collect it. I hardly had time to check what I was putting in there, so that's probably how come the boots turned up.'

'Ah. I did wonder. I thought perhaps you were intending for Geordie to wear them?' Melinda grinned and started to laugh.

'Well, you never know,' she said. 'I don't think he'd have been too keen on the spike heels, for a start, but I was intending to work on him a bit, soften up a few of his daft macho ideas, that sort of thing.'

'I think you might have quite a job on your hands,' Anna remarked drily. 'But I've known of stranger things. Thank you for the loan of the clothing, anyway.'

'Oh, you're welcome. Tell you what, why don't I pop along the passage and get some of my other stuff and we can try a few things on, see how we complement each other.'

'Oh, I'm sure we will complement each other quite nicely,' Anna replied, her eyes twinkling. 'But what about Sara?'

'Ah well, she never thought to organise anything,' Melinda said. 'The lads will bring some stuff back for her from Celia's. I don't think I've got anything here that would appeal to her much. None of my Milly the Filly stuff went in the crate, as I didn't think poor old Geordie would really want to risk me trotting around the island here, no matter how few people there are.'

'But what if she comes back in the meantime?' Anna persisted. 'She never had to go anywhere nearly as far as the men. She could be back by this evening.'

'Doubt it,' Melinda said. 'She told me she was going to get the money and then stay at a hotel overnight and time her drive back to get the first ferry tomorrow morning and then take a room in one of the hotels, in case anyone sees her coming in and out of here.

'If the lads time it right, they'll be arriving at the ferry early in the afternoon, with Celia in tow and we have to be over there to meet them.'

'So we all make the crossing together?'

'Except Geordie. He's going to charter a boat and bring it round the long way.'

'Does he know what he's doing?' Anna demanded. 'These waters are treacherous.'

'The boat comes complete with skipper,' Melinda explained. 'Another one of Colin's famous contacts is organising it, I think. The idea is that in case anyone's watching the ferry here to see who arrives, they'll see the four of us and then one of us going to collect a fifth friend who travelled up on her own.

'Geordie and his sailor chappie will then take the boat and lurk somewhere close enough to the two islands so they can move in quickly if they're needed. Colin's organising some radio gadgets and the boat itself will be able to get in touch with the coastguard, if the jolly old balloon should go up.'

'You do know this could be very dangerous, don't you?' Anna warned. 'I know it's all very exciting stuff, but this isn't a game. This Celia Butler is one thing, but from what I've already heard, the people behind this Healthglow operation play their games a great deal more seriously. They may even be murderers.'

'Yes, I do know,' Melinda said. 'But let's worry about that when the time comes, eh? Meanwhile, there's just us girls and a huge box of goodies to play with, so why don't I open a bottle of something and let's enjoy ourselves for the evening? Tomorrow is another day and we can handle that and anything else when we get over to those islands.

'Meantime, I reckon we deserve some fun, don't you?'

When Fiona finally reined him to a halt, Sol stood between the shafts, gasping for air and cursing the hateful bit that obstructed his mouth. His chest heaved and the tight corset girth seemed to have become even more vice-like and his legs and feet screamed out from the unaccustomed stretching of muscles imposed by the dramatically elevated hoof boots.

From behind him, Sol heard the sounds and felt the shift in weight and movement of the shafts as Fiona dismounted from her seat and walked slowly up and around in front of him. In her right hand, she still carried the long whip with which she had been urging him to even greater efforts, but it was the thing she held in her other hand that now held Sol's full attention.

'Time for your friend, Solly boy.' She snickered, waving the slim dildo under his nose. 'Let's see how fast you run with this for company, eh?' Sol groaned inwardly, but very shortly his groan became audible, as Fiona released the crotch strap sufficiently to allow her access to her intentioned target.

As she pressed the tapered end of the butt plug to him, Sol instinctively clenched his muscles, tightening his sphincter against the coming invasion, but Fiona simply cupped his sheathed testicles in her free hand and applied enough pressure to elicit a sharp cry from him.

'That's just a warning!' she hissed. 'Fight this and I'll twist your nuts so they turn every colour of the gothic fucking rainbow, understand?' Sol groaned again, but forced himself to relax and was surprised then at how easily the cold shaft penetrated him once the tip had effected its initial entrance. However, as she pushed it fully home and replaced the crotch strap, tightening it fiercely, Sol quickly realised that, slim or not, the dildo was long enough to instil in him a feeling of unnatural fullness.

At the same time, he also remembered her threat to use an even bigger phallus on him, once she had finished trying to run him into the ground. He closed his eyes and tried not to think about it.

Fiona, meantime, having double-checked that she could not cinch the harness any tighter, walked back around in front and inspected his tethered erection in its sheath, noting with satisfaction the tiny hole positioned in the tip of the leather sleeve.

'Excellent.' She beamed. 'That should be just about right. You see, Solly boy,' she continued, leaning closer in to him, 'once that little beauty starts bouncing around inside you, you're going to find yourself needing to pee and it's going to feel more urgent than you could ever imagine, but we shan't be stopping for such trivialities.

'So, my little pony-boy, if – when, rather – you need to pee, you're going to have to do it on the run, understand?' Sol stared back at her from between the blinkers, his expression sullen. Fiona laughed again. 'Oh, don't worry,' she said, 'you might try to fight it – I'm sure you will – but in the end you'll have to give in and the result should be quite spectacular . . . not to say amusing, of course.'

Anna Johnsson rose to her feet uncertainly. The boots Melinda had lent her had heels far higher than anything she had ever experienced before, arching her insteps unbelievably, so that only the very ends of her toes actually made any contact with the ground through the thin leather soles. The zipped inner sides were also augmented by laces on the opposite, outer, side, which allowed for an adjustment that Melinda had made full use of. The thick black rubber now clung to Anna's long legs from toe almost to crotch, offering a clinging support and bracing that she found almost disturbing.

'These must have cost your friend a fortune,' she gasped, peering down at her newly booted lower limbs. 'They really are spectacular. Mind you, I don't know whether I'll be able to walk in them,' she added, pulling a curious face.

Melinda sniggered. 'Boots like that aren't intended for walking in,' she said. 'Not for long, anyway. Just get used to balancing and standing in one place and then we can try the corset on you. You'd better remove your bra and panties first, though. Pretty as they are, they'll somewhat ruin the desired effect!'

'These must be even higher than the pictures of those pony boots you showed me earlier,' Anna murmured, but she reached behind her and began fumbling for the clasp that held the whispy piece of lace confectionery in position. Seeing this, Melinda stepped quickly forward and moved behind her.

'Let me help,' she said softly. Her eyes narrowed as she inspected the long back and the narrow waist at close quarters and she had to give herself a mental shaking to bring her attention back to the matter in hand. 'There,' she said, releasing the catch and passing the two ends of the straps around beneath Anna's armpits, the sides of her hands brushing lightly against the Norwegian girl's firm breasts as she did so.

She saw Anna's body stiffen slightly, but nothing was said and, by the time Melinda moved back around to face her, Anna was holding the discarded brassiere in one hand and making no attempt to hide what its removal had revealed. Anna smiled and let the flimsy garment drop on to the bed behind her.

'Do you approve of what you see?' she asked quietly. Melinda swallowed and nodded.

'Very much so,' she whispered. Their eyes met and for a few moments there was a heavy silence between them, the air heavy with electricity that seemed to be desperate to discharge itself.

'Better try the corset, then,' Anna said, at length, finally setting the mood aside, at least for the moment. 'I've worn something similar before, in leather,' she added, as Melinda ducked past her to pick up the rubber garment, 'but it wasn't particularly tight, to be honest. This one looks a little more fearsome, I think.' Melinda grinned at her and held it up for her to see again.

'It is,' she agreed. 'There are steel stays hidden inside the rubber seams and it'll lace down to around eighteen inches at the waist, though I've never quite managed to get it that far. I think your waist might be a little bigger than mine, unfortunately.'

'You may be surprised.' Anna chuckled. 'My height is very deceptive. Last time I measured my waist, it was fifty-three centimetres and I don't think I've put on any weight these past two or three weeks.'

'Fifty-three centimetres?' Melinda echoed. 'Let's see, that's – bloody hell, that's about twenty-two inches. It can't be.' She lowered the corset and peered closer again. 'Sheesh!' she exclaimed. 'It probably is, too. Well, this little beauty is going to fit you like an absolute treat and who knows, we might even get it to lace closed altogether!'

At long last, Fiona hauled on the reins and allowed Sol to stagger to a halt once more. On the point of collapsing now, he knew he dared not actually crumple, for that was regarded as the cardinal sin for a human pony and he was still desperate not to hand the ultimate victory to the tormentress he had once, so recently, tormented himself.

True to her earlier prediction, he had finally failed in the battle to control his bladder and she had roared with appreciation when he had finally given in, soaking himself thoroughly as the warm urine sprayed straight upwards, but there had been little he could have done to prevent that and they both knew it. To actually sink to his knees between the shafts would be a sign of complete surrender of a different nature and he knew he could expect no mercy in defeat.

Thus far, despite her threats, Fiona had confined her use of the whip to urging him on and guiding him as a supplementary signal to the ones transmitted via the reins to his bit, but if he refused to keep going, he suspected she would put the vicious lash to a much more painful use.

'You know, Solly boy,' she said, dismounting lightly and stalking up alongside him once again, 'with a bit more training, you could actually be quite good at this. I must admit, I thought you'd have gone down well before now.' She leaned across him, patting his sheathed and harnessed erection, ignoring the now damp leather.

'Still nice and hard, too,' she observed smugly. 'Whatever stuff it is they used on you in the stables, it's certainly very effective. Better even than Viagra. Be interesting to see how much longer it holds up, though.' She straightened up and began unclipping the traces and clasps that secured Sol to the shaft on one side and then moved around to repeat the procedure on the far side.

'If it does stay up,' she said, 'and if I decide you've performed satisfactorily, then I'll let you have a bit of a rest and then you can walk back to the stables. Much as I hate you for what you did to me, Solly boy, I don't really want to damage you permanently.' She laughed as the final clip fell away.

'No indeed,' she said. 'That would be a waste, especially as we can repeat tonight's performance on a nice regular basis, eh? Won't that be nice, Solly, eh? Oh, why the long face, then? I seem to remember you were quite keen on the fact that we could spend so many nights together not so long ago, don't you?'

She reached up, clipped a short lead rein to one side of his bit and gave it an experimental tug.

'Of course,' she said, 'that was slightly different, wasn't it? Then it was me doing all the work and you just giving me a quick shagging when it suited you, whereas now . . .' She left the sentence to hang in mid-air between them and tugged on the rein again, indicating that she wanted Sol to start walking forward. Almost immediately, he saw what she intended.

The punishment frame was one of the older ones, made from well-weathered timber and resembling a carpenter's sawhorse, except that the support legs at each of the four corners were much longer and the spar that ran across just above ground level on either side was designed to hinge open in two places; this afforded a crude set of stocks into which the victim's wrists and ankles could be secured and thus holding him or her bent over the wider upper crossbar in the perfect position for whipping or caning.

Sol himself had secured plenty of trembling slaves, including losing pony-girl contestants, into this and similar contraptions and now he began to understand their trepidation. Already helpless in his pony rig, once Fiona had him locked over this crude apparatus he would be even more completely at her mercy. For the briefest of moments, the urge to resist was overwhelming, but her quick reminder, a simple flick of the whip across the backs of his thighs, brought home to him the futility of such a reaction.

To struggle would delay the inevitable, nothing more, and then, once she had achieved what she was always going to achieve anyway, Fiona would almost certainly exact a terrible retribution for his daring to even consider such an action. Biting deeply into the soft outer layer of the bit, he shuffled forward and obediently placed his heavily shod feet so that his ankles sat neatly inside the waiting crescents.

He closed his eyes and tried not to listen as the two matching segments were swung solidly into place, but the sharp click-clicking as they were finally locked sounded to Sol like two mortally wounding pistol shots in the unnaturally still night air.

'That looks amazing!' Melinda exclaimed. She stepped back and reached out and up to take Anna by the shoulders, turning the taller girl around so that she could see her reflection in the mirror on the wardrobe door.

'It's very tight,' Anna said, but her eyes opened very wide when she saw the effect of the corset and all Melinda's efforts to lace it completely closed at the back. Her waist seemed almost to have disappeared and, in contrast, her slim hips now looked much wider. Her breasts had first been compressed and then, as Melinda had progressed, they had been squeezed and lifted upwards, forming two mounds out of all proportion to their original size with her nipples, protruding through two circular cutouts, swollen and distended beyond belief.

'Wow!' she exclaimed. 'What a difference.'

'Yeah, wow!' Melinda breathed. 'Wow and double wow! I think you should wear that on the island, when we get there. No one will take any notice of anything the rest of us get up to. They'll all be too busy ogling you!'

'The men will, perhaps,' Anna conceded. Melinda choked back a nervous laugh.

'Not just the men, darling,' she said firmly. 'Not just the men, believe you me. Now, how about some gloves and maybe a collar.'

'Not the mask hood?' Anna said, raising her eyebrows. 'The mask hood thing that you placed so discreetly just behind that pillow earlier?'

'Ah, well . . .' Melinda looked sheepishly up at her. 'I didn't know quite whether you'd want to go that far. It . . . well, it could be a bit intimidating.'

'Because there are rings there for fitting a gag, too, no doubt,' Anna said, keeping her face perfectly straight. 'Presumably you have the gag somewhere close at hand, too?'

'Um, yes well, I expect there's one in amongst this lot somewhere,' Melinda muttered. 'I mean, there's all sorts of things here, as you can see.'

'Yes, I do see,' Anna agreed, still expressionless, but suddenly her face softened and she leaned forward and kissed Melinda gently on the lips. 'I see quite a lot of things, actually,' she said. 'And I feel a lot of things, too.

'Go ahead, Melinda. Finish dressing Anna as you want to see her and yes, mask her and gag her and even manacle her hands, if that is what you wish. You can be sure that Anna will do the same to you, when it is her turn!'

Sol groaned into the bit and his arms and legs tensed, but he was spreadeagled so efficiently over the punishment frame that he knew there was no way he could prevent Fiona from completing the next stage of her humiliating revenge. She had made him watch as she had unzipped the crotch of her tight leather breeches, inserted the smaller half of the double-ended dildo into her and then secured it in position with the complex web of straps.

Then, with a calm deliberation, she had proceed to walk slowly up and down before him, all the while insisting that he kept his head lifted painfully, in order that he could see her moonlit parade the better, the larger phallus bobbing obscenely before her with every carefully choreographed step. The entire performance was studied and unhurried, a perfect example of prolonging the tension that preceded the eventual act and Fiona was proving herself an expert the equal of any of the stable grooms, or even the most practised of the dominant guests who frequented the island.

'And now I'm going to fuck you, Solly,' she hissed, taking the thick shaft in her right hand and massaging it as if it were alive. 'I'm going to put my big fat cock in you and fuck you as if you were a helpless little pony-girl. I want to see you squirm and squeal the way you forced me too, you arrogant little shit,' she growled, stepping closer, so that the black effigy was only inches from his eyes.

'I want you to really understand what it feels like to have someone shagging you till you think you're going to break in two. And then,' she added gleefully, 'I'm going to turn you over, unstrap that nice big cock of yours and we're going to go for a ride of a completely different kind.

'I said I'd let you walk home earlier, didn't I, Solly?' She leered. 'Well, I promise you this much, you'll be lucky if you can still manage to crawl there when I've finished with you!'

* * *

With the long latex gloves finally in place on Anna's arms, courtesy of a generous application of talcum powder and no little application of Melinda's patience, attention turned finally to the final two items of the ensemble: the close-fitting latex hood and the thicker rubber collar which would lock it in place. Melinda looked up into Anna's eyes uncertainly.

'You're sure?' she asked. The tall blonde nodded and smiled back.

'Yes, quite certain,' she replied huskily. 'I'll sit down on the bed and make it easier for you, shall I?' The smile did not waver one flicker.

Carefully, Melinda drew the fair tresses back into a high ponytail and deftly fastened this with a thick band. Then, taking the limp mask, she spread it out and raised it above Anna's head. The aroma of rubber was already heavy, as corset, dress and boots responded to the warmth of Anna's body, but very soon now, as Melinda knew only too well, the smell of it would seem overpowering to the Norwegian girl.

'OK, then,' she said. 'Hold steady. This will be a bit of a tight fit.' To her surprise, however, the latex moulded itself easily over the crown of Anna's head, the ponytail slipping through the rounded opening, so that she had to hold it clear with one hand when she finally came to starting the zipper downwards. Now the mask indeed began to tighten, pressing itself closely to Anna's features, forming snugly about her nose and chin and emphasising the bones of her eyebrow line and cheeks.

Finally, the zipper slid the final few inches to the base of her neck and Melinda picked up the collar. Anna remained motionless and silent as she wrapped it about her neck and slipped the two locking catches into place against her upper spine.

'There,' Melinda announced, standing back. 'Would you like to look in the mirror?' Two glittering eyes regarded her impassively through the acutely angled slits in the rubber and the full lips, compressed somewhat by the embrace of the latex above and below her mouth, moved stiffly.

'Perhaps you should finish everything first?' Anna suggested, her voice flat and emotionless. Melinda hesitated and then remembered.

'Oh, of course,' she said. 'Wait a moment.' She moved across to the small easy chair in the corner and lifted the cushion there, revealing the set of broad leather wrist cuffs she had secreted earlier, but in truth had not expected to be using like this. As she returned again, Anna dutifully stood, wavering unsteadily on the unfamiliar heels, before slowly turning about and placing her hands obligingly behind her.

Suddenly afraid that the tall girl might change her mind at the last moment, Melinda moved in quickly. With deft fingers she buckled the first cuff in place and slipped the small padlock through the reinforced slot that would prevent removal. A few seconds later she had repeated the exercise on the other wrist, so that the two were now fastened together with just a few links of steel chain, perhaps four inches long in total. Melinda heard Anna let out a soft sigh and now she knew just what was expected of her.

'Sit!' she ordered and turned quickly for the gag. It was shaped like a stubby penis, made of black rubber and attached to a short, wide strap, each end of which was perforated at intervals so that it could be matched with the corresponding buckles to either side of the mouth opening on the helmet. Without being asked, Anna opened her mouth and Melinda slipped the plug between her lips, secured it and stepped back again.

She was breathing quite heavily herself now, for the game had advanced too far not to continue to the ultimate conclusion. The tall, athletically built and superbly endowed blonde was now almost as helpless as it was possible to be and for a moment Melinda considered fettering her ankles, too. However, there were more pressing matters to attend to first and that, she decided, could wait until she, too was more suitably attired.

'I have left my outfit in the next bedroom,' she announced. 'You may continue to sit, as I know you are not used to those heels, but I expect you to remain perfectly still until I return. Do you understand that?'

Slowly, the mute head nodded, but the eyes that continued to glint from behind the all-enveloping latex looked anything but subservient. In fact, Melinda chuckled to herself, as she ducked out into the passage, they looked just as eager now as her own probably did.

Sol gasped as the thick rubber dildo finally filled him and he bucked wildly, only the thick mitten sleeves preventing him from tearing the skin of his wrists in the rough wooden stocks that held them. Behind him, he felt Fiona pressing hard up against his taut buttocks, her breath coming in harsh gasps as she thrust even deeper into him.

'There!' she almost shrieked, her triumph now complete. 'How does that feel, Solly boy? Do you feel like a girl now, eh, with your tight little cunt stuffed full with my big juicy cock?' She pulled back and Solly moaned with relief as the thick shaft began to withdraw from his stretched sphincter, but the relief was only momentary and never total, for at the moment when it felt as if the phallus would slip out completely, Fiona stopped, paused and then drove it back in again.

This time, as she completed the thrust, she fell across his back, her gloved hands coming around his torso, fingers seeking the rings in his newly pierced nipples, pulling viciously on them to stretch his tender teats. This time his groan was of a much higher pitch, but Fiona was unrelenting. Twice, three times, then four, she repeated the same movement, only this time as she worked the dildo in and out she used only her hips, keeping her weight on him and the rings tightly in her unrelenting grasp.

'Doesn't feel so good from that end of things, does it?' she grunted. 'Much more fun to be the one with the cock, isn't it? But then, I was forgetting.' She paused at the point of deepest penetration and her right hand, releasing the ring on the side, slipped down to enfold his own shaft, still tightly encased in the restraining straps and the softer leather sheath.

'I think I prefer you to come like this first.' She leered, increasing the pressure of her grip. 'All secure in your little pouch and with your cunt stretched to the full, I want you to come the way you like to make the girls come. And until you do,' she added, lowering her head so that she was leaning over and speaking directly into his ear, 'I'm going to carry on just like this.

'After all,' she said, laughing, 'that's the way you'd do it if things were the other way round, isn't it?'

When Melinda finally returned to the smaller bedroom, her outfit was the equal of Anna's in its erotic impact.

Spurning her usual choice of catsuits, she had chosen long stockings of a fine red mesh, held up to the hem of a matching red satin corset by a total of four garter straps on each side. The corset was not as severe as the rubber version into which she had laced Anna, but it shaped her usually lithe figure into much more dramatic contours and her uplifted breasts were left almost totally exposed by the lacy half cups that now supported them.

Red stiletto-heeled ankle boots and long, red satin gloves, together with a lace-trimmed red velvet choker completed the desired effect, with her eyes now peering out from behind a red leather highwayman mask. In her hand she carried a short leather quirt and she walked with a calculated swagger as she approached the still unmoving form on the bed.

Tossing the quirt to one side, she moved in and straddled Anna's outstretched knees, grasping her rubber-covered face in both hands and tilting it up to her. Gently, she lowered her mouth and planted a long kiss on the gag strap.

'Now,' she breathed, 'shall we see just how good a slave you make, Anna darling?' She leaned backwards and peered down into the raised eyes. 'Is this how you like it? Do you prefer girls completely, or do you like men to do this to you, too?'

She stepped back and brought her legs together, feeling the heat now in her naked crotch and the dampness between her closely pressed thighs. The combined scents of Anna's body and the rubber which it had now finished warming thoroughly assailed her nostrils and for a moment she experienced a heady feeling of disorientation.

Shaking her head, she breathed deeply again and reached forward, fingers and thumbs reaching for nipples that had now become impossibly elongated by the tight pressure of the rubber circles through which they were being forced as their owner became steadily more aroused. Bending lower, Melinda stretched her neck forward and deftly sucked the right nipple into her mouth. Anna's reaction was quite startling.

Arching her spine, the Norwegian girl threw back her head and a feral howl rent the air in the room, despite the muffling effect of the gag and its covering strap. Surprised, Melinda drew back, but a moment's inspection showed that there was nothing wrong with her captive lover. Quite the opposite, in fact.

The eyes that had shone in lustful anticipation so shortly before were now glazed over, the pupils dilated until there was almost no white left to be seen. Melinda gasped herself and shook her head again.

'Ye gods!' she whispered. 'And I haven't even started yet!' She opened her hands, fingers spread wide and carefully cupped the rubber-covered breasts, allowing her thumbs to trail lightly across the unprotected nipples and immediately she felt Anna's entire body beginning to tremble.

'Slut!' she hissed, but her lips formed themselves into a delighted smile. Firmly, she pushed against Anna, who made no effort to resist the pressure, falling heavily back across the bed, her legs sliding outwards and apart, exposing the gaping slash of a sex that was already glistening with expectancy.

'Oh my!' Melinda exclaimed. 'Oh my, but we'd better do something about that, I think.' She stooped again, pushing forward so that her knees forced Anna's outstretched legs even further apart and then leaned forward, taking her weight on her arms, her gloved hands gripping the fabric of the bed covering to afford her the purchase she needed.

Slowly, she lowered herself, pressing inwards until her own sex was touching Anna's. To her amazement, she sensed something that felt like a small penis pressing against her own nether lips and, when she pulled back again and peered down between them, she was rewarded by the sight of the longest clitoris she had ever seen, already projecting well clear of Anna's outer labia and still, it appeared, growing larger by the second.

'Well I never did!' was all she could find to say, but she quickly recovered, even though she continued to stare at the phenomenon transfixed by disbelief for several more seconds. At last, when the pink stem finally appeared to have reached its maximum size, Melinda squatted down again and examined it at much closer quarters.

'Well, I never did,' she repeated to herself softly. 'But that's about to change, I think.' Delicately, she extended her neck one more time, her tongue flickering between her lips, and lifted the long, booted legs carefully up to drape them over her shoulders.

'How come I'm getting the feeling that there's something bigger going on here than just a couple of coppers doing a bit of unofficial fishing? And no pun intended.' Geordie peered through the spray-covered wheelhouse screen at the grey waves and deeper grey sky above them. They had been at sea only half an hour, but already he was beginning to realise that there might be more to the trawler, *Essie*, than at first met the eye and the same might also be said for its skipper, the balding, bearded Angus Frearson.

Alongside him, Frearson sucked steadily on a pipe that had extinguished itself some time ago now and continued to stare steadfastly ahead into the growing swell. For several seconds it seemed that he might not have heard Geordie's question, but then, without turning his head, he grunted.

'Good friend of yours, Colin Turner?' he asked. Geordie regarded him with a sideways look.

'We're friends, yes,' he replied.

'Known him a long time, I hear?' There was the faintest burr of a Scots accent, but Angus Frearson had evidently spent many years away from his native land, if indeed it was his native land. Geordie detected several other dialectic influences in his voice, though he was unable to pin any of them down with any confidence.

'Long enough,' Geordie said tersely. 'We don't live in each other's pockets, but we still keep in touch.'

'Aye, that's the best kind of friendship.' Another heavy silence descended. Then: 'You did some undercover work, so I hear?' Geordie looked as surprised as he felt. That was a chapter in his eventful life that was supposed to be a closely guarded secret and the fact that Frearson seemed to know of it, if not all about it, suggested he was no simple, semi-retired fisherman.

'Must have seemed like the back end of beyond when they sent you up to these parts,' Frearson continued. 'Bet you'll be glad when the dust settles and you can get back to the bright lights, eh?'

'It's pleasant enough up here,' Geordie replied, non-commitally.

'Aye, it's a beautiful place and no mistake,' Frearson agreed. 'And far enough away from psychotic drug dealers so you don't have to go around all day with one eye in your arse, too.'

'There is that,' Geordie agreed. So Frearson knew about the contract that the Newcastle underworld, in the terrifyingly insane form of Bozzy Harper, had placed on him. Geordie studied the man closely. He was six feet four himself, yet he didn't dwarf Frearson, so the supposed trawlerman had to be at least six two and he was powerfully built, broad-shouldered with thick fore-arms and almost no fat to mark the passage of time, despite the fact that he had to be fast approaching sixty, at least.

'You going to tell me what's going on here?' Geordie suggested at last. 'I mean, this is all supposed to be strictly unofficial and, as far as I knew, you were just someone Colin knew from the past.'

'Aye.' Frearson sucked noisily again and his eyes flickered downwards, as if he had only just realised that his pipe was no longer alight. 'Right on both counts, laddie,' he murmured. 'Yes, this is all *very* unofficial and yes, I am someone he knows from the past. We've worked together twice before, as it happens.' He turned his head sideways and fixed Geordie with an unblinking stare.

''Course,' he continued, 'there's unofficial and there's unofficial, if you get my drift?'

'I think so,' Geordie said, though he remained unsure. Frearson looked back towards the plunging bow and continued.

'I'm not privy to the counsel of the so-called great and wise, you understand?' he said. 'So I may not know a whole lot more than you do yourself.'

'I wouldn't put your pension on that,' Geordie muttered. 'But go on. I'm all ears.'

'Well, all I know is this: yon islands we're heading for are a bit of a mystery and this isn't the first time they've come to the attention, as it were. Nothing dramatic, you understand, but little things – annoying little things and coincidences that didn't ought to happen.

'Mind you,' he added, with a gruff chuckle, 'that's the thing with coincidences. They shouldn't happen but they do and that's why we call them coincidences. Still, this lot have been stretching the point over the past few years and there are certain people who don't like that.

'Unfortunately,' he said, stressing the word with a heavily ironic tone, 'there are certain other people who seem determined that this first lot of people shouldn't get close enough to ask too many questions of the very first lot of people – the people who run this Healthglow place.'

'Friends and influence,' Geordie muttered.

'Aye, and in all the right and wrong places. Two words along the wrong lines and wallop, everything is shut down tighter than a drum. Nothing official is ever said, you understand and nothing is ever written down – nothing that could ever be considered incriminating if it all went pear-shaped in the future, at least.'

'But definitely heavy political muscle?'

'Political muscle or money muscle,' Frearson agreed. 'Which amounts to the same thing, usually, in my experience. You know yourself what happened when you tried to push things over the death of your sergeant lassie.'

'Yes,' Geordie said grimly. 'Very polite and very helpful. Model fucking citizenship, but just on the surface. When we considered trying to look beyond the obvious, which any half-decent copper would at least take a crack at, my governor was told very firmly to lay off and that the case was closed to everyone's satisfaction.'

'Except yours, of course.'

'Aye, except mine.' Geordie turned away from the screen and crossed the small wheelhouse to the swivelling seat that served the small collection of radar and communications equipment in the rear starboard corner. 'Technology,' he muttered. 'Can't even net a few fish without it.' He looked up at Frearson's broad back, but the skipper seemed to be concentrating on what lay ahead of his craft, not concerned with anything his passenger might be doing.

'You actually use this boat for fishing, then?' he asked innocently.

'Now and then, just for appearances,' Frearson replied, without turning round. 'We do the odd tourist trip, too. Lot less work involved. Mind you, the lad takes her out more than I do nowadays.'

The 'lad', Geordie assumed, had to be the thirty-something, flame-haired ogre who seemed to divide himself between the engines and the tiny galley space, where he was even now supposedly brewing tea to fill the huge tin mugs Geordie had seen hanging on a row of hooks in there.

'He's got a couple of younger brothers who help out sometimes, too. One's away at university most of the year, but he's around when he's most needed, in the summer holiday period.'

'Your lad back there,' Geordie asked, 'does he know what's going on here?'

'Some,' Frearson said. 'He knows what he needs to know, anyway.'

'But he's not a copper.' Not like you, he added, but only under his breath.

'No. And neither am I, for that matter.' Geordie looked at the man's back disbelievingly. 'Not in the strictest sense, anyway. Had fifteen years in the job, of course, when I was younger, but then I sort of transferred out.'

'Ah.' Geordie fell silent and pondered this for a few moments. It made sense, he thought. Top notch young copper with better than average brain, other skills that could be useful, not least the ability to look like a simple trawler skipper and probably with the sort of background that ensured he wouldn't look out of place in an area like this.

'So, what do you do mostly up here?' he asked again. 'I mean, OK so you do a bit of fishing and take a few tourists round the islands during the season, but that's not enough to pay for a boat like this and keep her running. This little electronic set-up alone must have cost a fortune and it all looks a bit new to me.'

'Aye, it is,' Frearson conceded. 'But then you'll find similar in quite a few other boats in these waters.'

'Even the sonar?'

'Useful for tracking the shoals.'

'Among other things?'

'Aye, among other things.'

'Meaning I should stop asking questions?'

'You ask all the questions you like, laddie,' Frearson said affably. 'It'll help pass the time, if nothing else.'

'But you won't necessarily give me all the answers, eh?' Geordie grinned at the broad back. 'Maybe I'll just go and see where that tea's got to. What did you say your lad's name was?'

'Not sure as I did,' Frearson said. 'But it's Mac.' Geordie shrugged and sighed quietly.

'Yeah,' he said, half under his breath. 'It would be.'

Sara was packed and waiting when Colin finally called to collect her, her case waiting at the foot of the bed. She had dressed conservatively – Celia had stressed that guests travelling to Carigillie never did anything to draw attention to themselves – in a smart jacket and skirt of navy blue, crisp white blouse and medium-heeled court shoes. She had rinsed a dark henna colouring into her hair and she looked very nervous. Immediately Colin began to have second thoughts about including her in the travelling party.

'I'll be all right,' she asserted quietly, when he probed her. 'I'm not afraid, not as such. I'm just . . . well, from what little I do know, this could be a somewhat unusual experience. You've got to remember, this is all as new to me as it is to you and there are going to be even more people out there.'

'Ah, I see.' Colin nodded his understanding. 'But there were people at Celia's,' he pointed out.

'Yes, there were,' she agreed. 'And even that made me feel a bit strange.'

'You'd rather stay behind?' Colin offered. 'We can always say you're coming down with a bad cold or something.' Sara shook her head, fiercely.

'No!' she said. 'No, I want to come.' Colin looked at her curiously, but she refused to meet his gaze.

'Fair enough,' he said at last. 'Then we'd better get a move on. They sent a car and driver to meet us from the ferry and it's waiting outside now. You've got everything straight in your mind?' She nodded and raised a hand to touch her hair.

'Does this colour work?' she asked.

'Fine,' he replied. 'Just in case there are any odd guests there who might have seen you in the past, that's all. It's surprising how a change of hair colour and style can alter a person's appearance,' he added, stooping to pick up her case. 'All this James Bond stuff about false moustaches and plastic surgery – it's all a load of bull, mostly. Unless we're unlucky enough to find someone who knows you really well, you won't be recognised.'

'And we have the back-up story,' Sara added. 'I got to know you at a seminar about a year ago and eventually you discovered my little secret passion.'

'And dear old Andy Lachan never knew that you and I were playing his own little games on the side.'

'Of course,' Sara agreed. She looked pointedly down at the case that was now in his hand. 'Don't you think I should carry my own bag?' she said. 'After all, you're supposed to be my master, aren't you?'

'No, I'll carry it,' Colin asserted. 'Nothing to draw attention, remember? Once we arrive on the island, that's a different matter, but up until then, we act as any couple might.'

'Fair comment.' She looked around the room for one more time, as if to make sure that she hadn't forgotten anything. 'You managed to organise things for me from Celia?'

'No need,' Colin replied. 'Apparently, the price includes the use of any facilities they have and according to Celia they're pretty extensive. Oh, by the way, let me have your mobile phone and I'll leave it at the desk till we get back. Celia tells me they insist on all phones being handed in on arrival.'

'Ah!' She opened her small handbag, took out the cellphone and handed it to him. 'You think they might try tracing the phones back to their owners?' He grinned.

'Depends how thorough they are,' he said. 'I know I might do it, so we'll bc just as thorough.'

'What about your phone?'

'No problem. It's been registered to Jason David Anderson for more than a year now and the bills are all settled through an account in the same name.'

'Another of your aliases?'

'A very useful one, actually. Jason Anderson is registered as a major shareholder in several fictitious companies, which by now that Healthglow lot will have checked into.'

'What if they realise the companies are bogus?'

'They won't,' Colin said firmly. 'A lot of trouble went into creating this particular identity string. I can't tell you too much, but I doubt whether I'm the first Jason David Anderson. In fact, I know for a fact I'm not.'

'What about if you run into someone who met one of the other Jasons in the past.' Colin shrugged and grinned.

'Not very likely,' he said, 'otherwise I wouldn't have been given the ID to use. And the last Jason is now masquerading under an entirely different name, working as an attaché in one of our diplomatic outposts in some obscure little African dictatorship.' Sara's eyes narrowed.

'I thought you said you were just a policeman,' she said accusingly.

'Policemen, my love,' Colin replied, turning towards the door, 'come in all shapes and sizes and there are more funny little government departments than you could count on all your pretty fingers and cute toes, which tend to overlap with each other when the need arises.' He raised a finger to his lips.

'But that's as much as I'm prepared to tell you at this stage, OK?' Sara hesitated.

'Your friend?' she said. 'Geordie? Does he know?'

'Know what?' Colin replied, with an innocent look. 'What's to know? I'm just a humble detective constable – a small cog in a very big machine.'

'Yes, and I'm the Queen of Sheba,' Sara muttered, shaking her head, but she let the matter drop and followed him dutifully out into the corridor.

Celia had mooted the idea for better disguising Sara, during the short wait for the helicopter that was to take the small party out to Carigillie Craig. As they stood in the lee of the small, brick-built single-storey building that appeared to serve as both oupost office and waiting room for Healthglow guests and services, she quietly drew Colin to one side and explained.

'Tell her now,' she urged, in an urgent whisper. 'And don't forget, once we leave here, never mention anything that might arouse suspicion. Out in the open, you should be all right, but I do know that there are cameras and microphones all over the interior quarters.'

'Every room?' Colin asked. Celia looked vague.

'I don't know for sure,' she admitted. 'Possibly not, but I wouldn't count on it. Their security is like something out of a spy movie, believe me, and there are guards patrolling on the outside, too. Better not to take any risks at all.'

'No risks,' Colin repeated to Sara. 'Just fit in with everything and act naturally. Leave the other stuff for me, though keep your eyes open, obviously.'

'You won't be with me all the time?' Sara looked alarmed at the prospect, but Colin laid a reassuring hand on her arm.

'I promise I won't leave you on your own for more than I have to,' he said. 'But I need to take advantage of whatever opportunities come up. We have to appear as if we're just out there for the jollies, same as everyone else who pays their extortionate prices, but at the same time we need to look around, see if we can find anything incriminating, or anything that might give us a clue as to why they'd risk killing a police officer.'

And probably a good few other people into the bargain, he thought, but he kept that to himself. There seemed no point in worrying Sara any more than she already clearly was and the doubts as to the wisdom of including her in the venture resurfaced with a vengeance. However, as the small dot appeared over the horizon and quickly magnified into the shape of a helicopter, rotors chop-chopping in the keen morning air, he knew it was too late to go back now.

For better or worse, if they were going to go, it had to be today. If they pulled out at such a late hour, suspicions would be sure to become aroused and, even if they did get a second opportunity, they would probably find themselves under even closer scrutiny than Celia appeared to think they would be already.

'Just pretend we're back at Celia's,' he whispered. 'No need to rush at anything. Let's just enjoy ourselves and let things take their own course. You don't have to do anything except look your usual gorgeous self.'

The trip was short and uneventful, although the helicopter bucked alarmingly on two or three occasions as it hit unexpectedly turbulent spots. The pilot, however, knew his job well and fifteen minutes after take-off they touched down on the concrete landing pad in front of a modern-looking building that could have been a small hotel almost anywhere in the world. Glass, brick and stone – modern, smart and totally without character, two storeys of practical efficiency triumphing over the aesthetic. But then, Colin mused, with an ironic grin, the people who came here sought their aesthetic kicks in ways that made innovative architecture superfluous.

Even before the rotors had stopped spinning, the glass doors swung open and a bevy of smartly uniformed attendants, both male and female, emerged and fanned out to form a reception party. Bags and cases were taken, nods and respectful greetings were directed towards Celia, and a black-haired, tightly skirted female in her early thirties attached herself to Colin, carefully ignoring the two younger women in the party, as if she was already aware of their assumed slave status.

'We've put you and your, er, companion in Blue Fourteen, Mr Anderson,' she said brightly. 'I think you'll find everything there to your satisfaction, but if not, just ring through to reception, or ask for me. I'm Sylvia, by the way, Guest Liaison Officer.'

'I'm sure everything will be fine,' Colin assured her. 'Miz Butler has waxed extremely lyrical over your facilities, believe me.'

'I'm sure we'll live up to her recommendation,' Sylvia purred, as they passed into the foyer. Colin noted the small reception desk, the door leading off into what he guessed was the entrance security office and the two discreet cameras that watched over the area from either side. No attempt had been made to disguise them properly, but then, he thought, that was probably a calculated move. It was an old trick: keep the cameras small but visible where it didn't matter if people saw them, but where it counted, that was a different matter.

'Miz Butler is an old and honoured guest here,' Sylvia twittered on. Colin raised an eyebrow and smiled at her.

'I shouldn't let her hear you use the "o" word, if I were you.' He chuckled. 'I think our Celia is only too well aware of the march of time, dear lady.'

'Oh, I didn't mean –' Sylvia began to protest, but left the sentence unfinished. 'I'll just collect your key for you,' she said, recovering her composure. 'Then we can go on up.'

There was nothing so far in the building that was at all out of the ordinary, Colin decided, when Sylvia finally left them alone in the suite. Even their effusive guardian angel was exactly what one might expect to find in a place set up to cater for the whims of the rich and idle who had decided to leave behind the more extreme trimmings of the good life in the name of good health and a trimmer figure.

'Go through, strip off and get yourself into the bath,' he instructed Sara tersely. They exchanged a brief glance and his lips twitched, belying the abruptness of his tone. Sara lowered her head, turned away and moved across to the wide double bed, already unbuttoning her jacket.

'Nice view,' Colin commented, standing in front of the wide expanse of glass and looking out towards the nearest stretch of coastline and noting how few trees there were to block the view to the sea. 'Still, we're not up here for the scenery, are we, Sassie? So move your arse and go get in that bath and make sure you shave your cunt nice and close, right?'

If anyone was listening in, or even watching, that should sound convincing enough, he calculated. After a moment's thought, he crossed the room again and picked up the telephone from its cradle on the bedside table. A polite female voice answered within three seconds.

'Coffee, please,' he snapped. 'And I wonder if you could rustle up a bottle of brandy. No rubbish, mind.'

'Of course, sir,' the girl replied. 'Anything to eat?' Colin added an order for roast beef sandwiches and replaced the phone, just as the knock came at the door. It was Celia and she was carrying a small, square-cornered case.

'I've come to help you prepare Sassie,' she said briskly, 'though you understand that her tack will have to wait until we get to the other side?'

Colin nodded. 'Of course. You've brought a cape for her, though? I don't want her back in her own clothes until it's time to leave again. I like to keep her on a strict rein, as it were.'

He looked steadily at Celia, whose own expression gave nothing away, save for a slight flickering of her eyelashes, and then turned away and walked back to the window. So far even his trained eye had not been able to spot any cameras, though he felt sure they were there somewhere, possibly secreted in one of the turned metal ends of the curtain track. Someone knew his business, of that Colin was certain; the miniature microphone disguised at a securing bolt in the head of the bed proved that.

'It's going to be a nice morning, Jangles.' Amaarini had dismounted and now she walked up to stand beside Alex, who was once again between the shafts in full harness and hooves, bit between her teeth and her voice deactivated. It was as though the previous night had not happened, except that Amaarini's tone with her was a little less harsh.

The tall alien reached out and took hold of the cheek strap, turning Alex's face towards her.

'You see, my pretty Jangles,' she said, 'it's not so bad a life here, is it? The air is fresh out among these islands and, when the sun shines, there is no more beautiful place. And as for you, there is no more beautiful pony. The doctor excelled himself when he produced these particular host bodies, I think.' She relaxed her grip and finally let go altogether, though Alex continued to look at her.

'Perhaps I could even arrange for you to transfer to an even better body,' Amaarini continued, almost absently. 'They are making new improvements all the time.' Her gaze was now fixed on the distant horizon; the early cloud and threatened mist had dispersed with the sort of haste peculiar to the speed with which the weather changed among the islands and now the sun hung brightly in the clear blue autumn sky. It was the sort of morning Alex had known many times in the past, though never under such bizarre circumstances as now.

The fishing fleets, or what remained of them, would be long put to sea by this time, she knew, anxious to take advantage of the weather break, keen to find one more worthwhile catch before the really bad weather started to set in. On the farms, the little tractors would be busily chug-chugging up and down, turning in the last of the stubble and breaking the ground ready for the winter frosts to perform its annual duty.

There would be few tourists among the islands now, though. She had only learned the exact date yesterday, from watching the television news bulletins and had been surprised how early it still was, but even so, the short Shetland summer season was already well past and the first snows could appear at any time, despite the mildness of the weather this morning.

Eventually, Amaarini seemed to remember she was still there and turned back, reaching out a hand to cup one of Alex's heavy breasts. Despite herself, Alex felt a wave of desire shudder through her and mentally cursed the way in which the woman was able to exert such a control over her body's desires and reactions.

'The doctor and his people are making even greater leaps forward now, you know,' Amaarini murmured. 'It really is quite remarkable what they have achieved so far and yet, they tell me, there are even greater strides to be taken. Perhaps they will even discover a way to produce a body suitable for our females, one at least that will last more than a few decades at a time.'

Alex raised her eyebrows quizzically, wishing she had the use of her voice again, if only for long enough to prompt the woman further. Amaarini, however, seemed to be in an unusually talkative mood and verbal prompting appeared to be unnecessary.

'Of couse,' she said, 'you don't know anything about it, do you? I suppose you think that just because we've given you and your kind bodies that will endure for centuries that we can do the same for ourselves. Sadly, my dear Jangles, that is not so, at least not at the present.

'I suppose it is quite ironic,' she continued. 'Whilst Ikothi Leenuk and his admirable team can clone bodies directly from among our own females, the resultant hosts are no more enduring than the originals and the bearing of a child hastens even that premature end still further. Eventually, they managed to produce a hybrid clone host, using a gene mixture that was part natural, part human, taking samples from the half-breed offspring.

'These are an improvement, but still far from perfect. The life span is still measured only in decades and the ageing process is only staved off for the first twenty years or so, necessitating regular body changes.' She stepped back and looked Alex up and down, as if seeing her for the first time.

'I think your body would provide an excellent host mother,' she observed casually. 'I shall speak with Leenuk on the matter. But whether to inseminate you naturally or artificially, that would be the big question. Would I want you to lie panting beneath some suitably husky Askarlani, or would I prefer to do it myself, eh?

'Perhaps the latter would be more fitting,' she went on, smiling strangely. 'An insemination kit used in my own bed, as a suitable consummation of our love-making? There would be a certain delicious irony in that, don't you think, Jangles? How beautifully perverse for me to inseminate my sweet pony lover in order to produce the child from which my next host body will be cloned.

'Oh, I see you look surprised by that, Jangles? Did you think that we would take the child itself for that purpose? My, but you must think us as barbaric as your own races, even to consider such a terrible thing!

'No, Jangles, any babies you bear will be treated well and brought up among us almost as if they were true blood Askarlani. Not quite, you understand, if only because the half breeds tend to exhibit certain flaws that mark them apart from us in some respects.

'Poor Sol is a half breed. I suppose you might have guessed as much for yourself now that I have told you what I have told you. Of course, we all tend to find ourselves slightly enslaved by our various bodies, as I already explained to you, but unfortunately the half breeds suffer that burden to a far greater extent and some, like Sol, are weak-willed into the bargain.

'There is a delightfully crude human expression that applies to Sol, I think.' She laughed, shaking her head in amusement. 'Our little Sol,' she said, 'too often follows where his cock leads!'

Fiona tightened the final lace on the penis sheath and gave the thin chain that led from the ring at its tip a sharp tug.

Sol grunted and bit into the gagging rubber, almost toppling forward at the same time.

'Excellent!' Fiona exclaimed. 'Quite the ideal thing.' She stood up, paying out the small coil of fine links and wrapping the last few inches about her gloved hand. Sullenly, Sol eyed her from between the heavy blinkers, wondering what new tortures her corruptly fertile mind had cooked up for him today.

His entire body still ached from the rigours of the previous evening and night and he had only been granted a scant four hours of respite since she had finally returned him to his cramped stall, but already she herself seemed full of energy again, bright-eyed and plainly eager to resume her quest to exact her revenge upon him.

'Unfortunately,' she sighed, 'I have had to endure one disappointment already this morning. Last evening I learned that a certain guest – one of the regular visitors – was arriving first thing today and I'd assumed she would be bringing her regular companion with her. I expect you remember Loin, don't you, Sol?'

Sol's eyes opened wide in horror and he gasped again, for he knew Loin only too well, had seen the strange fellow several times, his prodigious weapon and ability to sustain a prolonged assault with it already a legend on the island, among residents and visitors alike.

'Sadly, however,' Fiona said, putting on a deliberately sarcastic show of remorse, 'poor Loin has been laid low by some bug, so his place has been taken by a female slave. Not the same thing at all, of course, but there will be another time, I'm sure. I've had a quiet word with Loin's mistress and she assures me that he will be fit to travel again in another ten days at most. She's also agreed to lend me his services, which I thought was quite sweet of her, don't you agree?

'So that'll be something for us both to look forward to, won't it? I'm told you'll be staying down here for at least a month, so that leaves plenty of time for you two to get to know each other, doesn't it?'

* * *

The mask felt very cold as Celia pressed it to Sara's face. The gum adhesive sprayed over the inner surface gave the thin latex a slippery, dead fish texture and the combined smells were both acrid and sweet, bringing small tears to the corners of Sara's eyes.

'Hold very still, Sassie, and don't even try to speak.' Not that there was much to be said, Sara thought, as Celia continued stretching and easing the rubber over the contours of her features. They had all agreed earlier that they would stay strictly 'in character' at all times, so that anyone monitoring their movements would see nothing suspicious.

Melinda and Anna had assumed the roles of Celia's latest slaves. Melinda having been a regular participant in the events at Celia's various establishments, it had required no effort to provide her with a cover and Anna had simply adopted the identity of one of her female cousins, an artist who lived largely off a trust fund established by a long-dead great-grandmother and who globe-trotted at such a frantic rate that it would be nigh on impossible to establish her supposed whereabouts at any given time.

'That's got it,' Celia announced eventually. 'Now, just remain still for another few minutes, until the adhesive finishes drying.' The finished effect, when Sara was finally permitted to study it in the bathroom mirror, was quite startling. The mask was designed to cover only her face, leaving her dyed hair unimpeded and it had been made by a real craftsman. Only a very close inspection would betray its presence, Sara saw, and by the time a collar was added to disguise the lower edges, the illusion would be complete.

The face that stared back at her was unrecognisable as her own and the slightly darker skin tone went well with the dark reddish brown of her hair. What she now presented was the face of the greater East, a curious mixture of oriental Chinese features and the light, coffee-coloured complexion found among the native peoples in the Pacific islands.

The slightly slanted eyes, flatter-looking and broader nose, the wider mouth and fuller lips all combined to produce a quite flattering effect and Sara was reminded of the women she had seen on Bali a few years earlier, during a holiday tour that had been her reward for getting a double first at Cambridge. She opened her mouth to say something, but the words came out badly slurred, the inwardly curving rubber lips that covered her own lips proving a surprising impediment to coherent speech.

'No speaking from now on, Sassie,' Celia warned her. 'You're still a pony, don't forget, even though we haven't got you to the stables yet. Your new face will remain for the duration of our stay here, a reminder to you that you have no connection with your former personality without your master's permission.'

The entire mask had now taken on a stiffer quality, not completely rigid, but certainly restricting the face's ability to illustrate emotions. Tentatively, Sara tried an experimental smile; the lips curved slightly at either end, but no more and the rest of the features remained impassive. Almost the proverbial inscrutability, she thought, and definitely now unrecognisable as Andrew Lachan's former personal assistant. Even her own parents wouldn't recognise her like this, she realised, and, safe behind her new anonymity, she finally began to relax.

'Everything appears to be perfectly in order, Boolik Gothar.' The young Askarlani female passed the sheaf of print-outs to the security chief and sat back in her seat, looking up at him expectantly. Boolik took the reports, but did not look at them immediately Instead, his expression became suddenly and frighteningly ferocious.

' "Appears", Soobilini?' he growled. 'Only "appears"? Either these details are in order, or they are not!'

Soobilini Makanat looked flustered and confused.

'I only meant,' she stammered, 'that I have carried out all the required checking procedures and there is nothing to suggest any problems with these people in the Butler party.' Boolik made no reply, but he began to leaf through the papers, his keen eye scanning the various paragraphs at a surprising rate.

'An artist, eh?' he muttered, at last. 'Strange creatures, artists. And two little rich girls, probably spending ridiculous allowances from over-indulgent fathers. Or else the money is coming from this man, Anderson. He seems to be something of an enigma.'

'Most likely a crook who manages to maintain an aura of respectability,' Soobilini ventured. 'My checks indicate that his companies have attracted the attentions of the authorities on several occasions.'

'But no actions ever taken,' Boolik said. 'Insufficient grounds. Unfounded allegations.' He finished reading and handed the papers back. 'Looks like our Mr Anderson covers his tracks well. Or perhaps he is legitimate and just has a few enemies.'

'Should I investigate him further?'

Boolik shook his head. 'No point,' he replied. 'Our systems have found everything they are likely to find. Further searches would be fruitless, I assure you.'

'Then everything *is* in order?'

'It is,' Boolik confirmed. 'But transfer your results to my personal terminal. Anderson could prove useful to us in the future. He is exactly the type of human we may be able to make use of, so now all we need is to be able to establish just what sort of inducements or leverage will work best with him.'

When Celia finally returned to their room, Melinda and Anna were given a small package each. In her hand she retained a similar package and the girls saw that all three were wrapped in soft cloth and tied around with a thin ribbon.

'Don't open them yet,' Celia instructed. 'Just bring them with you and come with me.' Without further explanation, she turned and opened the door again. The two girls exchanged glances, but said nothing and rose to follow her out into the corridor.

They walked in silence, passing several closed doors and a stairwell, until, when they reached the end of the building, the passageway took a left turn. Twenty yards further on, they turned yet again and found themselves standing in a bare vestibule, with more doors leading off in three different directions.

'You may open the packages now,' Celia told them. 'You will see they are quite simple blindfold devices that fit over the top half of the head and face and fasten by means of a locking chin strap. I am also required to be blindfolded, before we go any further.

'When we are all ready, someone will come to guide us. Not even I am permitted to know where the entrance to the subway is hidden.'

'Subway?' Melinda looked puzzled, but Anna was already pulling the ribbon from her package. Celia gave her an exasperated look.

'The real action takes place on another island altogether,' she explained. 'Access from the sea is very dangerous at best, so there is a tunnel beneath the sea bed, connecting it with this island. However, the actual entrance is very well hidden and no guests are allowed to know where it is. Once we are in the tunnel itself, the blindfolds will be removed again, but for now we must put these things on.

'They're not uncomfortable, but you'll see that the soft padding and the way in which the outer fabric is cut to fit down over the cheeks ensures that not even a glimmer of light penetrates. There is also padding over the ears, though it doesn't block out all sound – just enough to prevent us recognising any background noise that might provide clues, so I'm told.'

As she drew the cap over her head and settled the padded section across her eyes, Melinda found herself suddenly pitched into total darkness and realised that Celia's assertion as to the efficiency of the blindfolds was well founded. Also, as the two thicker sections pressed over her ears, she began to feel alarmingly disoriented and completely alone, despite the fact that she could still vaguely sense, rather than hear, the nearby movements of her two companions.

Fingers reached out to assist her in fastening the chin strap and the click of the small lock sounded unnaturally loud as it was transmitted through the bones of her jaw and skull.

'Just stand perfectly still.' She heard Celia's muffled instruction from close by her left ear. 'As soon as I've secured my own blindfold, someone will be along to take us down. We don't usually have to wait more than a minute or two.'

True to her words, they were not left to wait for very long. Melinda sensed the new presence just a moment before the strong hand took hold of her wrist, but it was all she could do not to cry out in surprise, even so.

'Just relax,' a new voice – male – penetrated the ear padding. 'Just walk steadily ahead and turn whenever I tell you. I won't let you come to any harm.'

The next several minutes were a confusion of walking, turning, standing, turning again and yet more walking. To Anna, it felt as if some of the manoeuvres were nothing more than feints, designed to add an extra layer of perplexity to the journey, although she knew she had no definite grounds for that suspicion.

She sensed doorways as they passed through, but that too could have been only in her imagination. The thorough deprivation of senses taken all too often for granted could have strange effects on the human mind, as Anna knew only too well, but there was no mistaking the elevator when it began to descend, nor the jarring sensation when it stopped again after what seemed to be only a very short trip.

Again they walked, turned, walked and turned several more times and Anna realised that they were probably still on one of the hotel levels, either the ground floor, or perhaps a basement and this was soon borne out, for they entered a second elevator and this time the descent lasted a lot longer. This time, when the door slid open, there was a faint draught and the air felt cooler and considerably more damp.

The unseen guide urged her forward again and Anna felt the hard stone or concrete floor beneath her feet. They were definitely well below the ground level now and in some sort of man-modified, if not entirely man-made tunnel system. They went forward and she counted twenty-five paces, before they turned to the right, another fifteen paces followed by another right turn and then ten straight ahead and a final halt.

She felt fingers beneath her chin and a moment later hands were drawing the blindfold hood from her head, making her blink as her eyes were exposed to the harsh glare of overhead fluorescent lighting. Anna shook her head to settle her hair, blinked again and looked about her. To her left stood the man she presumed had been leading her and to his left again two more men were removing the hoods from Celia and Melinda.

They were all standing on a narrow, raised platform, just below which ran a narrow-gauge, single-track railway line, which led off in both directions, disappearing into a darkened tunnel in each case. As she listened, Anna heard a distant rumbling sound from the left-hand tunnel and, as it grew louder, she saw a faint glimmer of light from around what appeared now to be a gentle bend. A moment later, a small electric-powered engine came into view, its headlights dazzling when seen full on, and behind it, like something out of a fairground scene, came two open-topped carriages, each designed, it appeared, to carry up to six passengers at a time.

The journey through the tunnel was eerie, but uneventful. The engine's headlights lit up the way ahead, but above and behind them everything was black and impenetrable. Nervously, Anna peered up at the curving roof, wondering just how many feet of rock separated them from the full weight of the cold North Sea above, consoling herself with the thought that whoever had been responsible for creating this tunnel had to have had a good deal more engineering knowledge than she had and that if the water hadn't caused a collapse by now, it probably wasn't about to do so just because she was there.

The tunnel emerged eventually into a carbon copy of the 'station' where they had boarded the curious little train and squealed to a halt level with an arched opening, through which Anna could plainly see a wide flight of stone steps leading upwards. At the top of these stairs another tunnel waited, this time sloping gently upwards again, for about fifty yards, where a heavy door blocked the way, with a small camera set above it, a red warning indicator light flashing steadily next to the lens.

Whoever was monitoring their approach was apparently quite happy that all was in order, for the door slid noiselessly sideways as they reached it and they walked through into a rectangular area with a carpeted floor. From this room several more doors led off in different directions and a small, mirror-glassed window, set high in the wall opposite, looked down upon their arrival like an unblinking eye.

'We go this way, slaves,' Celia announced, pointing to the right. She turned to the three guards who had accompanied them and smiled. 'Thank you so much, gentlemen,' she said, nodding to each of them in turn. 'It'll never replace the Orient Express, of course, but it's always an engaging little trip.'

She led the way to one of the doors, opened it and walked on through, Anna and Melinda falling in behind her, single file. They were now in yet another corridor, a heavy duty, slate grey carpet underfoot, walls darkly panelled to waist height and painted a much paler grey above. After a further twenty paces or so, they began passing doors on either side.

'Our suite is right at the end,' Celia told them. 'It's much closer to the communal areas and the entrance down to the stables, but you won't be seeing much of either for the moment. I've arranged a special little introductory treat for the pair of you, whilst I spend a few hours helping to put Sassie through her paces.

'Come along now, slaves. There's a special little race meeting scheduled for two o'clock and I want to leave myself plenty of time to practise. Sassie may be a bit raw, but she has great potential, so I intend to drive her myself, as I'm a lot lighter than her master.'

* * *

The sea had become almost flat since they had first put out and the *Essie* made easy headway beneath an almost cloudless sky, her powerful engines throbbing dully beneath their feet.

'Don't often see it like this,' Geordie commented, 'not even in the middle of the summer, so I'm told, anyway.' Angus Frearson leaned against the binnacle, which was almost the only remaining traditional feature in the cramped wheelhouse, and grinned.

'Well, you were told right, laddie,' he chuckled. 'And it's as likely to turn into something else without a moment's notice, too,' he added, 'though I reckon we're set fair for a good few hours yet. Shipping forecast reckons this high will last sometime into tomorrow morning.'

'That's good, then,' Geordie said.

Frearson shrugged. 'Well, it makes for less work,' he agreed, 'and it means there'll be plenty of other activity to help distract attention, but it means we don't want to be getting too close too soon. A calm sea makes radar detection dead easy, you see. A few nice big waves and the *Essie* can disappear off the screens until we're almost on top of them.'

'You think they'll have radar on those islands, then?'

Frearson nodded. 'I don't think, son,' he said. 'I know so.' He tapped the side of his nose with the stem of his pipe. 'Those jokers aren't playing kiddie games.'

'You seem to know a lot about them,' Geordie observed drily.

Frearson grunted and shrugged again. 'Not as much as we'd like to know,' he replied. 'We did manage to get a couple of satellite pictures of the area from the Yanks, a couple of years back now, but then all of a sudden, when we wanted more, we're told they don't have a satellite passing over here any more.'

'Budget cuts, maybe?'

'Budget cuts my arse!' Frearson exclaimed. 'Someone doesn't want us, or anyone else for that matter, looking too closely out here. Someone across the big pond authorised an orbital shift some time back. New priorities was the official explanation, but if you believe that, then you'll believe the Pope's Jewish.'

'Friends in very high places, eh?'

'Very,' Frearson agreed. 'Gives you some idea of what we might be up against here. Takes a lot of clout to get a military satellite shifted, without anyone asking awkward questions.'

'What about the Russians?' Geordie suggested. 'Don't they have anything over the same area? I heard we were now swapping information with them on a regular basis.'

'We probably are,' Frearson said, 'but they don't have anything much left that isn't bloody clockwork driven. All their stuff is pretty ancient now, dropping out of the skies like rain, so I hear. No, laddie, our friends yonder are sitting in a nice blind spot and they know it.'

'So, how close are you intending to go?' Geordie asked.

Frearson leaned forward and picked up his chart board.

'We're going to round Herma Ness in about another hour,' he explained. 'That's the northernmost point of Unst, right? It also happens to be the northernmost point of the main Shetlands group, so then we swing around and go south-east and then east and eventually we start heading back on a south-westerly tack. That way, if we do show up on any screens, it'll look like we're coming down and across from Norway.

'After that, we'll just head back and forth, with some nets out, so if they've got anything in the air, it'll look like we're fishing. If we hold off twenty miles or so from them, they shouldn't get suspicious. That's plenty close enough for the emergency transmitters Colin's got with him.'

'And how long after he signals before we can get there?'

'An hour or so, depending exactly where we are when we hear the signal,' Frearson said. 'But that's not the point. If he does get into trouble, our first priority is to radio back and pass the message on. As for getting ashore there, that's something else altogether.

'If it stays fairly calm, then we could probably get on to Carigillie without too much trouble, but Ailsa is a different kettle, believe me. From what we do know, it'd need inflatables. The rocks around it would tear the bottom out of the *Essie* before we got within a quarter of a mile, unless we were very lucky and I don't believe in pushing luck that far, believe you me!'

'Do we have an inflatable aboard?' Geordie asked.

Frearson nodded. 'Aye, we do that, but there's no way we're going to try tricks like that, not unless things get really dire. No, our job is to go in and make our presence very obvious and wait till the cavalry arrives. There's a specially trained unit, exercising near Freswick, back on the mainland, a few miles south of John O'Groats.

'Three choppers and a couple of dozen crack men, laddie. They'll like as not arrive over the island about the same time we turn up and they'll do whatever needs to be done. Mind you,' he added, with a wry grin, 'if they go storming in there and they don't find anything, I'd hate to be the poor bastard who has to clean the shit off this fan!' He looked down, studying the compass for a few seconds.

'Personally,' he said, after a short pause, 'I hope young Colin manages to get in, find what he's looking for and get the fuck out again without getting into trouble. That way, when the glory boys do go in, they'll know exactly what they're looking for and, more importantly, exactly where to look for it!'

Celia's quarters in the rock beneath Ailsa Ness were much larger than their counterpart on Carigillie, comprising a lounge area, from which led off two bedrooms, a bathroom and one further room that had been extensively equipped to cater for a variety of bizarre activities.

From the ceiling hung several lengths of chain and rope; the end wall comprised a hanging rack, from which dangled all manner of harnesses, whips and other accoutrements whose purpose was not entirely clear to the two girls; the floor space contained a padded vaulting horse construction, complete with securing cuffs on each of the four supporting legs, a high-backed chair with enough straps and cuffs to ensure that the user could be totally immobilised in it and, strangest of all, a life-sized rocking horse.

Celia, however, gave them little opportunity to explore any of this further. Directing them into the smaller of the two bedrooms, she ordered them to strip and then went through to the bedroom she had selected as her own. In there, waiting at the foot of the bed, was a large flight case, the lid already thrown back to reveal a bewildering assortment of clothing. Rubber, leather and PVC, red, black, white and even an eye-searing turquoise shimmered enticingly, but Celia seemed to know exactly what she was looking for and, by the time Melinda and Anna were down to their panties, she returned, carrying a plain black latex catsuit over each arm.

'You'll find talcum powder in the bathroom,' she said, passing them a suit each. 'You can help each other, if necessary, but get those knickers off first. You're going to be my sweet little rubber pets today, so I don't want anything getting in the way.'

It took them about fifteen minutes to get into the suits. They were quite straightforward and held no mysteries for Melinda, who had soon wriggled and eased herself into her new skin, but for Anna it was more of a struggle, her extra height meaning that the latex had to be stretched that much more, an exercise that had to be approached with caution, for fear of ripping the thin fabric.

At last, however, they were ready and stood for a few seconds admiring each other. It came as no surprise to the more experienced Melinda that there was no crotch in either suit, the rubber having been cut away to leave the sex exposed, the edges reinforced to ensure that they did not split and also that they formed an additional pair of lips that squeezed the outer labia into even greater prominence.

The nipples were also left unencumbered, squeezed through reinforced round openings that gripped them in the same way the corset had gripped Anna's nipples before. Feet and gloves were welded extensions of the legs and arms, so that when the back zippers were drawn up to the high collars, both girls were sealed inside a one-piece extra skin, against which the paler colours of their exposed sexes and nipples formed a vivid and unmistakable contrast.

'Stand over alongside the bed,' Celia ordered, coming back into the room. One look at the complex arrangement of straps she had with her told Melinda exactly what was coming next and Celia, understanding that she was far more experienced than her Norwegian partner in slavery, passed the harness to her.

Arranging the straps carefully, Melinda stepped into it, drawing it up her legs and thighs, until one end of the double dildo pressed against her tightly compressed sex lips. Then, holding the waist strap in one hand, she flexed her knees and guided the tip of the phallus into its target, only to find that the additional pressure exerted by the rubber on either side meant that she really needed an extra hand.

'Help her, Ingrid,' Celia ordered, addressing Anna by her assumed name. 'No, don't just hold the straps. Get down on your knees and put the damned cock into her. Don't worry, it'll be her turn to do the same for you in a couple more minutes. Yes, that's it, ease her lips apart.'

Melinda sighed as the thick dildo slid slowly into her; no matter how many times she did such things, that first moment was always such a thrill. She shuddered slightly and stood with her eyes closed, holding on to the harness, whilst Anna pushed the formidable invader fully home.

'Right then, buckle up now!' Celia cried. Shaking herself out of her temporary reverie, Melinda quickly drew the various straps into place, buckling the waist belt and adjusting the crotch strap so that it sat snugly in position.

'Good. Well done, Millie,' Celia said, nodding her approval. 'Now then, put the other end into Ingrid. Ah no, wait a moment,' she added, apparently noticing the disparity between their heights for the first time. 'Ingrid, go through to my room and bring back the shoes you'll find on the end of the bed. I meant to bring them with me, but no matter. Come on, hurry up, girl! Don't stand there gawping at it – it'll be snug inside you soon enough and then you can start appreciating it properly!'

Colin finished cuffing Sara's wrists in front of her and carefully adjusted the long cape to cover both her nakedness and her bondage, joining together the artfully concealed hooks and eyes to ensure that the front of the all-enveloping garment did not come open when she walked. According to Celia, there was a strict rule in force that no guests should appear on Carigillie Island itself in a manner that would attract undue attention and the capes were provided in order that the various masters and mistresses could disguise any preparatory work they considered necessary for their individual slaves.

He stepped back and studied her thoughtfully, wondering exactly what was going on inside her head. Handicapped by the stiff outer lips of the mask, Sara had abandoned all efforts to communicate intelligibly and had fallen silent almost as soon as Celia had left them alone.

'My beautiful, inscrutable Sassie,' he whispered reverently. 'What a picture you make, my darling.' Her eyes regarded him unblinkingly from behind the emotionless mask, but he saw her breasts rising and falling beneath the cape and he guessed that she was already becoming aroused by the anticipation of what was to come. The point of no return had now passed and they were both about to venture into unknown territory once more, but for Sara the situation was far more fraught.

Securely cuffed and already denied effective speech, she was all but helpless and would shortly be rendered even more helpless still. From now on, whatever happened, there was nothing she could do to influence either events or her own fate and although they had said nothing to each other, both of them were only too well aware of the potential dangers that awaited them when they finally reached Ailsa Ness.

'Trust me,' he whispered, stepping forward to take her in his arms, his mouth close to her ear. 'I won't let anything happen to you, my beautiful Sassie.'

But as he turned to answer the expected knock on the door, Colin wished he felt as confident as he'd tried to sound. From here on, he knew only too well, the rules of the game began to change dramatically and the penalties for breaking them were potentially lethal.

* * *

Perched on the crippling six-inch stiletto heels, Melinda now found herself able to look Anna eye to eye and although the Norwegian girl's face remained impassive, the eyes definitely betrayed her mounting anticipation, flickering downwards momentarily to rest on the lifelike rubber penis that now reared up from between Melinda's thighs and the pendulous-looking scrotum that dangled from beneath it.

'That's better,' Celia said approvingly. 'And now, Millie, you may penetrate your lover. Ingrid – move your legs slightly further apart. Yes, that's it.'

Bending her knees slightly, Melinda shuffled foward, grasped Anna by the hips and began to straighten up once more, but once again the pressure of the reinforced rubber around the open crotch slot proved a handicap to easy entry.

'Help her, Ingrid,' Celia instructed. 'Hold yourself open, there's a good girl.' Awkwardly, Anna reached down, her latex-sheathed fingers groping for her sex, pressing in to separate her labial lips and then gently prising them apart. At the same time, Melinda freed one hand to guide the tip of the dildo and between them they now effected an entry for it. Anna exhaled with a muted little cry and closed her eyes, her hands coming up to grasp Melinda on either side of her waist and at the same time Melinda straightened again, so that the entire black length disappeared inside the moist sheath and the two girls stood with their hips pressed close together, the oversized ball sac hanging between the tops of their legs like a grotesquely misshapen pear and the remaining harness straps dangling to either side of them.

'Just stay like that,' Celia said curtly and moved in to complete the harnessing operation. Deftly, she buckled straps about Anna's thighs and waist and then drew the second crotch strap up and between her buttocks, tightening it to the back of the waist strap. When she had finished, the two rubber-suited female bodies were held together, joined at the hips, as surely as if their bodies had been melded there.

'Now, Millie, place your arms about Ingrid's waist,' Celia ordered. Melinda obeyed and a moment later Celia was buckling and locking leather cuffs about her wrists, a few inches of connecting chain ensuring that Melinda could not pull her arms back again. The operation was repeated with Anna's wrists and now they stood in an enforced embrace, like two lovers on a darkened street corner. Celia, however, was far from finished.

Now she opened a small box and took out four circular metallic clips, three fine links of similarly coloured chain joining them in pairs. Melinda recognised their purpose immediately, though she sensed that Anna did not understand until Celia sprung open the first circle and snapped it tightly about the base of her bulging nipple. As the tiny blunted teeth closed in on the tender flesh, Anna let out a startled squeal, but Melinda, more prepared for the sensation, remained silent as the other half of this first pair was similarly attached to her. Moments later, their nipples had been likewise joined on the opposite side, so that if they did allow themselves the full range of slack that their entwined and shackled arms still permitted, they would be pulling against each other's most tender flesh quite painfully.

The final stage of their joining was the most complicated of all. The two rubber hoods were joined together at the mouth, from the insides of which projected stumpy penises that were in reality two ends of the same rubber shaft. This time, Celia began with Anna, working the latex hood down over her head and face and forcing the first end of the rubber penis gag into her mouth and then closing the back of the hood with the rugged zipper.

Now Melinda had to push her face forward, so that her nose was all but touching Anna's, and Celia's task was made all the more difficult by the close proximity of the two heads. However, it was obvious that she had performed the trick before and very soon the other end of the double penis was pressing into Melinda's mouth and the back of her hood was being likewise zipped shut. Two locking collars, one about each of their necks, ensured that only the keyholder would now be able to free them.

'Like Siamese twins,' Celia said, smirking with satisfaction. 'Now, should I zip your eyes closed, or should I leave them?' she mused. 'No, I think I'll leave them, for the moment, at least. That way you can gaze into each other's eyes whilst I'm away. One more thing, though.' She stooped and reached between them for the rubber scrotum and, a moment later, Melinda felt the thick penis inside her come to life. The sudden change in Anna's eyes told her that she was experiencing the same sensation.

'The batteries are in the balls.' Celia chuckled. 'And they should last for around six hours.' She stooped down again and the vibrations ceased abruptly. 'I think,' she said quietly, 'there's something else I've forgotten. Just stay there and don't go away.' She chuckled at her own joke and disappeared back through to her bedroom, but she was back again within seconds, brandishing two more rubber penises, each of which had a flattened, flanged base. In her other hand she carried a small, unlabelled jar.

'We've plugged everything else,' she said cheerfully, 'so we might as well do the job properly.' She selected Melinda first, unfastening her crotch strap and dragging her thighs wider apart. 'I'm lubricating it well,' she muttered, 'so just relax.'

The butt plug penetrated with ease, filling Melinda completely and then the crotch strap was tightened back into place, ensuring that she would not be able to use her sphincter muscles to expel it again. Staring into Anna's eyes, Melinda saw the surprise register as the other plug was pressed into her and the fluttering of eyelashes as her strap was drawn up equally as tightly. A moment later and the larger dildos came to life again.

'Perfect!' Celia exclaimed. 'Now, let's get you both a bit more comfortable.' As she finished speaking, she raised her hands, one to each of their shoulders and, before either girl had time to anticipate her intentions, she shoved hard against them, sending them sprawling sideways across the big bed.

The violent sensations this produced added to the already building effect of the vibrators and, as Celia began dragging their legs round to settle them more squarely in the centre of the mattress, Melinda knew that she was already on the verge of losing control completely. One glance at Anna's tightly shut eyes was enough to tell her that she was not alone.

'There, then,' Celia said, finally satisfied with her efforts. 'That should keep you both out of trouble whilst I'm gone.' She smiled down at them, two quivering, anonymous female bodies, already succumbing to the inevitable and quite helpless to do anything about it.

'You can both thank me later,' she said and laughed, turning towards her bedroom again, 'if you've got enough strength left, that is.' She shook her head and her eyes danced with amusement. 'Enjoy,' she said. 'Do enjoy!'

Sara was already beginning to think like Sassie again, even before the little subterranean train pulled into its destination beneath Ailsa Ness. The feeling of complete detachment from her everyday psyche that came with the sort of helplessness and anonymity created by the cuffs and her nudity beneath the long cape and Celia's strange face mask had now taken over and she followed Colin and their guide in a serene world of her own.

The aroma of rubber and leather as they entered the stables section was overpowering and Sassie felt her entire body start to tremble with anticipation as Colin removed the cape and exposed her to the gaze of the two men who were waiting for them. What she did not expect was the way they quickly moved in to take charge of her, nor the unquestioning way in which Colin accepted this turn of events.

'You leave her to us, sir,' the elder of the two men said, giving Colin a mock salute. 'We'll have her turned out for you in no time at all. Will you be coming back for her, or would you like one of us to drive her out to the track when she's ready? There's a changing room for guests just up there on the left, before the main exit tunnel, by the way, or you can go back to your quarters. You'll be wanting to wear something more suitable, begging my pardon, of course?'

'Well, if it's all right, I'll leave her to you,' Colin said casually. 'And I'll have a look and see what's available down here, too. I didn't bring that great a choice with me, as it happens. My friend has already gone out to this track, I suppose?'

'Oh yes, sir, that she has,' the fellow replied. 'Miz B went through about ten minutes since, didn't she, Jonas?' The younger groom nodded confirmation and at the same time produced a short thong, which he looped through the chain between Sassie's cuffs.

'Do I hose her down first, Higgy?' he asked. Higgy looked at Colin for guidance, but Colin simply shrugged noncommittally.

'Well,' he said slowly, 'she's clean enough, but I'll go along with whatever the usual routine is here. Don't want to upset anybody too soon, what?'

'Well, she smells nice,' Jonas commented. 'Not that my sense of smell is up to much, of course.'

'You're lucky you've got one at all,' Higgy retorted darkly. 'You younger ones just don't appreciate your luck at times.' He looked Sassie up and down with a professional scrutiny that sent a chill through her.

'No need to hose her,' he concluded. 'She looks fine as she is and, besides, time's getting on and Miz B will want to have a few practice laps to get to know her before the racing starts proper.'

With that, Higgy nodded to his younger companion, who gave a sharp tug on the thong and turned to lead Sassie towards one of the few open stable doors. Momentarily, she felt a tiny pang of panic, but she fought against the urge to turn and look back at Paul, who was already strolling casually towards the changing room that Higgy had indicated.

Inside the stall itself, the smells were even more intense and Sassie saw immediately the main source, a wall-long rack that was almost groaning under the weight of harnesses, boots, whips and an assortment of other things whose purpose was a total mystery to her.

Jonas wasted no time on formalities. He quickly released the wrist cuffs and draped them over one of the few remaining empty hooks and then ordered Sassie to raise her arms high in the air, walking slowly around her whilst she held this position, making little grunting noises all the while.

'Not bad,' he said finally. 'Now all we need to do is to make a proper pony out of you. Don't suppose you've ever had a professional work on you, eh?' Uncertainly, Sassie shook her head, lowering her eyes to avoid meeting his openly leering gaze. 'Well, we do things properly here. Sassie, isn't it? Well, you've got a right sassy arse, gal, I'll say that for you. Good firm tits, too.' He turned away, reached out and took something down from the rack.

'Open your mouth,' he said. 'Wide open, now.' Sassie obeyed, feeling the rubber covering of her lips stretching reluctantly. Immediately, Jonas grasped her lower jaw and thrust something in between her teeth, something cold, hard and metallic. For several seconds he fiddled with it, apparently easing it into position and Sassie felt something pressing down across the back of her tongue and heard and felt a dull clicking sound as two small brackets slotted over her molar teeth.

'Hold still now, while I tighten it,' Jonas said. From his pocket he took a small tool, which Sassie initially thought was a screwdriver, but as he raised it closer to her face, she realised that instead of a slotted blade, the end terminated in a strange hexagonal cross section.

'Don't fret yourself,' Jonas chided her, seeing the uncertainty in her eyes. 'This is just what they call an allen key and I'm just using it to tighten the two bits that fit over your teeth. That way, even when you have your bit taken out for feeding, you don't get tempted to start talking.

'Mind you,' he added, grinning, as he inserted the end of the key, 'I reckon this mask does a pretty good job on its own. Nice piece of work, this is. Lovely full lips.' He chuckled to himself as Sassie felt a slight tightening of the right side bracket. 'I love to see nice full lips on a pony-girl,' he said. 'Maybe tonight we'll get the chance to see how you use them, eh?'

The inference was unmistakable and Sassie knew she should have been horrified at what he was suggesting, yet somehow she felt absolutely nothing. An hour ago, if it had been suggested to her that anyone other than Colin would be permitted to even handle her in this intimate fashion, she realised that she might well have refused to let things continue, yet now, here in this closed-in, oppressive environment, she was beginning to feel that nothing could shock her. She had entered willingly, aware that she was handing control of her destiny to others and now, she thought vaguely, she was finally experiencing the ultimate.

Jonas finished at last and pocketed the allen key just as Higgy entered the stall. Once again, Sassie had to stand with her arms high, as the senior groom performed his own inspection routine. Like Jonas, he appeared suitably impressed and Sassie realised immediately that there was probably going to be an element of competition for her services when the time came.

'Fitted the tongue snaffle?' Higgy asked. Jonas nodded. 'Right, well, get those shoes off her and get her into some hooves. Order of the day is for lightweight racing plates, but when she gets back tonight, put her in a heavier pair of training shoes. Twenty-four-ounce should be about right for her – build up those leg muscles a bit.'

'Don't look like they need much building up from where I'm standing,' Jonas muttered, but he turned away and began examining the row of long hoof boots that hung together at the furthest end of the wall rack. After a brief consideration, he selected a bright red pair, which he brought back, laying one on the ground before her and opening the front of the other and holding it out towards Sassie's left leg.

Immediately her foot settled into the boot, she realised that the elevation of the heel was more marked even than the highest pair she had so far worn, pushing and arching her foot so that her toes were left pointing almost straight down. Her small gasp of alarm seemed to amuse the two men.

'You'll soon get used to them,' Higgy said. 'By the time Jonas gets them nice and tightly laced and you've spent half an hour in here, another half an hour trotting and you'll be ready to run like you was born in them. And don't worry, all the pony-girls out there today will be wearing the same kind of thing. Your biggest problem will be trying to beat any of our full-time ponies, Sassie, but don't fret about that, either.

'There's only one other visiting filly besides you today, so no one'll expect you to win anything, no matter how well you might have done in the amateur stakes before now. Our girls run every day and they live in their hooves. You'll see the difference that makes when you run against them.'

'Most of 'em are more pony than human, now,' Jonas added, grinning as he began tightening the boot's laces. 'Try getting 'em to run in flat soles or bare feet and they look like a bunch of cripples. How about you, Sassie? You always wear high heels at home?' Whether he expected a response to this question or not, Sassie did not know, but she gave a curt half nod.

Higgy needed to steady her whilst she lifted her other leg for fitting, but as the laces once again closed the boot leather about her ankles, she found, to her surprise, that she was already able to maintain her balance quite easily and by the time Jonas reached the top of her thigh, the boots were beginning to feel almost a natural extension of her limbs.

'She's a fine-looking filly, no mistaking,' Higgy observed approvingly. 'And there's no exclusion notice on her pedigree, I noticed.' He grunted and aimed a half-hearted kick at his colleague. 'I suppose you noticed that, too?' he said.

'And I suppose you'll be pulling rank on me tonight, as usual?' Jonas retorted.

'When you've been down here as long as I have, son,' Higgy said, chuckling, 'then you'll maybe get a few of the privileges. Besides, now her bloody highness has put Jangles off limits, a change of scenery would be nice. Why don't you try Jessie, now she's on the free list again? She's still the finest mare we've ever had here, even if she does act a bit vacant at times.'

'I might just do that,' Jonas said. He dealt Sassie a playful slap across her rump as he stood up and stood looking past her towards the wall rack once again. 'No bloody red harness in here,' he muttered, turning accusingly towards Higgy. 'I could swear I left a red harness in here, all polished up and ready.'

'Except you didn't check it properly,' Higgy snapped back. 'There was a damaged buckle and some stitching coming loose, so I took it over to the repair bay. You'll find a decent tack two doors down, in the stable we're putting that Jade girl in when she finally gets here. Use that for now and then get your arse over to see whether the other tack's been fixed yet. Red seems to be the popular colour of the moment round here and we're getting a bit stretched.'

'Then why not just order some more?' Jonas sighed, turning towards the door. 'It's not as though this place can't afford it, is it?'

The taciturn Mac had taken over the helm and now Frearson was seated in front of the various electronic monitors, his brow furrowed in concentration. Geordie, who had volunteered to take over galley duties, at least as far as brewing tea and coffee was concerned, placed three fresh mugs on the high-sided shelf and looked over Frearson's shoulder.

'Everything all right?' he asked. 'Only you look worried.'

'Not worried, laddie,' Frearson grunted. 'Just a bit puzzled.' He jabbed a finger at the left-hand screen and reached with his other hand to turn one of the knobs beneath it. Immediately, Geordie recognised the soft pinging sound of the sonar.

'See that?' Frearson said. 'That contact there?'

'Yes, I see it. What is it? I know next to fuck all about this stuff, don't forget.'

'That there,' Frearson said, 'is a submarine. Originally, it could have been almost anything, including a large shoal of fish, but as it's got closer, there's no mistaking it.'

'How far off?' Geordie asked. Frearson adjusted another control and sat back in the swivelling stool seat.

'Fourteen thousand yards,' he said. 'And it's moving pretty quickly, on a course that'll take it straight between Carigillie and Ailsa.'

'Royal Navy?' Geordie suggested. 'They run a lot of exercises up this way.' Frearson shook his head emphatically.

'Wrong noises,' he asserted. 'Our mob only has a few conventional subs that produce that sort of engine noise imprint and right at this moment, I happen to know that every single one of them is out of service. Some major fault with the air intake systems; it was in all the papers a few weeks back.'

'Yeah, I seem to remember reading about it,' Geordie replied. 'How about a Yank?'

'No, not one of theirs. Too small and too bloody old, to judge from the racket. More likely a Russian, but if it is, they're well off their usual patch. Since the early nineties they've been keeping their conventional subs closer to home for training stuff. With their economy the way it is now, they don't like spending out on more fuel than they have to.

'Plus,' he added, 'nowadays they generally get a clearance and notify our lads if they're running an exercise anywhere this close to territorial waters. Saves embarrassing incidents and accidents. No, if it is a Russki, then it's just Russian built. Trouble is, same as our lot and the Yanks, they've sold off so many of their obsolete boats, that fish could have come from anywhere.'

'But what other navy would have business in these waters?' Geordie demanded.

Frearson grinned. 'A private one, maybe,' he replied. 'We know for a fact that a couple of the larger South American organisations have been using subs to bring drugs across. Trouble is, until they surface, we can't do anything about them, just in case they did turn out to be full of a load of Borises and Vladimirs.'

'You sound like you're a bit of an expert,' Geordie observed.

Frearson pulled a face. 'Me and the *Essie* get roped in to a lot of funny things,' he said. 'Years ago it was spy ships and the like. Now it's a case of sitting out here occasionally and looking innocent, just to see if anything unusual turns up. Next thing to being pensioned off, if you ask me,' he said, chuckling, 'but every now and then we manage to do something useful.'

'Like now?' Geordie suggested.

'Like now,' Frearson agreed. He pointed to a small locker further along the bulkhead. 'Take a look in there,' he said. 'Small file in the blue all-weather pouch. You'll find some photographs, though whether any of that lot is relevant to our little caper is another matter.'

Melinda had seen most of Celia's little specialities in the past, including the one in which she now found herself a major player, but never had she realised just how totally shattering the experience actually was. All her concepts of time and emotions had long since been shattered into a myriad useless shards, it seemed, and nothing now appeared to exist outside of herself and Anna and the two of them seemed to be melding more and more into just one entity with every passing orgasm.

Hopelessly and helplessly entwined in each other's arms, joined at hip and mouth by the two double-ended dildos, constantly stimulated both by the vibrator mechanism and by each other's reactions to it, pleasure pain tugs at their nipples serving as a constant reminder, if one were needed, that they were now so totally dependent on each other and were forced to remain so until Celia decided to release them from their shared bondage, they clung together, wrapped in their tight rubber skins and the world outside grew more and more distant.

Vaguely, Melinda found herself wondering if this had just been a ploy on Celia's part to take the two of them out of the equation and if the ageing dominatrix intended to betray them to their hosts, but it was all but impossible to concentrate on anything long enough, other than the squirming, spasming body to which she was so emphatically linked.

Besides, she told herself, before the brief moment of lucidity was swept away on another raging tide of lust, it was far too late now for either of them to do anything about it if she did, so there was little point in wasting time and effort on a losing battle with a reality that now seemed only the flimsiest of memories.

'It's all right to talk out here in the open,' Celia said, 'but not near the trees. I know they have security cameras in some of them.'

'Just so long as they don't have long-range directional mikes,' Colin said, 'or zoom lenses on the cameras and people who can lip-read.' He grinned. He had found Celia waiting for him at the edge of the oval race circuit and they stood together now, watching three pony-girls being put through their paces, pulling enthusiastic drivers on very lightweight-looking buggies. Away to the right, four more girls stood patiently between the shafts, their drivers gathered in a small knot, apparently deep in conversation.

'How many of these girls actually live out here?' Colin asked. He had selected a pair of tightly fitting black leather breeches and an equally tightly fitting leather jacket, with zipped front. Heavy boots and studded gloves completed his appearance. Celia smiled.

'If by "out here" you mean this island, rather than out here in the open air,' she said, 'then all of the ones I've seen so far today. There's supposed to be one other owner bringing his own girl with him, but the last I heard was that they'd missed the ferry, so they didn't make it to the helicopter that brought us over.'

'What about the drivers?'

'These are all visitors,' Celia said. 'None of the staff grooms or drivers are allowed to compete in this sort of challenge meeting. Everyone puts into a pot and the overall winner scoops sixty per cent of the lot. Second place gets thirty per cent and third gets ten,' she expanded. 'I've already put our pledge in. We hand the money over later, of course.'

'How much?' Colin asked. Celia made a rueful face.

'Five thousand per entry,' she said. 'And don't forget, you're the one paying.'

'I don't suppose Sassie has much chance of winning?' Colin mused. 'She's still very inexperienced.'

'And so are a lot of these drivers,' Celia retorted. 'Usually, of course, it's the pony herself that's most important and the driver doesn't really have much of an effect on the outcome, but a bad driver can wreck a good girl's chances. If they get too carried away, the girls just refuse to perform to their full potential. It makes little difference to them whether they win or not. Even the champion of the day knows she's going to end up getting screwed by her driver and quite possibly half the rest of them, once they've all got drunk enough.'

'So they get back at the drivers beforehand?' Colin chuckled. 'As a famous general once said: "Get your retaliation in first." I reckon he had a good point. But what about Sassie? How do you assess her chances – realistically, I mean?'

'Well, from what I saw of her at my place,' Celia said, 'she's fit and strong and she runs well in hooves, but then these are pro ponies, so they are hardly ever out of *their* hooves. On the other hand, they do try to make things as fair as possible here.

'For these type of races they use a different type of hoof boot. Apart from the lighter horseshoes – they call them plates, by the way – the heel is raised a good deal higher, so the pony is all but running on tiptoe. If the boots didn't give such strong support, most of them would probably end up with broken ankles. As it is, they can't run flat out as they normally might do. See the way those three are trotting now? That's not very far off full pace.'

'Looks very ungainly,' Colin said. 'Very stiff legged and awkward.'

'And makes their tits bounce nicely.' Celia chuckled. 'Which is very popular with the spectators, especially the men.'

'But very uncomfortable for the girls, I should imagine.' Colin sighed. 'But then, the ponies don't have a say in these things, do they?'

'Well, no one here will risk letting them do anything that might damage them,' Celia replied. 'They're all treated like valuable thoroughbreds, believe me. Anyway, is this what you came to see?'

'Not exactly,' Colin confessed. 'I mean, a few pictures of one or two of the faces that aren't hiding behind masks might cause some embarrassment in certain quarters, but none of this is actually illegal, not unless one of those girls alleged she was being forced into all this.'

'Which they won't,' Celia asserted. 'They're all here voluntarily and from what I hear, they receive a damned good cash backhander for their efforts. Like I said, they're well looked after.'

'I wonder,' Colin said thoughtfully. He paused for a moment, squinting against the sun, which it seemed never rose very high in the sky at this time of the year. 'Tell me,' he went on, 'does this crowd have a thing about twins?'

'Ah, you've noticed.' Celia chuckled. 'Yes, a perfectly matched pair of ponies for the team races is very much sought after. Makes twins a real bonus. They have quite a few here and one set of triplets I saw a few weeks ago.'

'Really?' Colin stroked his chin again. 'How very fortunate they are,' he said at last. 'Very fortunate indeed.'

Sassie stood quietly as Jonas finished tightening the straps on her harness, wondering how she was ever going to run for more than a few yards at a time, so fiercely had he buckled the wide girth section. Breathing had now become a real triumph of determination over expectation and the upper harness arrangement did little to improve matters.

The circular straps through which her breasts now protruded had also been cruelly tightened, so that the veins on the twin globes now showed clearly through the stretched flesh and the rings that encircled her nipples had been deliberately designed so that they could be reduced in diameter almost to the point of severing the now severely engorged teats.

She grunted and gasped as Jonas continued a further inspection of all the buckles, tugging at them to ensure that nothing was slack and that there was no scope for yet more adjustment. At last, satisfied that there was not, he turned his attention to her head.

First came a curious skull cap arrangement, from either side of which rose two very authentic-looking horse's ears. It was secured beneath her chin, in much the same way as the blindfold cap had been earlier, though there were generous cut-aways for the eyes this time and the section that fitted over her nose had been elongated and shaped to form two enlarged nostrils.

At the back, an oval cut-out, placed vertically, allowed for her hair to be drawn through and brushed down to form a realistic-looking mane and, after carefully matching it to her own hair colouring, Jonas attached a smaller hair piece that started from just above her eyes and ran back to where her own tresses appeared, so that the overall effect was that they were all one.

'And now your bridle, Sassie,' Jonas announced, lifting the intricate arrangement of leather and steel rings over her head. He hauled it into position as carelessly and easily as if she had been a real pony, jiggling and shaking it and then prising open her mouth to take the bit. A few more adjustments and he was finished; Sassie the pony was once again almost ready to be put through her paces.

All that now remained was her arms and hands, which the grooms had surprisingly left until last. This struck her as curious, for she would have expected them to immobilise her upper limbs as soon in the proceedings as possible, but then, as Jonas began sliding the first mitt sleeve up her right arm, he said something that she thought probably answered the mystery and at the same time explained a psychology that she had not expected to find in such a situation.

'You accept the harness and bit nicely, Sassie,' the younger groom said, smiling. 'It shows you're already well adapted, that does. Some of the new ones start thrashing around when we get working on them – shows they're not really ready for it all and they're really wasting everyone's time.'

So that was it, she thought. They had left her arms and hands free as a form of initiation test and apparently she had passed. Now, of course, it was too late for resistance and, as Higgy stepped up to slip the second sleeve into place and her arms were folded behind her and strapped together, forearm to forearm, she really was completely helpless.

She tried to relax. No going back now. She peered between the blinkers towards the open stall door. Out there lay her destiny. Out there among the other pony-girls, some of whom, if what she had been told was to be believed, lived as she was now on a permanent basis, stabled, fed and groomed and available to any man or woman who could pay the price.

A moment later, she was jerked from her reverie as Jonas delivered a sharp cut across her exposed buttocks with a short crop and the curious whinnying sound that she made as a result sounded shocking and totally alien. The two grooms saw her surprise and laughed.

'It's a new idea from our workshop people,' Higgy said, seeing her confusion. 'See this bit in your mouth? Well, there's a series of holes through it and a sort of reed thing in the middle. Same inside these nose extensions. When air's forced through them, it sounds just like a pony neighing. Well, almost, anyway,' he finished, with a shrug.

'Yep, you're the first visiting filly to be fitted with this gadget,' Jonas added. 'We reckon the guests will love 'em, don't we, Higgy?'

'Yep. Looks like a pony, prances like a pony and now sounds like a pony,' Higgy agreed. 'And later, Sassie, we'll find out what you shag like.'

Detaching himself from Celia temporarily, Colin strolled down to the trackside, where he had a much closer view of the pony-girls as they trotted past. They were a spectacular selection of femininity, he saw, all above average height, well-muscled and firm-breasted, though their features were largely obscured by the bizarre masks which gave them their equine look.

The drivers were a mixed bunch and Colin studied them more closely now, turning to watch as more carts arrived and watching their different techniques and ability to guide their human animals, both of which varied as much as their physical characteristics.

Quite quickly, Colin decided he could discount at least four of the opposition. The drivers in question were all male and all considerably overweight, one of them at least three hundred pounds of fat that bulged grotesquely against the rubber shirt and breeches he was wearing. For any girl to drag that sort of weight around would be a handicap that no amount of fitness training and experience could possibly hope to overcome.

There were only two other women drivers besides Celia so far. One of these was also carrying a lot of excess flesh and the way her bosom heaved around in the low-cut latex bodice made Colin feel quite queasy after only a few seconds. She wore a half face mask and a headdress from which a purple plume sprouted ridiculously, but even the mask could not disguise that she was probably nearer sixty-five than fifty. Discount one more, he thought.

The second woman was much younger, to judge from her physique, for her face and head were completely enclosed in a leather helmet. She had legs that were the equal of any of the pony-girls and broad, well-muscled shoulders that contrasted with a trim waist and hips. She also employed a driving technique that was minimalistic, hardly using her long carriage whip at all, other than to flick it alongside her pony's face as an additional indication that she wanted her to turn or pull wider on the track.

'You could be a danger, madame,' Colin whispered out loud. 'Young, fit, strong and experienced, by the look of things.' He nodded appreciatively as she drove by his vantage point and he saw her head turn briefly towards him. 'And you know you're good, you arrogant bitch,' he added, as her back disappeared towards the bottom bend again, the wheels of her cart spewing dust and small pebbles to either side as it bounced along.

Geordie leafed carefully through the black and white prints, studying each of them in turn, but none of the six faces seemed familiar to him.

'Attractive-looking bunch,' he commented, shuffling the photographs back into order. 'Who are they? Should I know any of them?'

'Probably not,' Frearson said. 'You were dealing with the chains a lot further down. This little lot are at the top of their trees, believe me.'

'Drugs?' Geordie guessed. 'They all look vaguely Latin. South America?'

'Three out of three and give the man a coconut,' Frearson confirmed. 'These are the big noises from Central and South America, known to have supply routes directly into the United Kingdom and half of Europe.'

'Big enough noises to run their own submarines?'

'Well, one submarine, at least.' Frearson grinned. 'According to our intelligence, they work as a sort of loose cartel when the need arises and they are supposed to run one sub between them.'

'Makes sense.' Geordie nodded. 'You can stash an awful lot of expensive gear on even a small submarine, I reckon.'

'Several hundred million every trip,' Frearson agreed. 'Maybe even billions, except they wouldn't risk that sort of money in the one big basket.'

'And you reckon that blip there and all that noise stuff could be the very submarine in question?'

'To use your words,' Frearson said, 'it would make sense. This isn't the first sighting, either, but it's one thing to get a fix on it and quite another to keep proper tabs on the damned thing, assuming it is the same boat, of course. These islands make perfect screening devices and a good skipper can run any surface ship ragged here.'

'What about our navy subs?' Geordie suggested. 'I thought they could track just about anything?'

'Just about,' Frearson said. 'Trouble is, trying to convince their lordships at the Admiralty to stick a couple of billion quid's worth of their latest pride and joys up here to play policeman for us, especially as they wouldn't dare try to apprehend the damned thing anyway.

'They'd have to lie low and wait for it to surface and start offloading and although they're supposed to be able to run invisible, it isn't that easy. The skipper of our sub out there is a canny bastard and we could tie up all that defence budget money on a three-month wild-goose chase.'

'Surely, if it's that big, your people could get the go-ahead to raid any of these islands. The Healthglow crowd can't have that much influence.'

'Well, we'd have to be damned certain the stuff was actually on the island and be able to move in straight away,' Frearson explained, 'and whilst they might not have enough pull to actually prevent us mounting a raid, they could well have enough to delay it and even a few hours would be enough for the people on the island to clean house.'

'And if you draw a blank the first time –'

'– we won't be given a second crack at them and meantime the shit will be flying everywhere,' Frearson finished for him. 'Aye, you've got the picture. Besides that, of course, there are a hundred islands in this group and eighty per cent of them aren't populated, so that sub could make dummy runs and we could end up having a dozen lumps of rock to choose from.'

'Except you think it's got to be Carigillie or Ailsa,' Geordie said. 'And this is as good an opportunity to try to get a look from the inside?'

'Aye, when Colin told our department the sort of goings-on out there and said he had a perfect little team who could blag its way in, our governors were quite happy to go along with it.'

'And finding out what really happened to Alex Gregory is just a secondary objective.' Geordie looked pensive and began working his way through the photographs again.

'That one,' Frearson said, as he was about to go past the third face again. Geordie pulled the picture to the top of the pile and studied it more closely.

'Who is he?'

'Well, he's one of the few of them who ever sets foot outside home territory,' Frearson said. 'He goes by a variety of names, but his real one is Valerez – Ramon Valerez. Nasty piece of work, but that goes without saying in his line of business. Trouble is, no one can pin anything on him, so he comes in and out of Europe as and when he pleases. Doesn't even bother using an alias most of the time, the cheeky bastard.'

'So, is he the first among equals, or what?'

'Something like that. Our sources have it that he's working up to trying a sort of coup – take the whole lot over on his own. That sort of thing could end up destabilising several small countries in a very iffy strategic region, plus a lot of relatively innocent bystanders could get wiped out by the waves it causes.'

'I see. Anything to connect him with our friends on the islands?'

'Not directly, no,' Frearson admitted, 'but indirectly, through various front companies and certain supposedly charitable organisations, his footprint is likely all over the place.'

'You reckon he could be the real power behind Healthglow then?'

Frearson looked dubious. 'Probably not,' he said. 'But they could well be fronting this end for him, though so far there's nothing to connect Healthglow itself with any drug-based outfits on this side of the big pond.'

'Maybe they're laundering his cash for him?' Geordie suggested. 'Submarines can be used to smuggle other things than drugs.'

'Other things like people,' Frearson said. 'That girl the Norwegian trawler picked up definitely came from friend Ramon's neck of the woods. Shame we haven't been able to get to talk to her directly yet, though we've got people working on that, as soon as Colin mentioned her.'

'Some sort of slave trade, you reckon?'

'It's a possibility,' Frearson conceded, 'though it's a bit off the usual Valerez operation. Besides, why bring Indian girls all the way across the Atlantic when they would be better off used as slave labour back in their own countries? At a risk of sounding racist, most of those little lassies wouldn't be to the tastes of your average European.'

'And why bring only two of them over?' Geordie added. 'Or do you think there could be more of them involved?' Frearson shrugged and picked up his pipe again.

'Who knows?' he replied, noncommitally. Geordie stared back down at the sallow features of Ramon Valerez. After a few seconds, he tapped one finger dead in the centre of the man's forehead.

'He does,' he said quietly. 'He does.'

When Higgy finally led her from her stall, Sassie saw that there were now four more pony-girls in various stages of being hitched to a string of identical lightweight carts and she could not help but study each of them as she was led past them to her own vehicle.

Every one of them looked to be in the peak of physical condition and they wore their bridles and harnesses with evident pride, their heads held even higher than the stiff neck collar dictated was necessary. They, in their turn, eyed Sassie with coolly appraising stares and she could sense them evaluating her potential as an opponent.

Lifting her chin deliberately, she made no effort to control the swaying, swivelling motion of her hips and buttocks that the high hooves and tight girth encouraged. No matter if she was the newcomer here, she thought fiercely, her body and poise would stand comparison with any of theirs she had seen so far and she was determined not to let herself become overawed by them.

Besides, she reasoned, none of them could know anything about her, other than, perhaps, that this was her first visit to the island. For all any of them knew, she could be as experienced as they were, if not more so. Win or lose – and she was realistic enough to admit it would probably be the latter – she would give a good account of herself. She owed it to herself and to her master . . . and she wanted so much for him to be proud of her.

Leaving Celia to await the arrival of Sassie, Colin turned and wandered away in the general direction of the trees that ran behind the area where the various pony-girls, drivers and early spectators were assembling. He had no definite plan in his mind as yet, though he was fairly sure that he wouldn't find anything much above ground, but he reasoned that it could do no harm to try to establish some sort of picture of the geography in his head whilst he had the opportunity.

Not wanting to draw any attention to himself, he kept his progress sporadic and apparently random, drifting around on a curving course that took him close to the tree line, but then back again until he was standing close to the end of the line of carts and ponies. Here he paused, apparently admiring the soon-to-be contestants, but at the same time allowing his gaze to flicker beyond them, fixing various points of reference and identifying them with the mental image of the map of the island he had studied over the past two days, not that there was all that much to memorise.

At last, satisfied that he had got as much as he could hope to without leaving the immediate area, he began to study the pony-girls properly and now, following the example of several of the other people, began to stroll slowly along the growing line of near-naked female flesh.

They made an impressive display, he could not deny it, yet he knew also that Sara – his Sassie – would not look out of place in their company and he felt a thrill of anticipation at the prospect of seeing her arrive to take her place in this superbly erotic phalanx.

As Colin paused before the first girl, a towering brunette in her skyscraper hoof boots, her perfect body lightly tanned in contrast to the pure white leather of her tack, a leather-clad and balding fellow in his mid-forties detached himself from the nearest group of men and women and came over to him.

'What d'you think of her?' he asked conversationally. Colin looked the girl up and down again and nodded.

'She's beautiful,' he said truthfully. 'Is she yours?' The balding man guffawed loudly at this.

'I wish!' he exclaimed. 'No, I just drew her in today's lottery. Had my eye on her for a while now and taken her out a few times, though this is the first time I've got lucky for an actual race. Her name's Emerald. See? Look at her eyes.'

'Very green,' Colin agreed. The balding man nodded enthusiastically.

'She's got a twin sister here too,' he babbled on. 'Name of Gina, but she never comes to the stables. Works in the upper levels as a personal maid, if you know what I mean? Not considered suitable for all this stuff.'

'No, I can see it wouldn't appeal to every girl,' Colin conceded. 'You don't have a girl of your own – away from here, I mean?' The man looked wistful.

'Nothing regular,' he said. 'There was Marnie for a few years and we belonged to a small club; used to meet every month at this remote old farm place in Herefordshire, but then some nosey newshound got wind and there were some pictures printed in a couple of weekly rags and it all fell apart. The pictures were shit, all grainy and you couldn't really recognise anyone from them, but the couple who ran the club were spooked and shut down. Since then, I go to another place every now and then, when the money allows. Pretty good crowd, run by a woman who really understands. Didn't I see you talking to her over there just now?'

'Yes,' Colin confirmed. 'She's actually the one who introduced me here. This is our first visit.'

'Ah well, this place is a different class altogether,' the man said earnestly. 'You won't find anything better anywhere, for my money.'

'You come here a lot, then?' His new companion suddenly looked quite mournful.

'If only,' he said sadly. 'Business has been shit these past three or four years, so it's a bit of a juggle getting the readies for just a couple of visits a year. This place doesn't come cheap, as you must know yourself by now.'

'Well, you get what you pay for in life,' Colin replied neutrally. 'And maybe business will be better next year, eh?'

'I won't be holding my breath,' the man said. 'Oh, I'm Tom, by the way. And which girl did you draw, or aren't you racing today?' Colin introduced himself by his assumed name and then smiled.

'Actually,' he confessed, 'I've got my own girl, Sassie. They're preparing her in the stables, but she should be here soon. And no, I'm not racing her myself. To be honest, I'm still a bit of a raw novice and she's not that experienced, either, so my friend over there, the one I came with, she's going to drive her this afternoon.'

'Lucky bastard.' Tom laughed. 'Mind you, if I had my own girl, I don't think I could bear to let anyone else race her, even if we lost everything.'

'Well, I was brought up to play to win every time,' Colin said. 'Mind you,' he added, 'perhaps I should have entered for the lottery and driven one of the stable ponies. Too late now, I suppose?'

'Probably,' Tom agreed. 'Still, there's always tomorrow. C'mon, Jason my friend, let's have a look at the opposition together and see if I can remember all their names without looking.'

'Without looking?'

'Yeah, didn't you know? All the stable ponies have their stable names tattooed on them. Very delicate and discreet, but if you lift the left tit like this,' he said and demonstrated by reaching out and hefting Emerald's left breast in one hand and twisting the leather strap beneath it slightly, 'you can see her name underneath. There! See it?' Colin peered closer and, sure enough, in a dark brown ink, the girl's stable name was just visible in letters little more than a quarter of an inch high.

'Neat,' he remarked. 'OK then, Tom, let's see how good your memory is and I'll do the checking to see if you're right.'

'Where's our submarine now, then?' Geordie peered over Frearson's shoulder, trying to differentiate between the various flickering illuminations on the screens, but they still meant nothing to him. Frearson, however, had no such problems.

'There he is,' he said, jabbing a finger at a cluster of return signals. 'Right bang on course for Ailsa, now he knows there's nothing watching him closely.'

'What about our sonar signals?' Geordie asked. 'I thought submarines could tell when someone was echo-sounding.'

'Aye, they can that,' Frearson agreed. 'But see there . . . and there . . . and there? All trawlers and they'll all be pinging away, same as us. Just so long as we don't venture any closer, we're just one of the crowd. Trouble is, he'll be out of accurate range in a few more minutes.'

'You mean we can't track him to where he finally stops?'

'Nope, not properly.' Frearson scratched his chin. 'I'd stick a month's money on Ailsa, or perhaps Carigillie, if he changes course at the last minute, but that's as good as it gets. On the other hand,' he continued, sucking on his pipe, which as ever seemed to have gone out again, 'he's not our main problem, is he? Picking him up was just a bonus. Our job is to stay around for Colin's signal, if and when it comes. Until then, we stay put and wait.' He turned to Geordie and grinned. 'You'll get used to that, laddie,' he said. 'We do a lot of waiting in this job.'

'I'll go below and put the kettle on then, shall I?' Geordie suggested.

The skipper nodded. 'Good idea,' he said and turned once again to the screens.

'You still haven't told me where the girls are,' Colin said, when Celia finally rejoined him. Having inspected the impressive line-up of waiting pony-girls with Tom, Colin had finally managed to extricate himself from his new acquaintance's attentions and wandered safely out of earshot of the steadily growing crowd.

Celia flashed him a strange smile. 'Oh, I just made sure they couldn't get into any trouble,' she replied. 'They're quite safe, in my quarters and they won't be tempted to go poking around whilst we're out here. They've got much more important things on their mind now, in any case.'

'You wouldn't be trying to double-deal me here, would you?' Colin hissed. 'You try anything stupid and I'll make it my business to wreck you, your reputation and any chance you might have of ever being accepted in this damned scene again!'

'Shhhh!' she cautioned, laying a gloved hand on his shoulder. 'Don't get so worked up, dear boy. The girls are perfectly safe and probably enjoying themselves far more than if we'd dragged them out here with us just to keep an eye on them.'

'And why would we need to keep an eye on them?' Colin challenged her. 'The idea was that we took every opportunity to poke around wherever we could.'

'Exactly,' Celia snapped. 'And so you'd quite happily let that air-headed Millie go blundering about and draw attention to us? And as for the Viking princess, she may think she's some sort of super sleuth, but she could be a problem, believe me. No patience, that one, no patience at all. Either that, or she's just easily excitable. I was watching her on the ferry and again at the helicopter pad. She was like a cat on hot bricks. I don't know what she told you and your friend, but I reckon she's no more than a glorified pen-pusher.'

'Not from what I've heard of her,' Colin asserted. Celia raised one eyebrow and looked at him disparagingly.

'Men!' she sighed, shaking her head. 'You always see what you want to see and believe what you want to believe. Listen to me, my sweet, I'm doing you a big favour here and taking a hell of a personal risk, so believe me when I tell you, those two girls are a liability.

'I'll do all I can to help you, but that includes giving you straight advice, so trust me – those two are better off where I left them. You need to snoop around here – I'll help you all I can, but leave them out of it. I'll make sure they stay out of trouble and if you leave Sassie in the stables, the two of us are less likely to arouse suspicion if I start showing you around this evening. I know my way around here quite well, don't forget,' she reminded him. 'So, let's just enjoy the racing and then, after dinner, we can get on with it. I can't honestly say I've ever seen anything out here that would interest your people, so the sooner you see that for yourself, the sooner we can get this nonsense over with, right?'

'Right.' They looked at each other for a few seconds.

'Right, then,' Celia said at last. 'Now, where's that bastard Higgy got to with our Sassie? If he's fucked her just before a race meeting, I'll twist his balls off with my bare hands!'

Sassie trotted slowly along the pathway, gradually accustoming herself to the unfamiliarly high hooves and thrilling to the feel of the gentle sea breeze as it caressed her exposed flesh. Behind her, Higgy sat on the elevated driver's saddle, handling the reins with a light touch, allowing her to navigate the few gentle bends herself, calling out the occasional word or two of encouragement.

'That's it, Sass! Chin nice and proud there. Good girl!' Sassie felt herself tingling with pride and anticipation, all else forgotten as she focused her entire being on her body and the coming challenge and, as they rounded the final bend and emerged from behind the screening foliage, her breath caught as she saw for the first time what really lay in store.

As she trotted closer, she began to count and had reached a total of eleven ponies by the time Higgy guided her out on to the surface of the track itself. The crack of his carriage whip, a few inches from her right ear, brought her back to concentrating on the task in hand, the sharp tug of the bit in the left hand corner of her mouth signalling for her to start turning sharply left.

'Two laps, Sassie!' Higgy called out. 'Let's get the blood flowing in those lovely legs. Step it up a bit now! Hup!' He shook the reins and cracked the whip again and Sassie responded immediately and without thinking. From a gentle trot, she now extended her stiff-legged stride into something more akin to a canter, sensing the firmer surface of the gritted track beneath her, even if she could not really hope to feel it through the thick soles and the thin racing plates that separated her feet from the ground.

Ahead of her, she saw the back of another racing cart and driver, the pony-girl pulling it, pale blonde mane fluttering behind her as she ran. Twelve, she registered. That made twelve and she was thirteen and there had still been pony-girls being prepared when they had eventually left the stables. She shivered and sucked in more air; so many girls, so many beautiful pony-girls and she was going to be running with and against them.

She felt her vaginal muscles go into a sudden spasm and heard the faint whinnying as her breath forced its way past both bit and nostril reeds and, in a blatant show of arrogant pride, she tossed her head and deliberately forced an even louder neighing call to the watching spectators.

Boolik Gothar turned away from the monitor screens and unclipped the vibrating communicator from his belt. He recognised Major's voice instantly and his body seemed to stiffen in an unconscious salute of respect.

'Yes, Rekoli Maajuk,' he replied quietly. 'We have the submarine on screen. We have been monitoring its approach ever since it came into range.'

'The captain informs Señor Valerez that they have encountered nothing suspicious. Can you confirm that?' Boolik cast a sideways glance towards the screen banks again.

'We have nothing apart from a few trawlers, sir,' he said. 'The fine weather has brought the fleets out in numbers, so they're spreading themselves quite wide today. None of them reacted when the submarine came through, so it should be safe to assume they think it a Royal Navy boat on exercise.'

'Good.' There was a short pause. 'Boolik, most of the guests are outside this afternoon, of course, but I want extra guards posted to ensure that none of them wanders too close to the docking-pen area. The submarine will have to surface in order to dock, so make sure the headland above is cordoned off.

'And post extra personnel in the control room there. Special attention to air traffic, Boolik. First sign of anything in our air space, warn the submarine immediately. It's on Channel Forty on the UHF band this time. Establish contact now and keep it open until the submarine is safely under the netting.'

* * *

By the time Sassie was coming up to the completion of her second practice lap, there were another seven pony-girls on the track, spaced out at irregular intervals around the long oval. Added to those now waiting at the trackside, she calculated a total of twenty-two, though as she reached that conclusion, two more girls emerged from the direction of the stables.

'Easy now, Sassie,' Higgy called out, pulling back lightly on the reins and then tugging twice to guide her off the track and across the grass towards the waiting area. Sassie tossed her head again and slowed as she turned and now, for the first time, she was able to pick out Colin. He was standing with Celia, a little away from the two main groups of people and they seemed to be deep in conversation, but then Celia looked up, saw her and nudged Colin.

'There's your master, gal.' Higgy chuckled. 'Stick your tits out for him, there's a proud pony. Yes, that's the way. Show him what a lucky bugger he is!'

'Everything all right, Higgy?' Celia asked, as the groom finally reined Sassie to a halt. He draped the reins over the bar in front of the driving seat and jumped lightly down.

'Everything's fine, ma'am,' he said cheerfully. 'She's taken to the high hooves like she was born to 'em and for an amateur, she's not bad at all. Had her long, have you, sir?'

'Not that long,' Colin replied casually. 'Just long enough to recognise potential when I see it.'

'Oh, she's got plenty of that all right,' Higgy asserted. 'Put her with us for a few months intensive training and you'd have a top filly on your hands.'

'And she'd probably be running bow-legged, if I know you, Higgy.' Celia laughed harshly. 'She'd spend more time on her back than she would on the track.' Higgy tried to look affronted.

'That's a bit hard, Miz B,' he retorted indignantly. Celia looked straight at him and nodded.

'It always is in your case, Higgy,' she said. 'And that's the problem, isn't it?' She turned to Colin again. 'I'll take her round again myself, if that's all right with you?' she said. 'Nothing too strenuous. She's blowing a bit now, so I just want to get the feel of her and let her get the feel of me.'

'Fine woman that, sir,' Higgy said, when Celia had headed Sassie back out on to the track. 'Knows her girls, too, if you know what I mean?' He winked outrageously and Colin was unable to suppress a smile.

'Yes, I think I know what you mean,' he replied. 'But tell me, how do you rate Sassie's chances, honest answer, mind.' Higgy drew in a deep breath and turned to look along the line of waiting pony-girls.

'All depends, sir,' he said cautiously. 'She's running against experience here, as you can probably see, but then – and this is strictly between you and me – experience isn't everything. Some of these girls may be naturals for this, but that's only up here, see?' He tapped a forefinger against his temple. 'Some of them don't really have the legs for proper competition.

'I mean, they're all lovely-looking legs, of course, but beauty doesn't always mean speed. See the one on the very end there?' He pointed down the line to the girl Colin had first admired.

'You mean Emerald?' Higgy nodded.

'Yes, Emerald,' he confirmed. 'Beautiful filly and very placid, but she runs like she's got her hooves in a big bowl of rice pudding. Very attractive style, in its own way, but she's never won anything and it's my opinion she never will. The smaller blonde one two down from her, though – now, that's another thing.

'With the right driver, she'll run like the very devil and she's not even a full timer. She spends more time on the upper levels, where she's very popular among certain of our more influential guests, or so I'm told, but she always volunteers for race days. Her real name is Kelly, I think, though her stable name is Gem.'

'She's the best, is she?' Colin asked. Higgy winked again and grinned.

'Nah,' he said, shaking his head. 'Gem's good, but she's not the best. That's Jessie, that is.'

'Jessie?' Colin's ears seemed to tingle at the name. 'Which one is she?'

'Well, as it happens, she's not racing today. Not been herself these past few weeks, so we're letting her rest. Besides, she'll need a bit of working first. Got a bit too used to the same driver for a few years, so we'll need to make sure she hasn't picked up any little foibles before we let her go out with anyone else.'

'I see,' Colin murmured. 'No chance I could maybe run her myself in tomorrow's events?' Higgy fell silent for a moment and appeared to be considering his boots. 'I could make it worth your while, if you know what I mean? Maybe I could even take her out for a little practice run after this lot's all finished?'

On the back straight, Celia suddenly reined Sassie to a halt, dismounted from the cart and walked up to take her head.

'Just walk on, girl,' she said quietly. 'Let your breathing come nice and easy and just listen to me.' They began to walk together, Sassie in her huge heels now towering over Celia by three or four inches. The older woman waited for a minute or so, before speaking again.

'You know I'm going to be driving you for the races, Sassie?' she said. 'Well, looking at what we're up against this afternoon, it's going to be a tough event, but I want you to realise that it could have been a lot tougher. Three of their best four girls aren't running today, for various reasons, though little Gem's out and raring to go as ever, I see.

'Out of the rest of the field, one is a relative novice, like yourself, except she's built all wrong for racing, whereas you're perfect for it. Half a dozen of the others are only part-time stable ponies, like Gem, though none of them could get near her on the track.

'I've been asking around and the way the ponies have been drawn, most of the better ones have got the worst, or heaviest drivers, whereas I am a very experienced driver and weigh less than a hundred and forty pounds, which gives us seventy pounds and more in hand over the most potentially dangerous runners.

'Seventy pounds is a lot, Sassie, as I'm sure you know. In fact,' Celia continued, 'it's not just a lot, it's a hell of a lot and over four laps translates into a lot of drained energy. What this all means, in case you haven't caught my drift yet, is that I think we have a genuine chance of at least getting in the prize money.

'Not that the money seems to matter much to your master, but I'm sure you'd like to give him the pleasure of seeing you perform well, wouldn't you?' Mutely, Sassie managed to nod her assent to this. 'Good. So would I,' Celia went on. 'I like to win, you see,' she said. 'And if I don't win, I hate it to be for lack of trying.

'So, when the serious fun starts, I want you to be alert and on your toes.' She paused, glancing down at Sassie's feet and then laughed. 'Of course,' she said, 'you can't actually be anything *but* on your toes, but we both know what I mean. So now, Sassie, my dear,' she breathed, reaching out with her free hand to stroke Sassie's left breast, 'we're going to talk tactics.'

Jess stirred and turned over on to her side as the inner stall door opened. On the opposite bed, Bambi did not stir, the sedative Jonas had administered earlier having taken a firm hold within minutes. Jess yawned, looked up and saw Higgy looking down at her.

'Hello, Jess,' he said quietly. Jess eased herself into a sitting position and swung her heavily shod feet over the side of the bed on to the carpeted floor. 'I see your little stablemate is fast off?' Jess yawned again and nodded.

'He – she's still very upset,' she said. 'She's very sad, too. I've tried everything I can, but –'

'Don't you worry about her, Jessie,' Higgy said. 'She'll get used to it in time. Shouldn't have tried such a bloody stupid stunt. Idiot!' Languidly, Jess rose to her feet and held out her arms for the anticipated mitts.

'Not yet, Jess,' Higgy said. 'We don't need that between us, do we?' Jess regarded him impassively, her large dark eyes unblinking as ever.

'No,' she said, 'not if you say so.' Higgy reached out and took her hand, patting the back of it affectionately.

'We'll just have a little walk down to my private tack room, eh?' he said. 'There's a new visitor I was telling all about you and he's keen to work you out after the races are finished, so I said I'd have you ready when he came back. But there's plenty of time yet, I reckon.'

Jess turned and looked back at the slumbering form of her genetic twin and for a moment a sad cloud seemed to pass across her beautiful face.

'Yes,' she murmured. 'Plenty of time.'

Colin stepped back among the non-racing spectators and watched with interest as the drivers and three females who seemed to be members of the island's staff began to organise themselves. A small motorised buggy, carrying two male staff members, bumped into view along the track and Colin saw that there was some kind of board propped up on the back.

The driver swung the vehicle around alongside the course and now Colin realised that it was to be used as a mobile scoreboard. The surface was covered in some sort of white plastic veneer and, as one of the female organisers consulted her clip-board and began calling out, the vehicle's passenger began to print names on it using a thick marker pen.

Moving closer, Colin studied the names and the way in which they were being set out. Alongside him, at the front of the orderly semicircle that had formed facing the board, a red-haired female dressed in a white leather catsuit pressed against him, then looked up and smiled apologetically, her green eyes studying him from behind a narrow strip of mask. Colin found himself staring past her smile and down into the chasm that had been formed between her substantial breasts.

'Cost my last husband five grand for those.' She grinned, seeing his interest. 'Now I have to have my corsets and bras specially made, or I end up with crippling backache! I'm Cheryl, by the way.'

'Jason,' Colin said. He nodded towards the board. 'What exactly's going on?' he asked. 'I'm here for the first time, you see,' he added, by way of explanation.

'They're just finishing the preliminary draw,' Cheryl said. 'Twenty-four ponies this afternoon, so they can't run a straight knockout eliminator. What they're doing now is sorting out six groups of four as the initial heats stage. The winner of each group goes through automatically, plus the two fastest losers.'

'And then a straight knockout?'

'Sometimes, but not today,' Cheryl said. 'I just heard them say they're going to have a second group stage, with four runners in each. Winner and second in each group qualify, winner of group one then runs against the second in group two and vice versa.'

'To give two finalists, I presume? What about third place? Or does the third place prize money get split between the losing semi-finalists?'

'No.' Cheryl smiled. 'The losing semi-finalists have a run-off before the final. Makes a nice little curtain-raiser.'

'You don't race yourself, then?' Cheryl grinned again and shook her red curls with great emphasis.

'Not me,' she said. She placed her hands beneath her bosom and lifted it slightly. 'Those carts bounce around something dreadful and these things aren't fitted with shock absorbers. No, I don't mind the odd gentle trot out, but this is serious stuff and I could end up with a dislocated neck!'

Colin could not think of a suitable reply and instead turned back to study the growing list of names. He saw Sassie's name near the bottom and craned his neck to see who she had been drawn against, smiling with a mixture of satisfaction and relief when he saw the names of the other three in the final group.

One was Emerald, the tall brunette Tom was so proud of, the apparently beautiful but lazy filly, if the groom, Higgy, was to be believed. The other two were named Gigi and Diva and, as Colin looked across to where the different groups were being assembled he saw that whilst both girls looked as splendid as any of the others here, Gigi seemed a trifle lackadaisical in her attitude, and poor Diva, a raven-haired girl with a Mediterranean tanned-looking skin, had been handicapped by having the largest of all the drivers.

'Not a bad start,' Celia commented, strolling back over to rejoin him. 'The fat bastard puts the dark girl well out of it; the blonde looks as if she's come here off a hard night and the other one is the girl with the crap action. I reckon we should win this one.'

'Well, second wouldn't be so bad,' Colin suggested.

Celia snorted. 'Second in this group would be a disaster,' she snapped. 'Only the two fastest losers go through and this is going to be one of the slowest heats. Don't worry, though,' she added, 'I've whispered a few words of wisdom in Sassie's ear. We'll do the business, as they say in racing circles.

'And if you want to cover some of your money, the tall guy down by the board is running a book. Last I saw, he's offering two to one against Sassie. He's made Gigi the favourite at slight odds on, but he can't have looked at her as closely as I just did.'

Sassie stood now on the track, just a few yards back from the white painted line that marked the official starting point, blood already beginning to pound in her temples, the heat spreading out from her freshly plugged sex, the black rubber dildo seemingly pulsing in time with her own heartbeat.

The dildo was now a traditional refinement, Celia had quietly explained, after Sassie had stood patiently, legs parted obligingly whilst one of the female 'stewards' slackened her crotch strap and fitted the thick phallus with a practised professionalism that was as detached as it was efficient.

'It helps create a very special kind of energy,' the dominatrix told her. 'You'll understand when you start to really run, my sweet. Your hooves will fly over the turf and you'll gallop as though on a cloud!'

And now, as they waited for the signal to approach the line, Sassie was already beginning to believe her. Every nerve end tingled; every sinew was stretched like a bow string and yet she felt a curious relaxation beginning to overtake her. To either side, the other competitors shuffled and jingled in their harnesses, two to her left, one more on the right, her outside, but Sassie remained completely and serenely unmoving.

At last, the female steward who had taken on the role of starter mounted the small wooden dais and raised her flag, the signal for the four pony-girls to move forward and form a straight line across the track. Celia had explained that, despite recent widening, there would not be much width to spare with four contestants and warned Sassie to remember that whilst she might think she had plenty of room, not to forget that the buggy cart was considerably wider.

The flag went up again and came down with a flourish and the line surged forward, but Sassie, remembering her instructions, allowed the others to forge ahead and settled instead into a steady trot at the rear, noting with satisfaction how the wheels of the two carts immediately in front of her clashed against each other several times before they had even reached the first bend.

By the time they emerged into the back straight again, the four carts were strung out in single file and Sassie was able to lope along comfortably and watch as the tall, dark pony-girl and the shorter blonde began a duel for position which lasted a full lap. Immediately ahead of her, the raven-haired girl was now beginning to feel the additional weight of her driver and as they entered the home straight for the second time, Celia flicked her whip and shook the reins as a signal for Sassie to pull wide and overtake her, which she did easily, with no more than a slight lengthening of her stride.

As they drew level, the blinkers prevented Sassie from actually looking at her beaten opponent, but she could hear the girl's rasping breath and the whinnying sounds she was making and realised that the girl would do well to even complete the course, but she quickly put the girl's problems from her mind and concentrated on the remaining two carts that were now some twenty yards ahead of her.

'Easy, Sassie!' she heard Celia's voice from behind. 'No need to force it yet, gal. Nice and steady still.'

Sassie relaxed again and for another three-quarters of a lap she focused on the steady pulsing of the dildo, which now seemed as if it were setting a stride patter for her, two beats to the stride, two beats to the stride, two beats to the stride.

They now crossed the line to begin the final lap and still Celia refused to make a move, although now Sassie's flying hooves were almost kicking against the trailing anti-tip rails at the backs of the two leading carts. Around the top bend they went, the two leaders duelling shoulder to shoulder, Sassie hot on their heels and still she felt as if she had hardly begun to run.

In the back straight, the blonde girl suddenly fell away, leaving the tall brunette alone at the front. Seeing this, Celia shook hard on the right rein and cracked the whip above Sassie's head, the signal she had warned her to expect.

'Go, girl!' Celia cried. 'Round her and on!' A surge of adrenelin hit Sassie's brain like a charge of electricity. Incredibly, the failing girl and cart seemed suddenly to be going backwards as they passed it and now she was closing fast on the one remaining buggy as they went into the bottom bend.

'Steady!' came Celia's restraining shout. 'Wait for it, Sassie, my beauty. Wait for it now. We've got them now . . . and *go*! Go, girl!' As they came into the home straight for the final time, Sassie accelerated yet again and, breasts bouncing wildly, snorting loudly as she filled her lungs, she swept past the tall brunette and through the tape with a full cart and shaft length to spare and such was her wild elation that even Celia was unable to rein her to a halt until she had almost reached the top bend again.

'That was tremendous!' Colin enthused, as Celia guided Sassie back to the trackside. 'She looks pretty whacked, though.' He reached out a hand and gently wiped it across the sheen of perspiration on Sassie's shoulder. 'Shouldn't we dry her off or something?'

'There are blankets available over there, by the score board truck,' Celia said, pointing a finger. 'If you'd like to fetch one, I'll just jump down and ease her bit for a while, let her get her breath back.

'Well done, Sassie,' she said, as Colin headed for the truck. 'That was a very nicely timed run and you followed my signals perfectly.' She reached up, unclipped the bit from one of the side rings and drew it out from between Sassie's lips.

'She'll probably get about forty-five minutes rest before her next race,' Celia said, as Colin returned and began draping the blanket about Sassie's shoulders. 'We'll be drawn in the second group race, as we've only just run and there'll be a bit of a rest period before the first one starts. I'll just go over and check who's in which group, if you stay here and keep hold of her.'

'How are you feeling?' Colin asked, when Celia had walked off. 'That looked like it was hard work.' He gazed down at her feet and shook his head in wonderment. 'How the hell you managed to run like that in those, I'll never know. You *can* talk, you know,' he added, looking around to make sure they were well away from any of the other pony-girls and drivers, 'as long as you just whisper. It's just the two of us at the moment.'

Sassie shook her head and made a strange guttural sound in the back of her throat. Colin looked at her, perplexed for a moment, so she repeated the noise. His face took on a strange expression and he leaned forward, placing two fingers between her lips to prise her jaws wider.

'Ye gods!' he exclaimed, as he saw and felt the tongue plate between her teeth. 'They don't mess about here, do they? I'm sorry, Sassie, I didn't know they were going to do that to you. I'll get them to take that out.' He made as if to turn away, but Sassie stopped him with an urgent grunt and a fierce shake of her head.

'No?' he queried, astonished. 'You want that to stay?' She nodded and fluttered her eyelids. Colin looked at her in disbelief. 'Well,' he said, 'if that's what you want . . .'

'She wants to be a proper pony-girl,' Celia said, when Colin pointed out the plate to Celia and related Sassie's reaction to his suggestion. 'They all wear them here now and they all run with their pussies plugged. Sassie wants to be the same as the rest of them, don't you, girl?' Sassie lowered her eyes and, after a slight hesitation, gave a curt nod.

'Anyway,' Celia continued, smiling at her, 'the good news is that we've got probably the weaker of the two groups. For a start, Gem isn't in it. She'll almost certainly end up as overall winner anyway, but at least we get a chance at the semi-finals.

'I've just had a look at the others in our half of the draw. That very pale-looking girl with the white hair is in it.' She pointed out a slender-looking pony-girl standing about fifty yards further along the trackside. Next to her stood her female driver, a young woman with closely cropped dark hair.

'Her name's Phoenix,' Celia said. 'Her driver is Libby something-or-other. Hard bitch. Thinks she should have been born a man. No tits and a really spiteful personality. I just heard someone say she's threatened Phoenix she'll offer her up to the entire bloody crowd if she doesn't qualify from this round.

'The other blonde girl, just behind her, that's Daisy. She's not one of the regular stable girls, but she's pretty fast. Driver's that muscular fellow behind her. No finesse. The last one is that tall girl at the end. She qualified as one of the fastest losers.'

'She's the only black girl here, I see,' Colin remarked. Celia nodded.

'Yes, she's the other visitor.'

'Do they not have any black girls on the island itself, then?' Colin asked. Celia pursed her lips.

'D'you know,' she replied thoughtfully, 'I don't think they actually do, now you come to mention it. I mean, I've seen black and Asian girls around the place, but they've all come here with their masters and mistresses. Curious I never noticed that before.

'Anyway,' she continued, 'that one's name is Marsha. Finished a close second to Gem, though how much Gem had in hand we don't know.'

'Sounds like she's the big danger, then,' Colin said. Celia shrugged.

'Maybe,' she said, 'but she may well have gone too fast in her heat. There was no way she was ever going to beat Gem, but her driver kept whipping her on, even though she was nearly half a lap up on third and fourth at the finish. He should have eased up on her and let her conserve some energy. We'll see what she's got in reserve when the time comes.'

'Well, I made four hundred quid from the first heat.' Colin smirked. 'I put a couple of hundred on you two at two to one. I wonder what odds they're offering for this round.'

'Same again.' Celia smiled. 'I already checked. Oh, and by the way, there's another little refinement in this round. I forgot to tell you before.'

'Oh?' Colin looked at her, intrigued.

'Yes,' Celia said. 'They fit little ear plugs to all the runners and clip bells on their nipples and their bridles. Stops them hearing any shouted instructions clearly, so they have to rely on whip and rein signals only. There'll be a steward over in a bit to do the necessary.' She reached out and patted each of Sassie's breasts in turn. 'Musical tits time for you, my pretty,' she said, laughing.

Soobilini's fingers flitted over the keypad in front of her, while her eyes remained fixed on the split screen above it. She studied each of the graphic representations as they appeared, using the touch-sensitive facia to home in on certain areas and compared the changing read-outs in the bottom panel each time.

At last she paused, sat back in her seat, her right hand cupping her chin and continued to stare at the figures for several minutes. Finally, her hand moved again, this time flicking the communicator controls. The voice answered in her headset almost immediately.

'Yes.'

'Soobilini, Boolik Gothar.'

'Yes, I know. What is it you want?'

'I wondered if I could run something past you, sir.'

'Is it important? I'm busy supervising the unloading team at the moment.'

'I – I'm not sure, sir.' Soobilini hesitated. 'It could possibly wait, but it concerns the new visitors. I have a possible anomaly here and I think you ought to check it out.' There was a silence from the other end that lasted fully half a minute and Soobilini was about to check that the link had not been broken when Boolik finally spoke again.

'I'll be down in half an hour,' he said. 'In the meantime, run a check to make sure you know where they all are at the moment. I don't think they can get into any trouble in the meantime, but it pays to be careful.'

There was a dull click and this time the link was broken.

With the ear plugs now in place, Sassie felt curiously isolated from most of what was going on around her. To her surprise, fitting the sculpted soft rubber pieces had taken hardly any time at all, for there were strategically placed little zips in her horse-head helmet that allowed easy access for the female steward.

When the zippers were closed once again, the slight padding of the helmet itself added an extra layer of sound insulation that had barely been noticeable before and although the combination did not cut out all sound totally, the addition of the two sets of bells ensured that Sassie would certainly no longer be able to hear anything from Celia once they were out on the track again.

Two metal projections were clipped on to the bridle straps just above the blinkers, so that the bells themselves hung right over Sassie's ears and the second pair, attached to her already swollen nipples by thin circular clamps, were really superfluous and probably, Sassie guessed, just there for the benefit of the onlookers.

The first of the groups at last began making their way out on to the track and Celia took up a running commentary, mainly for Colin, but standing with her mouth close enough for Sassie to just make out what she was saying, so long as she kept her head still and the bells quiet.

'Gem should canter this one really,' Celia said. 'The main challenge ought to come from Tara, the one with the dark auburn mane. But the next one, Tammy, she's a bit of an unknown. She's only been a regular stable girl for a week or two, so I hear, but she ran very well to win her preliminary heat.

'I'm not sure, what with the horse masks and everything, but I think she might be Gem's sister. They've both got the same coloured manes and the lower half of their faces look identical to me. Could be they're twins and they got Kelly – Gem – to recruit her sister to the cause, as it were.

'The last one, the really dark mane and the green tack, that's Fliss. I know for a fact she can't be fully fit, as she hurt her leg in an accident about a month ago. Quite nasty, it was. Damn fool driver tried to overtake on the bend and get her to accelerate at the same time. Got all his weight wrong and flipped the cart.

'Brought poor Fliss down rather badly and she tore a hamstring. God knows how she wasn't more badly injured, but they seem to be a tough bunch, these girls. I wouldn't have let her race again for at least another two or three weeks, but I suppose they know what they're doing.'

The four contestants lined up. Fliss and Tara had the inside, with the two blonde pony-girls outside them, Gem in her gold harness on the very wide outside. As the flag dropped, Gem made no attempt to vie for the lead before the first bend, dropping into third place, with Tammy, in red, right on her heels and hanging slightly wide. However, as they came into the straight, Gem seemed to change up a gear, cruising past Fliss and Tara easily, with Tammy following her through. It appeared to Sassie that the favourite was determined to set a stiff early pace, probably hoping to run the legs out of the opposition and by the end of lap two her strategy seemed to be taking its toll.

A few yards further on, Fliss, who was clearly beginning to struggle badly, limped to a halt and, after a furious barrage of insults from her driver, together with several vicious swipes of his whip, the nearest steward went running over and the injured pony-girl was led from the track, her racing finished, not only for that afternoon, but probably for several weeks to come.

Meanwhile, Tara was also losing ground, but Tammy was once more beginning to close the gap on her doppelgänger.

'The cunning mare is going to let Tammy win, I think,' Celia hissed. 'No, she's just taking a breather. I must say, though, that Tammy has great potential. My, what a pair they'd make, too. Look at them go. What a fantastic sight!'

Celia's enthusiasm was now being echoed by the other spectators and, as the leading pair came past the finish line to begin their final lap, shouts of encouragement erupted from a crowd which had now grown to well over a hundred people. On and into the top bend they went, with only a single length between them still and they stayed that way down the back straight and around the bottom bend.

Then, as they straightened out for the line, Tammy moved wider and made her challenge. Again the spectators became very vociferous, several of them running forward to the edge of the track and waving their arms wildly in an effort to encourage the girl of their choice. Even Sassie found herself holding her breath, watching as the two blondes battled it out for the line and for a moment she thought Tammy would pull it off.

However, the favourite seemed to have just a little extra in reserve and knew exactly what was needed without her driver needing to move a muscle. She lengthened her stride slightly, stuck out her chest and, nipple bells bouncing wildly, went through the finish with a yard to spare and a yard that it was now obvious that Tammy had never really had a chance of catching up.

'Excellent finish!' Colin said, clapping his hands. 'Couldn't get odds on the winner, but I put two hundred on the second girl at even money.'

'Sensible bet,' Celia said approvingly. 'She was never really in it at the end, even if it did look close, but I reckon that Tammy ran her a lot harder than she expected. That's good for us, as long as we get through, of course,' she added with a wry grin.

'It's so frustrating, just having to sit out here like this,' Geordie muttered. Frearson shrugged.

'They also serve who stand and wait, laddie,' he said. Geordie stared out towards the southern horizon, the flat line between sea and sky broken by four small darker outlines, beyond which again lay Carigillie and Ailsa and, unless it had changed course after it had dropped off their screen, the unidentified submarine.

'Can't we go in just a bit closer?' he said sullenly. 'Another mile or two wouldn't hurt, surely?'

'It wouldn't do much good, either,' Frearson retorted. 'If that sub was headed for either island, he's docked by now, probably in some little cove that doesn't show on our photographs and probably safe under a load of camouflage netting. Might even be a cave there, for all we know.'

'So we just sit here until he puts to sea again?'

Frearson nodded. 'That's about it,' he confirmed. 'Same as I said, he's not our priority this time. Your friends are our main responsibility and we're their lifeline if anything goes wrong.'

'Can't you at least radio in and see if there's anything can pick up his trail again when he leaves?'

'Too risky,' Frearson said. 'If that crowd have got their ears on, they'll know something's up. And before you say it, yes, the *Essie* has got burst transmission capabilities and a satellite upload, but this close in they could pick up spurious emissions and they'd pinpoint them to us in a flash if they've got the latest DF stuff over there.'

'I just feel so bloody useless,' Geordie muttered. 'I hate having to leave it all to Colin and those girls. Shouldn't have let the three of them go in with him.'

'Good cover, though,' Frearson pointed out. 'Almost perfect, in fact.'

'Maybe,' Geordie conceded grudgingly. 'I just wish I knew what was going on over there.'

'Well, from what I've heard,' Frearson said, 'I wouldn't mind being a fly on the wall there myself. But then I'm just a dirty old man.' He chuckled.

As predicted by Celia, there was a break between the two second-round races and every second of inactivity seemed like a lifetime to Sassie. She stood impatiently, shifting her weight from one foot to the other, the sound of her pulse and breathing seeming to thunder inside her head.

All around her, the crowd milled back and forth, but she scarcely noticed any of them, for her attention now was focused exclusively on the track and on the white starting line that she almost imagined was now reaching out for her like a magnet drawing in a bright steel nail. Eventually, Celia replaced and secured her bit, but still there was no move towards the track.

Then, at long last, she felt Celia climbing up into the seat behind her and the signal was given to start forward. Two of the female stewards came towards the girls and began guiding them into their drawn positions and this time Sassie found herself on the tight inside. She waited as patiently as she could, one eye towards the starter, her sharp-edged steel racing plates scraping the ground as she continued to exercise her leg muscles.

The flag went up and down once and the ragged line became a straight one, hooves a few inches shy of the white paint. Sassie shook her head, bells jangling and her long mane swishing across her shoulders and neck, breathing now steady and regular.

Flag up. Flag down. And the race was on again.

Once more, Celia settled her in at the rear, adopting the 'holding up' tactic that she apparently favoured. Ahead, the black pony-girl, Marsha, took an early lead, with the blonde, Daisy, just wide of and behind her as they entered the top bend for the first time. The white-haired Phoenix, her crop-haired female driver standing clear of the seat, ran third, clearly also being held back for a later effort.

The pace this time, however, was much faster. Marsha's driver kept his lithe black pony-girl up to her work and her long legs flashed back and forth in a near blur and, by the end of the first lap, Sassie began to feel as if her lungs would surely burst. She hoped the effort was taking the same toll of the other three girls, yet still Marsha showed no sign of flagging.

To her surprise, however, as they went down the back straight for the second time, Sassie found she was getting a second wind. Blood ceased to pound so loudly and the vague red mist that had been hovering about her eyes cleared abruptly, leaving her with the sharpest vision and the satisfaction of feeling her legs striding out in an easy rhythm once more.

All the way now, the jangling of her bells accompanied her, the weight of the nipple bells tugging at her teats with every step, the dildo deep inside her seemingly sending her messages of comfort and concentration.

Into the third lap she began to sense that the black girl had gone off too fast after all. Out in front, she was taking the full force of the stiffening late afternoon breeze, whereas Sassie, with the two girls still running shoulder to shoulder immediately in front of her, was able to enjoy a certain amount of protection. Then, down the back straight, Phoenix responded to the whip cracking of her driver and accelerated past the flagging pacemaker. The darker blonde Daisy tried to follow her, but became trapped on the outside all the way around the bottom bend and although she finally moved into second as they entered the home straight, it was more because Marsha was now seemingly spent than from any real acceleration on her part.

Seeing this, Celia shook out the reins and her whip flicked lightly across Sassie's back. It was the signal Sassie had been waiting for. Throwing her weight further forward still, she swept past Marsha as they went through the line for the penultimate time and was just in time to pass Daisy before the bend was on them once again.

All around the long curve, Sassie ran with her eyes fixed firmly on the back of the leading cart. Her blood was thundering through her veins and arteries again now, but every inch of her tingled with excitement and determination. Out of the bend and into the back straight for the final time and this time Celia was leaving nothing to chance. With the other two girls apparently now well beaten, she was going all out for the win that would secure them the easier semi-final draw.

The whip flashed out again and now Sassie bit deep into the rubber snaffle and summoned everything she had left. For several yards, nothing seemed to be happening, for Phoenix's driver, sensing the challenge, urged her pony to respond, but the extra effort appeared to be too much for her and suddenly, to Sassie's surprise, she was passing her easily, taking the lead into the last two bends and knowing she was not going to surrender it now.

'Brilliant!' Colin almost screamed as she cantered to a halt and he ran out on to the track to throw his arms about her. 'You were marvellous, Sass! Unbelievable.' From behind her, Sassie heard Celia say something in reply, but the ear plugs and padded helmet muffled it too much for her to hear what. A moment later, however, Celia had jumped down and now she came around to hug her, too.

'Well run, my gel!' she trilled, in a voice so excitedly pitched that no ear plug ever made could have blocked out. 'What a bloody good show that was! Now, c'mon, let's get you rubbed down and watered. We run against the runner-up of the last heat, but she's still a damned fine pony. This'll be a real challenge for us, at last!'

Sassie, however, barely registered any of this, for as Celia continued to shake her fiercely in her triumph, she felt her knees beginning to crumple and, if it had not been for the tightly laced support of her hoof boots, she would have collapsed in the throes of the ferocious orgasm that rose up to overwhelm her.

'You did right to bring this to my attention, Soobilini,' Boolik said. He leaned closer to the screen and peered at the scrolling rows of figures and symbols. 'That's a ninety-nine per cent bone structure match and seventy-four per cent on the distinguishing features. It could be no more than a coincidence, perhaps – some of these human females tend to look almost alike as our good doctor's clones, but the name suggested by the system is too much of a coincidence.'

'The system's file photograph isn't as clear as it might be,' Soobilini pointed out. 'It was taken from a company brochure, nearly two years ago now.' Boolik pondered this for a moment and then shook his head.

'No,' he said, 'we have to assume that the girl in the Butler party is Sara Llewellyn-Smith, though my records indicate that she was never privy to Lachan's activities here.'

'Could your records be wrong, do you think?' Soobilini waited for an outburst, but it never came. Instead, Boolik pursed his lips, as he usually did when he was concentrating.

'Possibly,' he conceded. 'Maybe Lachan had contacts with Butler outside that we had no record of. Maybe he played his little games with the girl when he couldn't be here with his beloved Jessie.'

'Perhaps she came to like it so much that she contacted the Butler woman after Lachan's death?' Soobilini suggested. 'Butler could easily have found her a new master.'

'Yes, that's true,' Boolik replied. 'She has introduced several very good clients to us, but all this is conjecture, especially when we can ask Lachan direct. Unfortunately, I believe the grooms have him sedated at the moment, as he is still having trouble coming to terms with his new body. Such a shame, really,' he grimaced, 'considering how attached he was to virtually the same body on Jessie.'

'What should we do then, Boolik Gothar?'

'For the moment, nothing,' Boolik said calmly. 'Just keep a close watch on the two in Butler's quarters, though from what I see on the screen there, they won't be going anywhere without her help. Also, keep a close watch on the race track. Make sure none of the others manages to slip away from the crowd.'

'I don't think that's too likely just at the moment,' Soobilini said. She pointed to one of the screens to her left.

'The Smith girl seems to have qualified for the final stages. That means they'll be occupied for a good while yet.'

'I see,' Boolik mused. 'That *is* interesting. Maybe the girl is one of their pony freaks after all. Final stages, eh?' He turned away and walked to the door, where he paused and looked back at Soobilini.

'Call me if you see anything suspicious,' he instructed her, patting the small transceiver at his belt. 'The unloading has finished now and the submarine will be under way again in a few more minutes, so my work there is finished. Now, I think I shall take an hour off to go to the races. This could be quite interesting.'

The first of the semi-finals pitted the favourite, Gem, against Phoenix and her brutal driver, Libby, but it was something of an anti-climax and nearly a disaster for both pony-girls.

The race began predictably enough, with Gem's driver allowing Libby to take Phoenix into a narrow lead and make all the pace. Libby, however, was having none of this and reined Phoenix back. However, when Gem's driver also slowed, it seemed that things would continue at little more than a brisk walking pace, with everything saved for a mad sprint at the very end.

Quite how the collision actually occurred was hard to say, but it was the unfortunate Gem who came off worse, as the wheels of Libby's cart crashed into her legs and sent her sprawling, her driver having to jump clear as she pulled the cart over with her. Immediately, the stewards started flagging for Libby to stop Phoenix and a heated argument followed, but any chance of restarting the race vanished the moment Gem was lifted to her feet.

As she was unhitched and led slowly back to the track side, it was obvious that she could barely put any weight on her right leg. The spectators were mostly unimpressed and not just, it seemed, because many of them had lost money on backing the injured favourite to win the tournament outright. Libby, it appeared, was not the most popular visitor ever to set foot on Ailsa.

At least, Sassie thought vaguely, poor Phoenix would be spared the prospect of having to service maybe half the spectators after the meeting ended. Even if it was by default, she had managed to make it to the final.

'With Gem out injured,' Celia said, 'we're guaranteed third place automatically now.' She smiled at Colin, who was grinning hugely. 'Looks like you've come out of this trip with a profit, my dear,' she said. Colin continued to smirk.

'Yeah,' he said smugly, 'I'd already worked that one out for myself.'

There was no Gem now, but her look-alike, Tammy, who had performed so bravely against her in the previous group clash, was now the crowd favourite and bets began changing hands furiously, both for the second semi-final and for the final itself.

'Different tactics this time, my pretty filly,' Celia said, placing her mouth close to Sassie's ear. 'We don't want a repeat of that last fiasco, so we'll just have to see if we can't catch them napping. That Tammy is good, but her driver isn't that cute, believe me. We also have maybe a stone and a half weight advantage, so I intend to make that tell.'

Once again, Sassie found herself kicking at the ground as she waited for the starter to signal them forward. To her amazement, despite her earlier efforts, she felt full of running again and so, when the flag fell, she had no trouble at all in loping into an early lead and settled into a long stride that opened up several lengths by the time they turned into the back straight. Her mouth felt so sensitive now and every tiny signal transmitted through the reins to her bit seemed crystal clear.

For a full lap, she held roughly to the same pace, accelerating just slightly and then settling again as Celia dictated. How far behind her opponent was, she had no idea, but she did understand what Celia had explained to her and now was the time for her to put her complete faith in her driver's experience.

For another lap and a half she ran without a care in the world, glorying in the rushing air, the feel of her bosom as it bounced against her ribcage, the bells singing to her as she went. She tried to see Colin as they passed by the spectators, but the blinkers obstructed her vision and when she tried to turn her head, she received a sharp flick across the left shoulder for her troubles.

In the back straight for the final time, Sassie suddenly caught a glimpse of hooves coming up on her outside, visible just beneath the lower edge of the right blinker. Her instinct was to accelerate again, but the steadying pull on the reins reminded her just in time. Slowly but surely, Tammy eased up alongside her, but now they were swinging left on the bottom bend and the blonde girl was forced to run wider, adding several yards to her course.

As they hit the home straight for the final run-in, Sassie knew that she had won, even before Celia's signal for the additional surge. Tammy's driver had fallen into Celia's trap so easily and had left it far too late to try to close the gap, so that the effort of finally drawing level, combined with the extra yards Tammy needed to cover on the outside of the bend had left the people's new choice without any reserves for a finishing burst.

This time, however, as she crossed the winning line, Sassie dug her teeth deep into the rubber bit and managed to control the overwhelming rush that had almost brought her to her knees following her last victory. Panting and heaving, she turned proudly about and trotted arrogantly up to the waiting Colin, even the bit and rubber lips of her face mask unable to disguise her pleasure.

'I'm going to ask the stewards if they'll consider a weight handicap for the final,' Celia announced, jumping down and slapping Sassie across her quivering buttocks. 'That bitch Libby only got through on a default and her pony barely walked a third of the course, which gives her an unfair advantage. Mind you, she won't like it.'

Her words proved prophetic. The argument raged for several minutes and though the final ruling was technically in favour of Celia's objection, Celia was far from pleased.

'Five bloody pounds extra!' she stormed, coming back to rejoin Colin and Sassie. 'The cow is seven pounds lighter than me anyway. Still,' she continued, her features taking on a determined aspect, 'we've got an extra ten minutes before the final. Considering they don't have to have the third place run-off now, that was the least they could agree to.'

'That looks like our submarine on its way back already,' Frearson said. He pointed to the screen, but Geordie continued to stare out at the slowly gathering mist. 'Whatever he was delivering, it didn't take long.'

'Then why not just radio in and hit both islands at the same time?' Geordie demanded. Frearson tapped his pipe against the side of the binnacle.

'So,' he said, 'you know exactly what he was delivering, do you?' Geordie half turned and looked over his shoulder at him.

'Whatever it was,' he growled, 'it's got to be illegal.'

'Is that so?' Frearson replied, trying to conceal a smile. 'Oh for the confidence of youth.' He shook his head sadly. 'I must be getting old,' he said quietly.

'You mean we wait,' Geordie snapped back at him. Frearson remained impassive.

'Yes,' he replied. 'We wait.'

'I agree, Boolik,' Richard Major said. 'We wait. Wait and watch. See what they do. They can't get off the island and everything is well concealed. Let them have their fun and maybe, when they find nothing other than a crowd of fellow humans enjoying their little perversions, they'll leave us alone.'

'I've issued instructions to the grooms,' Boolik said. The two Askarlanis were standing on a small rise, looking down at the final stages of the afternoon race meeting. 'All the girls with the new voice boxes will have their vocal abilities disabled,' he continued. 'The rest will have tongue plates fitted. All the pony-girls out there have already been taken care of in that respect, of course.'

'Excellent.' Major nodded. 'I believe the man has arranged to take Jessie for a little solo run later this evening?'

'I wasn't aware of that,' Boolik confessed. 'That was an oversight on my part. I apologise, Rekoli Maajuk. I shall give instructions to prevent that, of course.'

Major waved his hand dismissively. 'Not at all,' he said lightly. 'Let him take Jessie for the run. And no tongue plate, either. I've already spoken to Higgy and he will speak to her in turn. The cart will be fitted with a microphone and she will know that the first thing she says to give even the slightest hint that all here is not as it seems, her precious stablemate will be taken back down to the laboratory level and terminated immediately.'

'You think that will be enough?' Boolik asked uncertainly.

Major nodded his balding head emphatically.

'Oh yes, Boolik,' he said. 'Apart from the fact that Jessie has an almost child-like loyalty to us, she also still loves that fool Lachan, even though he now has a body identical to her own. Curious species, these humans,' he sighed.

'Oh yes,' Boolik agreed. 'A very curious species.'

Celia unzipped the horse head helmet over Sassie's right ear and reached in to prise the small plug free.

'Now listen, Sassie,' she said quietly, 'we're already guaranteed second place, whatever happens, so your master is very proud of you and a large amount of money to the good. So, even if we lose this final, it doesn't matter and none of us wants to risk injuring you the way that other poor girl was hurt.

'We've got the outside draw and that Phoenix is a bit fresher than you, in theory at least, but her driver worked her hard in the earlier rounds, so she won't be feeling that full of life, whatever you might think. And as for what I think, well, I think you can beat her, but that bitch Libby is ruthless, so we have to make sure she can't pull another stroke like she did just now.

'Oh yes,' Celia continued, dropping her voice even lower, 'I'm pretty sure that was a deliberate attempt to run Gem off the track and if we could prove it, she'd be banned from running in competition for at least a year. We can't prove it, of course, but we're not the only ones who know what really happened. The pony herself knows and she was put at risk by that stupid manoeuvre, too.

'Therefore, she won't put herself on the line to do Libby any favours now, whereas you want to win for Colin, don't you?' Sassie gave a terse nod and Celia patted her cheek. 'Good girl,' she whispered and replaced the ear plug and closed the zipper over it again.

The final was to be run over an extra two laps, making six in all. This time, as she approached the line, Sassie felt strangely calm, yet still with the same physical tingling that she had experienced before the start of the earlier races. Even the dildo now seemed to be an integral part of her, its bulging presence reassuring and warm and the steady throbbing of her clamped nipples acted merely as a reminder to her that this was the ultimate test for her, her greatest challenge so far.

She tossed her head and waited for the subtle tensioning on her reins, relaxing herself and peering straight ahead beneath lowered eyelids. Now was the moment, she realised, to see if she had what it took to be a proper pony-girl, for if they were to triumph, she had to be able to place her fate completely in the hands of her driver. She drew a deep breath, her breasts rising proudly and moved up to the start line as the flag was raised for the first time.

Libby had clearly watched Celia's tactics in the previous race, for she seemed determined not to let Phoenix fall behind from the off and the two girls ran shoulder to shoulder towards the first bend. Seeing that they could not challenge further without the disadvantage of running the wider course, Celia signalled to Sassie to drop in behind and she tailed along closely into the back straight.

Once again, Libby urged Phoenix to increase her pace and Sassie followed suit, keeping the gap between them to a minimum. They ran in the same fashion for two laps and then Libby decided it was time to try for the first break. Her whip flailed mercilessly and even Sassie could see the red weals that sprang up across Phoenix's shoulders. The squealing pony-girl threw her head back and made to respond, but Sassie quickly matched her increased pace and after another half lap, the pace slowed again.

Resolutely, Sassie dogged the back of Libby's cart, refusing to be left, Celia refusing to let her make a move for the lead. At last they came up to the final lap and the starter waved her flag to signal the fact. Still Sassie loped along, the gap between her flying hooves and the safety board of the cart in front never more than inches away and, as they swung around into the top bend for the very last time of the day, she realised that the pace had now fallen off considerably.

Peering ahead, past Libby's solid form, she could see Phoenix clearly, clearly enough to see that the pony-girl's shoulders were beginning to roll from side to side and she guessed that Celia would have seen this too. Sure enough, as they hit the back straight, Celia gave a sharp shake out of the reins, the signal for Sassie to have her head.

Whinnying madly through mouth and nostrils, bells jingling and jumping about as if they had suddenly developed a life force of their own, she summoned every last reserve from her singing body and wanted to scream for joy when she felt it respond. She moved out, drew alongside Phoenix and passed her within a matter of yards, pulling clear into the bottom turn and, although she could not see what was happening behind her, knowing that she was increasing her lead with every stride.

The roar from the crowd reached her ears even through the soundproofing and the ribbon that two of the stewards were holding across the winning line wrapped itself about her breasts, flapping behind her like a jetstream . . . and still she ran, snorting, squealing, her mane flying from side to side as she rejoiced and this time, when the orgasm came, it carried her with it and she, in turn, carried it with her and did not break stride once as she continued around on a lap of honour that was scarcely slower than any she had run in competition all afternoon . . .

'Whoever she is,' Amaarini said, with an ironic smile, 'she's certainly stolen the show out there this afternoon.' She had joined Boolik and Major on the rise beneath the trees in time to see the final race of the meeting and had watched Sassie's convincing victory and spectacular lap of honour with interest.

'Friend Lachan certainly had an eye for his human ponies,' she continued. 'That one is a potential equal to Jessie, in my humble opinion.' Boolik shot her a sideways glance and decided to choose his next words with care; there was nothing humble about Amaarini, not in her opinion, nor in anyone else's and he knew that whilst she had supported him after the Lachan raid fiasco, she would not risk her own position by helping him to cover up a genuine mistake, no matter what the excuse might be.

'I, er, ordered the further checking procedures as soon as we had their arrival pictures,' he said. 'Until then, of course, all we had were the details supplied by the Butler woman and they all checked out perfectly. Perhaps we should insist on seeing pictures before we accept new guests in the future?'

'That would be a good idea, Boolik,' Major said. 'Meanwhile, even if there is more to the girl than meets the eye, no damage has been done. Your new security arrangements are a great improvement and this afternoon's operation was a model of efficiency. You are to be congratulated, Boolik.'

'Thank you, Rekoli Maajuk,' Boolik replied, trying to appear suitably modest. 'I am constantly reviewing everything now. But I wondered,' he said, avoiding Amaarini's eyes, 'if there is anything in particular you would like me to do about Butler and her party?' Major sighed and began to turn away from the scene before them.

'I think you are doing all that needs to be done at the moment,' he said. 'Just keep a very close eye on them and make sure none of them gets even remotely close enough to anything they should not see. I would rather we sent them packing than had another disposal problem to deal with, but I would also rather we did not do that too soon.

'If they aren't what they seem to be, we would only be giving them cause to suspect we are hiding something here.

Meanwhile, when Lachan wakes, question him under the hypno medication. Find out about the girl and about the others and also monitor the male when he goes out with Jessie later.

'If he tries to talk with her, that may tell us everything we need to know. Report any new developments immediately to me,' he added. 'In person.'

Colin stood in the doorway to Jessie's stall and for several long seconds he neither moved nor even breathed. As dark as Sassie was fair, the statuesque pony-girl was simply one of the most stunning visions of unspoiled sexuality he had ever seen and her languid posture and large, unblinking dark eyes sent a shiver of raw desire rippling up his spine.

She had been prepared for him in advance, bitted and harnessed, her large nipples ringed and belled, her arms drawn back behind her and securely pouched in the curious bag-like devices he had seen used on several of the other stable girls already that afternoon and yet she radiated an aura of anything but helpless servility. No wonder Lachan had named a yacht after her and had been building his own stable for her, Colin thought.

At last, he found his tongue again.

'Jessie?' he said. Slowly, she nodded, her dark mane rippling like a black stream in the moonlight, but her features, unencumbered with the rubber pony mask that had been de rigeur for the racers earlier, remained as immobile as if they had been chiselled from the finest marble. Hesitantly, Colin took a step closer to her.

'God, but you're beautiful!' he breathed. A flicker of something moved across the huge eyes, but was quickly gone again. Another step forward and he reached out a hand, touching her gently on the shoulder and then letting his fingers trail softly downwards, feathering the side of one breast and then withdrawing again.

This was impossible, he told himself. It was as if he was afraid to make any physical contact with her and yet Higgy had made it quite clear that Jessie was his to do with whatever he wanted for the evening. He closed his eyes and breathed out deeply, trying to block out the image he had just left behind in the nearby stall, of Sassie standing proudly in her own equine regalia, eyes burning with fierce pride at her newly proven status.

When he looked again, Jessie appeared not to have moved so much as a single muscle and only the gentle swell and fall of her magnificent breasts indicated that she wasn't, in fact, simply a statue and the pinnacle of some erotic sculptor's lifetime achievements.

'You're beautiful,' he said again. This time she did move, lowering her eyes from his gaze and taking a half step forward, so that now he could feel the warmth radiating from her and smell the faint musk mingling with the more tangible odour of her leathers.

Tentatively, he reached for her again, this time placing his hands to either side of her tightly girthed waist and she made no move to draw away again. He could feel the hardness of her nipples, with their rings and bells, even through the thin leather of his shirt jacket and was immediately conscious that the bulge in his tight breeches was beginning to swell with embarrassing rapidity.

'I shouldn't, I know,' he whispered, his hands moving back and down to rest on and cup her firm buttocks. 'But I think we both know I'm going to, Jess, don't we? Not in here, of course, and not just yet, not with Sassie so close. It wouldn't feel right, you understand?' He drew back from her again, shaking his head fiercely.

'What am I talking about?' he almost sobbed. 'I shouldn't even be thinking of any of this! I must be losing my mind, or something.' He looked down for a moment, but his eyes were quickly drawn back up to her again. Still she remained impassive, not even the slightest tic of a muscle. Colin sighed.

'I'm going to hate myself if I do,' he muttered, 'but if I don't, I know I'm going to spend the rest of my life regretting it. Either way I win and lose, don't I, Jessie?' He shrugged in resigned acceptance and held out a hand to her again.

'C'mon, my gal,' he said, his voice barely audible in the silence of the stall. 'Let's get you hitched up and out of here, before something explodes.' Jessie hesitated, fixing him with her unblinking stare, her wide, full lips framing the black rubber of her bit. For several more seconds, it was as if time had been frozen about them and then, with a liquid grace that brought a painful knot to Colin's stomach, she glided past him and out into the main concourse area.

Soobilini turned from the screen bank with a barely disguised smirk and looked up at Amaarini, who appeared similarly amused.

'These human males are all so alike and so predictable.' She chortled. 'He'll be coupling with Jessie inside half an hour, I suspect.' Amaarini, her eyes still on the monitor that showed Colin now fumbling to hitch Jessie to one of the carts, let out a little snort of derision.

'Slaves to their hormones,' she said. 'Look at him. Barely minutes ago he was in with his own female and now he can barely co-ordinate his actions because of Jessie. Yes, you're right, Soobie, he'll have her bending over the back of that cart as soon as he thinks they're far enough away from the entrance area.

'Nevertheless, keep the audio channel open and stay alert. You know which patrols are in which areas out there tonight? The first sign of Jessie saying anything that might arouse his suspicions, call the nearest squad and have them intervene.' She looked up at the digital clock display.

'I'll make sure Boolik sends someone to relieve you in another hour,' she said. 'You've been on duty far too long already.' She turned and looked around the control room. One uniformed male officer sat on the far side, flicking through several cameras in sequence.

'There should have been someone else in here to share your watch anyway,' she said. 'I'll find out what's happened and rectify that situation immediately. Meantime, you have done very well today, Soobie. Your work has been noted.'

Colin reined Jessie to a halt at the side of the track leading down to the race circuit, dismounted and walked around in front of her. The air smelled heavily of an impending mist, but the few wisps that had made their way in from the sea so far were just that and the moon hung high in the sky above them.

By its light, Jessie looked even more ethereal than she had done inside and he found it hard to believe that she would not just melt away before his eyes if he even touched her again. She stood watching him, breath drifting in tiny vapour trails from her nostrils.

Slowly, deliberately, he reached up and unclipped her bit from one side, drawing it from between her teeth and lowering it to hang gently against the side of her jaw. He saw her tongue run lightly over the inside of her top lip, but she made no attempt to speak and he wondered if she, like Sassie and the others earlier, wore an internal plate across her tongue.

'Do you talk?' he asked huskily. There was a long pause and then, finally, she spoke, her voice as sultry and silkily smooth as the rest of her.

'I talk when I am required to by my master,' she replied. Colin felt his fingers trembling at the sound of her and swallowed hard.

'And who is your master?' he prompted her. She smiled, very slowly.

'You are my master,' she said simply. Colin tried again.

'You must have many masters, then?' he suggested.

'I have many masters,' she agreed, 'and many mistresses. I am a pony-girl and I serve as and when required.' The smile flickered and widened briefly. 'I serve you tonight, master,' she said. 'You have only to command and your pony-girl will obey.'

'Tell me, Jessie,' he urged, 'do you enjoy being a pony-girl? Is there nothing else you wouldn't far rather be doing?' Her face grew serious again.

'You don't think I am a beautiful pony-girl, master?'

'Oh, believe me,' Colin said, 'you're a beautiful pony-girl all right. In fact, you're probably the most beautiful pony-girl I've ever seen – or am likely to see,' he added. He thought briefly of Sassie and a pang of guilt stabbed at his heart, but he forced the image of her aside. 'But you're so beautiful, you could be anything you want to be,' he continued. Jessie regarded him with a look of mild surprise.

'But I *want* to be what I am,' she said. 'That makes me lucky.'

'Lucky?'

'Do you want to be whatever it is you are?' she countered. 'I do – and that makes me lucky.'

'Even though you're available to anyone and everyone?' he said. 'Even though I could just fuck you here and now and then just stick you back in your stable?' His eye flickered to the row of brass bolt heads near the end of the shaft on this side of the cart. Someone had done a good job of concealment and camouflage, but his trained eye could tell that the bolt furthest from where the shaft joined the pivot on the cart was unnecessary.

Of course, he thought, he could be wrong, but . . .

'You wish to fuck me, master?' Jessie said, without emotion.

Colin turned his attention away from the bolt that he was sure was some sort of microphone and his gaze flickered along the nearby line of trees, but if there was a camera among them it was too dark for him to have any hope of locating it.

'I'd like nothing better, Jessie,' he admitted. 'But –'

But she was so cool and detached from the obvious reality . . .

'Will you remove my harness strap – down there?' Her eyes dropped momentarily and Colin looked down, staring at the point where the broad leather crotch strap covered her sex. 'Please?' she said, seeing his hesitation.

'It just seems a bit . . . clinical,' he replied. Jessie's eyes suddenly came to life.

'Please?' she repeated and now there was an edge to her voice that hadn't been there before. 'I promise you won't be disappointed, master.'

'No,' Colin whispered, as he stepped forward and reached for the buckles that secured the strap to the front of her girth, 'I'm damned sure I won't be.' His fingers fumbled over the brass fittings and he stifled a curse. 'The problem is, Jessie girl,' he continued, as the straps and pin yielded at last, 'will you be?'

'All on your own, Sassie?' At the sound of Celia's voice, Sassie rose from the narrow strip of bench that afforded the only seating in the cramped stall and turned towards her. The older woman stepped inside and pulled the two halves of the door closed behind her.

'Still got your tongue plate in, have you?' Sassie nodded and Celia smiled wickedly back at her. 'Well, never mind,' she said. 'It may stop you talking, but I know for a fact it won't stop you doing other things with your tongue.'

Sassie stared back at her. Celia had changed into an ankle-length dress of dark red latex, with high neck and long sleeves, the thin fabric clinging to her upper body and limbs and cascading about her legs in rippling folds. Sassie herself was still in full harness, except for her bit.

'Your dear master is a bit occupied elsewhere at the moment,' she said. She was standing immediately in front of Sassie now and her hands came up to cup the blonde pony-girl's harnessed breasts. 'However, I couldn't stand the thought of you down here, all on your own,' she continued, as her thumbs found Sassie's projecting nipples. A tiny whinny escaped through Sassie's rubber nostrils.

'You did so well today,' Celia said, 'I thought you deserved a special reward.' She leaned forward and her lips brushed Sassie's rubber mouth. 'And so do I,' she whispered. She lifted her hand and took hold of the ring that lay against Sassie's left cheek and pulled her head down gently.

'Come,' she said. 'My quarters are just at the top of the inner corridor. I think we'll be a lot more comfortable there. Tomorrow we race again, but tonight we celebrate our victory.'

'Nothing so far,' Boolik muttered. Amaarini walked across to join him in front of his personal console. On the screen, a ghostly green picture indicated that it was currently connected to one of the outside cameras. Boolik jabbed a finger at the writhing figures. From the small speaker came the faint, but distinctive sounds of grunting and harsh breathing.

'He never mentioned Lachan once,' he said. 'I think he's probably feeling guilty because he wanted to do that with Jessie, but that's all.' Amaarini smiled and nodded.

'Well, I think Jessie would tempt any one of their so-called saints,' she said. 'What about the others?'

'The two girls are sleeping now,' Boolik said. He flicked a key and the picture changed to show two rubber-clad female forms. They were no longer forcibly coupled together, as they had been when he had watched them earlier, but they remained in each other's arms as they slumbered.

'And Butler herself?' Another flick and another picture. Amaarini studied it for a few seconds and then let out a short laugh.

'Everything quite normal then?' she said, shaking her head. She pondered the scene for a few more seconds. 'Well, maybe there isn't anything for us to worry about after all,' she suggested, 'and if there is, it won't be until the morning. Leave the surveillance to the control room watch and get some sleep, Boolik. I doubt there will be any further revelations tonight!'

To be continued . . .

But there, dear reader, we must for the moment leave our little band of intrepid adventurers. Perhaps their subterfuge will continue undetected, but then again, perhaps it won't; nothing is certain in life, except, as the man said, death and taxes.

Find out what does happen in the next volume in this series, *Slave Acts*, which will be coming to a bookstore near you soon. In the meantime, perhaps you already have some suspicions of your own and the saga is far from over yet, so . . .

In this interactive world of ours, why not write and let me know what you think might happen next, or even what you'd like to happen next? I'd be more than happy to receive your thoughts, as well as your reaction to the *Slave* series so far.

You can contact me via my website, *The Storybook World of Jennifer Jane Pope*, which you can find at www.avid-diva.com, where you will find extracts of all my other published books, news of forthcoming publications and a tempting little collection of my short stories, all free for your enjoyment. My e-mail address, which you will also find in my site, is jenny@avid-diva.demon.co.uk and I guarantee you a personal reply.

Meanwhile, I'd like to thank you for buying this book and hope that you've had as much enjoyment reading it as I have in writing it. Thank you all.

NEXUS NEW BOOKS

To be published in July

PENNY PIECES
Penny Birch
£5.99

Penny Pieces is a collection of Penny Birch's tales of corporal punishment, public humiliation and perverted pleasures from nettling to knicker-wetting. But this time Penny lets her characters do the talking. Here she brings you *their* stories: there's Naomi, for instance, the all-girl wrestler; or Paulette, the pretty make-up artist who's angling for a spanking. Not least, of course, there's Penny herself. Whether finding novel uses for a climbing harness, stuck in a pillory, or sploshing around in mud, Penny's still the cheekiest minx of them all.

ISBN 0 352 33631 5

PLEASURE TOY
Aishling Morgan
£5.99

Set in an alternate world of gothic eroticism, *Pleasure Toy* follows the fortunes of the city state of Suza, led by the flagellant but fair Lord Comus and his Ladyship, the beautiful Tian-Sha. When a slaver, Savarin, appears in their midst, Comus and his ursine retainer, Arsag, force him to flee, leaving behind the collection of bizarre beasts he had captured. Their integration into Suzan life creates new and exciting possibilities for such a pleasure-loving society. But Suza has not heard the last of the slaver, and its inhabitants soon find that Savarin's kiss is more punishing than they had thought.

ISBN 0 352 33634 X

LETTERS TO CHLOE
Stefan Gerrard
£5.99

The letters were found in a locked briefcase in a London mansion. Shocking and explicit, they are all addressed to the same mysterious woman: Chloe. It is clear that the relationship between the writer and Chloe is no ordinary one. The letters describe a liaison governed by power; a liaison which transforms an innocent young woman into a powerful sexual enigma. Each letter pushes Chloe a little nearer to the limits of sexual role-play, testing her obedience, her willingness to explore ever more extreme taboos until, as events reach their climax, the question must be asked: who is really in control? A Nexus Classic.

ISBN 0 352 33632 3

To be published in August

THE LAST STRAW

Christina Shelley

£5.99

When Denis Mann loses his job, his life hits a hiatus of junk food and daytime TV, much to the consternation of his wife Helen and her wealthy mother Samantha. Soon, the women realise that he would be more use to them as a feminised sissy maid, and set about enforcing their will with the aid of the mysterious Last Straw Society. It seems the women have found the way to mine the seams of Denis's dark perversity forever. Will his contempt for the aims of the Society prove a match for the waves of masochistic desire its members have awakened in him?

ISBN 0 352

THE MASTER OF CASTLELEIGH

Jacqueline Bellevois

£5.99

When Richard Buxton is forced to leave the delights of nineteenth-century London, marry, and run a country estate, he assumes that the pleasures of the whip are no longer his to be had. Both the estate and his new wife Clarissa, however, provide unexpectedly perverse opportunities, and he is diligent in making the most imaginative use of them.

ISBN 0 352

PARADISE BAY

Maria del Rey

£5.99

Paradise Bay is an idyllic resort on a remote and beautiful island, where sex and desire are taken to extremes. It is the place where Alice, secretary to the beautiful and powerful Joanne, comes to terms with her inner feelings of submission. It is the place where icy journalist Amanda Trevelyan discovers the shocking erotic secrets of the famous and temperamental artist Jean-Pierre Giradot. A Nexus Classic.

ISBN 0 352

NEXUS BACKLIST

This information is correct at time of printing. For up-to-date information, please visit our website at www.nexus-books.co.uk

All books are priced at £5.99 unless another price is given.

Nexus books with a contemporary setting

ACCIDENTS WILL HAPPEN	Lucy Golden ISBN 0 352 33596 3	☐
ANGEL	Lindsay Gordon ISBN 0 352 33590 4	☐
THE BLACK MASQUE	Lisette Ashton ISBN 0 352 33372 3	☐
THE BLACK WIDOW	Lisette Ashton ISBN 0 352 33338 3	☐
THE BOND	Lindsay Gordon ISBN 0 352 33480 0	☐
BROUGHT TO HEEL	Arabella Knight ISBN 0 352 33508 4	☐
CANDY IN CAPTIVITY	Arabella Knight ISBN 0 352 33495 9	☐
CAPTIVES OF THE PRIVATE HOUSE	Esme Ombreux ISBN 0 352 33619 6	☐
DANCE OF SUBMISSION	Lisette Ashton ISBN 0 352 33450 9	☐
DARK DELIGHTS	Maria del Rey ISBN 0 352 33276 X	☐
DARK DESIRES	Maria del Rey ISBN 0 352 33072 4	☐
DISCIPLES OF SHAME	Stephanie Calvin ISBN 0 352 33343 X	☐
DISCIPLINE OF THE PRIVATE HOUSE	Esme Ombreux ISBN 0 352 33459 2	☐

DISCIPLINED SKIN	Wendy Swanscombe ISBN 0 352 33541 6	☐
DISPLAYS OF EXPERIENCE	Lucy Golden ISBN 0 352 33505 X	☐
AN EDUCATION IN THE PRIVATE HOUSE	Esme Ombreux ISBN 0 352 33525 4	☐
EMMA'S SECRET DOMINATION	Hilary James ISBN 0 352 33226 3	☐
GISELLE	Jean Aveline ISBN 0 352 33440 1	☐
GROOMING LUCY	Yvonne Marshall ISBN 0 352 33529 7	☐
HEART OF DESIRE	Maria del Rey ISBN 0 352 32900 9	☐
HIS MISTRESS'S VOICE	G. C. Scott ISBN 0 352 33425 8	☐
HOUSE RULES	G. C. Scott ISBN 0 352 33441 X	☐
IN FOR A PENNY	Penny Birch ISBN 0 352 33449 5	☐
LESSONS IN OBEDIENCE	Lucy Golden ISBN 0 352 33550 5	☐
NURSES ENSLAVED	Yolanda Celbridge ISBN 0 352 33601 3	☐
ONE WEEK IN THE PRIVATE HOUSE	Esme Ombreux ISBN 0 352 32788 X	☐
THE ORDER	Nadine Somers ISBN 0 352 33460 6	☐
THE PALACE OF EROS	Delver Maddingley ISBN 0 352 32921 1	☐
PEEPING AT PAMELA	Yolanda Celbridge ISBN 0 352 33538 6	☐
PLAYTHING	Penny Birch ISBN 0 352 33493 2	☐
THE PLEASURE CHAMBER	Brigitte Markham ISBN 0 352 33371 5	☐
POLICE LADIES	Yolanda Celbridge ISBN 0 352 33489 4	☐
SANDRA'S NEW SCHOOL	Yolanda Celbridge ISBN 0 352 33454 1	☐

SKIN SLAVE	Yolanda Celbridge ISBN 0 352 33507 6	□
THE SLAVE AUCTION	Lisette Ashton ISBN 0 352 33481 9	□
SLAVE EXODUS	Jennifer Jane Pope ISBN 0 352 33551 3	□
SLAVE GENESIS	Jennifer Jane Pope ISBN 0 352 33503 3	□
SLAVE SENTENCE	Lisette Ashton ISBN 0 352 33494 0	□
SOLDIER GIRLS	Yolanda Celbridge ISBN 0 352 33586 6	□
THE SUBMISSION GALLERY	Lindsay Gordon ISBN 0 352 33370 7	□
SURRENDER	Laura Bowen ISBN 0 352 33524 6	□
TAKING PAINS TO PLEASE	Arabella Knight ISBN 0 352 33369 3	□
TIE AND TEASE	Penny Birch ISBN 0 352 33591 2	□
TIGHT WHITE COTTON	Penny Birch ISBN 0 352 33537 8	□
THE TORTURE CHAMBER	Lisette Ashton ISBN 0 352 33530 0	□
THE TRAINING OF FALLEN ANGELS	Kendal Grahame ISBN 0 352 33224 7	□
THE YOUNG WIFE	Stephanie Calvin ISBN 0 352 33502 5	□
WHIPPING BOY	G. C. Scott ISBN 0 352 33595 5	□

Nexus books with Ancient and Fantasy settings

CAPTIVE	Aishling Morgan ISBN 0 352 33585 8	□
THE CASTLE OF MALDONA	Yolanda Celbridge ISBN 0 352 33149 6	□
DEEP BLUE	Aishling Morgan ISBN 0 352 33600 5	□
THE FOREST OF BONDAGE	Aran Ashe ISBN 0 352 32803 7	□

MAIDEN	Aishling Morgan ISBN 0 352 33466 5	☐
NYMPHS OF DIONYSUS £4.99	Susan Tinoff ISBN 0 352 33150 X	☐
THE SLAVE OF LIDIR	Aran Ashe ISBN 0 352 33504 1	☐
TIGER, TIGER	Aishling Morgan ISBN 0 352 33455 X	☐
THE WARRIOR QUEEN	Kendal Grahame ISBN 0 352 33294 8	☐

Edwardian, Victorian and older erotica

BEATRICE	Anonymous ISBN 0 352 31326 9	☐
CONFESSION OF AN ENGLISH SLAVE	Yolanda Celbridge ISBN 0 352 33433 9	☐
DEVON CREAM	Aishling Morgan ISBN 0 352 33488 6	☐
THE GOVERNESS AT ST AGATHA'S	Yolanda Celbridge ISBN 0 352 32986 6	☐
PURITY	Aishling Morgan ISBN 0 352 33510 6	☐
THE TRAINING OF AN ENGLISH GENTLEMAN	Yolanda Celbridge ISBN 0 352 33348 0	☐

Samplers and collections

NEW EROTICA 4	Various ISBN 0 352 33290 5	☐
NEW EROTICA 5	Various ISBN 0 352 33540 8	☐
EROTICON 1	Various ISBN 0 352 33593 9	☐
EROTICON 2	Various ISBN 0 352 33594 7	☐
EROTICON 3	Various ISBN 0 352 33597 1	☐
EROTICON 4	Various ISBN 0 352 33602 1	☐